Death at Rainbow Cottage

Death at Rainbow Cottage

Jo Allen

Author Copyright Jo Allen 2020

Cover Art: Mary Jayne Baker

The moral right of Jo Allen to be identified as the author of this work has been asserted in accordance with the Copyright, Designs and Patents Act of 1988.

All rights reserved. No part of this publication may be reproduced, stored in a retrieval system, or transmitted, in any form or by any means, electronic, mechanical, photocopying, recording or otherwise, without the prior permission of the copyright holder.

This story is a work of fiction. The characters are figments of my imagination and any resemblance to anyone living or dead is entirely coincidental.

Some of the locations used are real. Some are invented.

Dedication

To my lovely Beta Buddies. Thank you xx

Prologue

Natalie Blackwell stood stock-still in the pool of blood, her eyes as wide as those of the stranger sprawled like a doll on the ground in front of her, her jaw as slack as his, but with stupefaction rather than mortality. She drew a hand across her eyes as if to waft this gruesome vision aside, but when the shadow had passed nothing had changed. The man still stared up at the blank white sky, the puddle of his blood still lapped at the soles of her muddied running shoes, and the deep scarlet stain had bled a few threads further into the Sunday-best starched white front of his shirt.

From somewhere nearby, a forlorn whimper penetrated the fog of confusion that had descended over Natalie's brain. Her fear intensified. It took a second to understand that she was alone in the lane, quite alone, and the sound was only her pitiful cry for help.

He was dead. Surely he must be dead? But what if he wasn't?

Clenching her teeth, she dropped to her knees on the edge of the grassy lane and, closing her eyes, laid a hand upon his chest as she'd seen paramedics do on the telly. His skin rippled under her fingers, the faintest rhythm of life showing he was no corpse. 'You poor man,' she whispered into the still March air. 'You poor, poor man.'

No-one should die alone. She must do something, if it was only to cradle him while he died;

but when she tried to lift him she succeeded only in pulling his dead weight against her. Fighting for balance she saw a macabre vision of herself, trapped under the body of a dying man, and pushed him away from her. He flopped onto his back in the emulsion of mud and blood and muck that had accumulated in the lane. It took a second attempt before she managed to cradle him against her.

'I don't know what to do,' she whispered to him. 'I'm so sorry. I don't know what happened. I don't know what to do.'

Even as she whispered, she knew. His body hung limp and unresponsive in her arms, and she could do nothing. After a moment of futile hope she let him fall. Her blood-stained fingers searched for some sign of life, but the throb of the pulse at his neck had stilled. The last whisper of this stranger's mortal soul had left his body.

She bounced up to her feet and looked down at her bloodied hand in fascinated horror. Her breathing, which had been rapid as she'd run through the countryside of the Eden Valley, had slowed as she witnessed this death scene and now she became starkly aware of her own isolation. The closest building, a barn, was derelict. The fields around her were empty but for a few curious sheep nibbling at turnips. The hum of traffic along the A66 a bare quarter of a mile away might have come from the Moon.

A rainbow shimmered above Beacon Hill. She drew a deep breath, vibrantly conscious both of being alive and of how quickly life could slip into death with scarcely a sigh, and placed her hand on her chest like an actress in a Victorian melodrama.

'Claud!' she shrieked into the emptiness. 'Claud, help me!'

The scream faded to an empty echo lost in the sky, in the traffic, in the song of the birds. Unable to take her eyes from the freshly-slaughtered corpse in front of her, she backed away towards the path along which she'd come and, reaching it, turned and ran for home, leaving a trail of bloody footprints on the dry gravel track.

Chapter 1

The promise of a bright spring Sunday had faded into thin, cold drizzle, under whose shadow the soft green of the grass had lost its electric brightness and dulled to grey. From a distance of a dozen yards, outside the line of blue and white tape that marked the inner ring of a crime scene, Detective Chief Inspector Jude Satterthwaite stood with his hands plunged deep in the pockets of his Barbour jacket and a customary frown of deep thought upon his face. Around him the police swung into the action that always accompanied the discovery of a body — uniformed officers steering away the odd interested onlooker whose curiosity impelled them to approach though they knew they shouldn't; white-suited forensic investigators photographing the scene from every angle before beginning a fingertip search; a van bearing the white tent that would protect the scene from both the weather and the prying eyes of the public — but Jude, having issued his instructions, remained still at the edge of its frantic activity.

There would be no shortage of images available to remind him of every detail but he scanned the scene for a long moment. In the freshness of the golden hour after the crime there might be something to give him a head start in the hunt for a vicious killer. A man, about five foot seven and, as far as he could judge, in his late forties or early fifties, lay lifeless on his back in the middle of the rutted track, suit jacket flung open, the front of his shirt stiff with semi-dried blood. His thin face, drained and grey, bore an expression of appalled surprise and his dark hair, showing signs of salt-and-pepper ageing at the temples, stood out in damp spikes. One arm trailed wide across the stain of blood which must mark the place where he'd died and the other lay limp across his body. The white VW Golf in front of which he lay had been parked carefully on the verge facing towards the main road. The driver's door stood open.

Jude stared for a moment longer before turning east, where another set of blue flashing lights, late to the party, scythed along the A66 from Penrith. A flock of crows, startled by the activity, rose up from the freshly-ploughed field beside him and into the grey sky.

If only the birds could talk. He shook his head and turned his attention to the ground. Someone, presumably the police officer first on the scene, had used a plastic bag weighted with stones as an improvised cover for the blurred and bloody footmarks that led away from the scene towards a path across a field, but they'd petered out by the time they met the soft turf.

Something told him they were less of a clue than he might first have thought. He looked further. Three hundred yards beyond, on the far side of the field where the footsteps led, stood a stone bungalow, its picture windows facing towards them. That was where Natalie Blackwell lived, and the footmarks almost certainly belonged to her. Most murderers were too careful to leave so obvious a trail, and to his mind the main exit route for the killer almost certainly led along the lane towards the A66. From there, traffic permitting, someone could have made it a long way in the half an hour since the crime had been reported.

The man was very recently dead, he noted, grimly. 'Tammy.'

Tammy Garner, the CSI in charge of the crime scene, had been working within the taped-off area. Handing her camera over to a colleague, she stepped towards him with care. 'Hello again, Chief,' she said from behind her forensic mask. 'Not looking good, this one.'

Murder never looked good, or not to anyone with a shred of conscience or humanity. 'What do you reckon?'

She ducked under the blue and white tape and, once securely outside it, pulled down the mask in a movement that blended into a shrug. Tammy, who was the best of the CSIs on the Cumbria force, had been short with him on the last couple of occasions they'd passed one another in the corridor of the police headquarters and today she avoided his eye, but whatever he'd unwittingly done to offend her wasn't serious enough for her to carry it over into the professional arena. 'First thoughts?'

'Body's been moved.' She extended a gloved forefinger towards the pool of blood a few inches from the dead man.

'I'm told he was still alive when he was found. That's why.'

'Curse those well-meaning civilians, eh?' she said, cheerfully. 'Have you spoken to whoever found him?'

'Not yet. But she lives locally. Over there.' He gestured to the cottage, separated from the village of Temple Sowerby by the A66 and with access via a narrow bridge.

'Ah, okay. Then those might be her prints.' Dissatisfaction creased Tammy's brow as it always did at the first review of a disturbed crime scene. Later, she'd relish unravelling the puzzle. 'You know I never speculate.' She sniggered, a half-laugh at a running joke. 'But it looks like whoever it was did a runner via the A66. There's a second set of tyre marks just there on the verge. Fresh.' She gestured up the farm track. 'And they overlie the marks from this car, so I'd say our victim was here first and someone joined him, by accident or design.'

The lane wasn't wide enough for two cars. The second must have blocked in the first. 'If it's his car.'

'Yes.'

Both the track and part of the inside carriageway of the A66 had been closed off and Jude had parked in the village of Temple Sowerby and approached across the bridge, picking his way with care past the cottage and along the edge of the ploughed field. 'Then our killer could be miles away by now.'

'I expect so.' She allowed herself a fractious sigh, and turned her back on him. 'I'd better get on. I'll get back to you when we've had a proper look.'

She was usually more chatty that that, even when there was work to be done, but he shrugged her coolness off, and turned back to the constable who had been standing just behind him. 'Do we have anything on the car?'

'It's registered to a Leonard James Pierce.' She jerked her head towards the east, along the A66. 'A businessman. He lives in Appleby.'

'Anything to suggest that's Mr Pierce lying next to it?'

'Yep. That's Len Pierce.'

She'd been holding a tablet device which she tilted towards him. Modern policing gained from modern means, and she'd gone straight to social media for her information. Len Pierce's Facebook profile, open in front of them, didn't tell Jude everything he needed to know but it confirmed the identity of the corpse. In the image the middle-aged man smiling on the bridge in Appleby on a sunny day was lit up by the spark that death extinguished but it was unmistakably him who lay yards away, his empty eyes tilted up to a grey sky.

Jude flicked a finger and swiped through the life Len Pierce chose to make public. Pictures of a garden, bursting with blossom, of cupcakes and traybakes, of a grey-muzzled collie dog, tongue hanging out as it lay flopped down on the grass. Len's life, it appeared, was anything but people-centred. 'We'll need to find someone to give a positive ID.'

'There's nothing in his profile to suggest he has family. But we'll find someone.'

'Get on to that, would you?'

'Right away.' She folded the cover on the tablet.

Jude allowed himself another moment to check over the scene, to make sure that everything was running smoothly so that he could move on. 'DI Dodd is coming over. He'll be here any minute and he'll take over.' Doddsy, his best friend and deputy, lived in one of the new houses that had blossomed behind Temple Sowerby's medical centre. 'One last thing. The woman who found the body. What was she doing?'

'Jogging.'

'And she was the one who called the police.'

'No. Her husband called them. She didn't have her phone with her, so she went home.'

So he'd been right, and that would explain the bloodied footmarks. 'Did she move him?'

'I don't know for sure.' The policewoman turned to look at Len Pierce, sprawled on the floor, and her mouth twisted a little, as if she was fighting to

15

keep a severe expression in front of a senior officer. 'No-one's interviewed her yet.' She held up a quick hand as if to justify a failure in procedure. 'I tried to get a statement out of her but she was barely coherent. I thought I'd better let her calm down. Didn't want a breakdown on my hands. Poor woman.'

Jude spotted Doddsy striding past the Blackwells' cottage. 'Okay. I'll speak to her. You carry on.'

Leaving those on the scene to get on with what they were doing, he headed towards the building, intercepting his friend halfway. 'One day we might get a whole weekend off,' he said to him, by way of greeting. 'You can take over here. I'm going down to chat to our only witness.'

Pausing by the wall, Doddsy snatched at the opportunity for a quick cigarette. It would be a while before he had the chance of another. He was in his suit on a Sunday afternoon. 'A Lent lunch after church,' he said, spotting Jude looking at him. 'Up at Skirwith. Or I'd have been here sooner.' He unclipped a cross-shaped lapel pin from his jacket and slipped it into his pocket. 'We have an actual witness?'

'Not a witness to the deed. The woman who found him. She lives in that cottage.'

'Natalie Blackwell?' Doddsy said, nodding. 'Ah. Okay.'

'You know her?'

'I know of her. The Blackwells are recent arrivals in the area. I've met her husband, in passing. Interesting couple, if you believe the local gossip.'

'Oh?'

'Half of what I hear won't be true.' Doddsy looked at his half-smoked cigarette with obvious regret. 'Folk think they're a bit odd. The village gossip is that she used to be a ballet dancer.'

'Is there a lot of talk about them?'

'Not a lot, but they came up in conversation over lunch. He's a bit of a crusader. I get the impression he likes to take people out of their comfort zone. That never goes down well.'

For a moment Jude had toyed with the idea of handing the witness interview over to Doddsy but at the mention of the Blackwells' oddness he decided against it. Doddsy was an organiser *par excellence*, but sometimes he missed the clues that hid under people's idiosyncrasies.

'It's a pity Ashleigh isn't here.' Doddsy must be thinking the same. 'She's always good with interesting people.' He ground out the cigarette on the wall.

Doddsy's sly smile brought a matching smile to Jude's lips. Ashleigh O'Halloran was one of those rare detectives who seemed somehow to charm confidences out of the least willing of witnesses, to persuade the most stubborn of people to part with secrets they never even knew they possessed. Quite how she did it even she didn't seem to know, asking the same questions as her colleagues and yet reaping greater, and often instant, rewards. 'She'll be back in tomorrow. We'll get her straight on to the case.'

'Missed her, have you?'

Even under the sombre circumstances, Jude allowed a beat of pleasure to creep under his guard at the prospect of Ashleigh's return. She was his girlfriend as well as his colleague, and they hadn't been together long enough for him to regard her long-planned family holiday as a chance to do his own thing. It wasn't love — God knew, neither of them was prepared to take that kind of risk — but the relationship worked just fine without it, and he'd felt her absence more than he'd thought he would. 'She'd certainly be some use to us today.'

'And in the meantime we'll have to make do with you. Right. I'll get on.'

'When I've spoken to Mrs Blackwell, I'll go back to the office. Let me know what resources you think you'll need.'

'Sure.' Doddsy strolled off up towards the buzz of activity in the lane, unruffled.

Rainbow Cottage stood at the end of the rutted track from Temple Sowerby, a track whose vehicular capability petered out at the Blackwells' cottage though the route itself stuttered on into the path on which they stood. The pedestrian link it offered to the dead end where Len Pierce had been slain, and so directly to the A66, was so frail that it wasn't marked on the map, and no-one could have used it from that direction without passing the cottage. The Blackwells could only reach the main road by car by going through the village. As Jude had walked past it earlier the nervous twitching of curtains told him the occupants were watching and waiting to play their part in the investigation.

The cottage was a century or so old, built in traditional style but with a modern glass extension on two sides. The sign announcing it as Rainbow Cottage was new and boldly carved on green Coniston slate. The garden was well tended, its borders a carpet of fading crocuses among the blue of grape hyacinth and glory-of-the-snow. Jude turned through the gate and up the path. Behind the opaque glass panel in the front door a figure shimmered, wrenching it open and interrupting his survey of the property.

'The police?' A man some six inches shorter than Jude himself but with a physical presence more than reinforced by a barrel chest and a bull neck, bounced onto the doorstep. He was probably in his forties, once-dark hair dusted with grey and receding at the temples. The rolled-up sleeves of his checked shirt revealed capable forearms. Energy sparked from him, every movement short, sharp and full of purpose.

Jude flashed his warrant card. 'DCI Satterthwaite. I'm sorry to have left you hanging around. I needed to get the investigation up and running before I spoke to you. Mr Blackwell, is that right?'

The man held out his hand as if it were a social visit. 'Yes. Claud Blackwell. No worries, Chief Inspector. Your people did offer to leave us a policewoman when they saw how upset Nat was, but I guessed you'd need every hand to the pump up there. And there was no way Nat would have been able to tell them anything. Anyway, she has me to look after her.'

'Is your wife all right?'

'I think so. Very shaken up to start with, but she's calmer now. She's taken something.' Claud Blackwell stepped back and held the door open, motioning Jude through the narrow hallway. 'She's in the living room. Would you like coffee?'

Jude declined the coffee and headed through. Natalie Blackwell was sitting straight-backed in an armchair by the unlit fire, gazing across the dual-aspect room and out towards the village. Her face was turned away from the flurry of activity at the end of the lane. When Jude entered the room she rose and turned towards him, extending a hand. She'd showered and changed, and was dressed in jogging bottoms and a baggy sweatshirt. Her dark blonde hair, twisted into a tight bun, was damp and the fresh aroma of shower gel, mint and strawberry, clung to her. She looked ageless, anywhere between fifteen and fifty but judging her — probably inaccurately — by the age of her husband, she might have been in her forties.

'Chief Inspector.' Her voice was barely a whisper, but he heard music in it.

'Mrs Blackwell.' He shook her hand. She was as tall as he was, a good six feet, and she looked him calmly and levelly in the eye, a gaze from which any curiosity had been wiped away by shock and medication. 'Are you all right?'

Her hand fluttered in front of her breast. Despite the shower, the fingernails on the right hand were still picked out in red and she spotted him looking at it and held it out, as if for inspection. 'I'm like Lady Macbeth, aren't I? *What, will this hand ne'er be clean*?' Her eyes were veiled, her soul hidden. 'Yes. Very shaken. And I'm so sorry. I moved the body.'

'Oh?' He took the seat to which Claud motioned him, and watched Natalie as she resumed her seat in the armchair, snatching a fearful eye at the goings-on outside before returning her attention to him.

'Yes. I know you aren't supposed to touch anything, but I'm afraid I panicked.' She folded her hands on her lap. 'He was still alive. I thought I might need to do CPR. Then I realised there was nothing I could do and he was going to die. I wanted to hold him, so he didn't die alone, so he knew there was good in the world as well as evil. The poor man. A stranger.' A tear glimmered in her eye. 'He died and I panicked. I don't remember exactly what happened.' Her hand fluttered upwards again, but whatever she'd taken to calm her had rubbed the inflections from her voice as easily as it had wiped the nuance from her expression, so her whole statement offered nothing but a sense of emotionless anti-climax. 'I was covered in blood. So much blood.'

'Did the police officer who spoke to you ask you to keep your clothing?'

Claud twitched in what looked as if it might be vindication but Natalie's look was blank. 'She did, but I put it in the washing machine. Claud said I should keep it like she said, but I couldn't bear to see the man's blood. And it doesn't matter, does it? It isn't as if I killed him.'

'I'm sure it doesn't matter, Nat.' Jude sensed resignation in Claud's voice. 'I'm sure it was just a precaution.'

Just a precaution. Who knew what forensic evidence had clung to Natalie's clothing as she'd cradled Len Pierce in his death throes? In the background, the hum of the washing machine made a mockery of procedure, but there was nothing to be done. 'Don't worry about moving him, Mrs Blackwell.' It happened. It was frustrating, and sometimes it cost a conviction, but Jude was human. The clothing was different — infuriating, evidence contaminated or lost — but you couldn't blame someone for trying to save a life.

She was still gazing down at her hand. 'Did I kill him?'

'I beg your pardon?'

Claud's expression was somewhere between outrage and stupefaction. 'Nat—'

'I moved him, but he was so badly hurt. Did I kill him? Tell me he didn't die because I moved him?' She turned her blank expression towards Jude and that fluttering gesture of desolation ghosted once more in front of her body.

Jude shook his head. He didn't need a medical report to tell him Len's injuries had been so severe they'd have been almost instantly fatal. Nevertheless, he struggled to suppress a sigh of irritation as he flipped open his notebook. 'I don't think there was anything anyone could do for him.' He paused. 'Can you try to talk me through what happened?'

'Of course.' She paused.

Claud slid a cup of coffee on the table at Jude's elbow, regardless of the fact that he'd turned the offer down. 'I'll step outside.'

'No. Don't go!'

Jude sighed, but nodded his acceptance and Claud sat down next to his wife, taking her hand. Her fingers were bony. Jude hadn't noticed before how thin she was, because her shirt was too big and her jogging pants baggy, but as she sat so still the fabric settled over her body and drew attention to the sharpness of her shoulders and her collarbones. Too thin, he said to himself, unable to stop himself contrasting her unfavourably with Ashleigh O'Halloran's strikingly different form.

'You were out for a run?' he prompted. Now he had Ashleigh in his mind he might at least try and work out how she wound witnesses so completely around her little finger, but all he could see when he reviewed her interview techniques was that she somehow managed to look them in the eye in a way that promised them her every action was in their best interests.

Natalie got a grip. 'Yes. I'm a marathon runner. No, that's not strictly true. I run a lot because I like running. I've run marathons.' She gave Jude a watery smile that lit her face. 'Claud has a lot of work to do at home at weekends, so I went for a long run. I left around noon, I think. I have a circuit. Culgaith, Skirwith, Langwathby and back along the river.'

Natalie looked so frail that Cumbria's infamous Helm Wind might have blown her away so Jude, a runner by inclination but restricted by time and the demands of his job, was impressed. 'That's a fair way.'

'It's more than a half marathon. I could do it in under two hours, if I wanted to. I never do, though, because I have a routine. I stop at the beginning to do some stretches, as soon as I'm out of sight of the cottage, and I stop again near the end to do the same, just before it's back in sight.'

'Nat has a touch of OCD,' interrupted Claud. 'Hence the importance of routine.'

'Yes. Everyone laughs, but I can't—'

'No-one's laughing at you, sweetheart.'

'I know you aren't Claud, but the chief inspector will think it's odd. And odd is suspicious. Isn't it?' She looked at him, in a gesture of appeal. 'It's why I had to put my clothes in the washing machine, even though your policewoman said I shouldn't. Claud said we should do as she said. It's not his fault. But I couldn't bear the thought of that poor man's blood in the house.'

Claud sat back and gave Jude an extravagant shrug, then turned to Natalie, soothing her as if she was a child. 'Tell the chief inspector about your run.'

Obediently, she turned back to Jude, like a child repeating a lesson. 'I ran as normal. I stopped where the path goes under the A66, for ten minutes.'

'Also as normal?'

'Yes, ten minutes to the second. I did some stretches and some breathing exercises, and then I set off for the last part. I ran along the river to the end of the lane... I'm not sure exactly when. There was a car parked. A white one.' She stopped, gathered her thoughts, carried on. 'The door was open but I couldn't see anyone in the car. I thought that was odd.' She took her hand from Claud's and spread her fingers out on her lap. 'So I stopped. The bank is crumbling just beyond there and not safe, or I would have gone that way. But I had to go down the lane to get home. I was a little nervous.'

'What made you so nervous, Mrs Blackwell?'

She threw her husband an anguished glance, and he came to her rescue. 'Nat suffers from anxiety, Chief Inspector. Don't judge her by everyone else's standards.'

Jude lifted an eyebrow. 'I was just asking.'

'Anything unusual bothers me,' she went on, in a bright, forced tone. 'I need routine. If there was any threat to me—'

'There was no threat, Nat.' Claude squeezed her hand.

'I see that now. But there was in my mind. When I'd got to Langwathby I realised I didn't have my phone and that put me on edge. I was sure something terrible was going to happen so when I saw the car everything felt wrong. I thought about running past it and breaking for home, and I was going to do that. But then I saw the man.' She licked her lips.

Claud placed an arm around her shoulder. 'It's okay, Nat. We're here. But you have to tell the police what you saw.'

'I don't remember exactly. I had a panic attack. I don't know how long I was there. Everything went black and time stopped. I must have shut my eyes. I knew I had to concentrate on my breathing. I closed my eyes and I breathed, but I don't know for how long.' Her breathing lengthened in the present, as she spoke of it in the past.

'When you opened your eyes, what did you see?'

'I was kneeling down next to him. I touched him and the blood was pumping, so I knew he was alive, and I just held on to him. I couldn't bear the thought that he'd die, but he did. I had blood all over me. I stood up and looked about but I didn't see anyone. I screamed.' She turned to her husband in mute appeal.

'Can you be sure there was no-one else there?'

'Oh God. Do you think they were hiding?' If possible, she grew even paler. 'No. I don't remember looking for anything, really. I just looked round and I looked at the body.'

If Tammy was correct, the attacker had probably arrived and left by car. The lane was a dead end, connected to Rainbow Cottage and Temple Sowerby only by the track through the field that he'd taken to reach them. The only alternative was across the open fields, or on foot via the track. 'Did you see any other vehicle?'

She shook her head.

'Was there anyone else on the path?'

'No.' It was Claud, this time. 'I was looking out for Nat, because she was a little later than I was expecting. You can see where it happened from the window. I saw the white car but I didn't see another, though it could have left before I started looking. But if anyone had come past on the track I would have seen them.'

'And I didn't have my phone,' said Natalie, like a child repeating a lesson. 'So I ran home and told Claud and he called the police.'

'What time was that?' Jude looked to Claud.

'Just after two.'

Jude's eye was drawn to the thick rubber bracelet on Natalie's fragile wrist. 'Your running route will be on your fitness tracker, I take it?'

'Yes.' She looked alarmed. 'Surely you don't think I—?'

'No.' Jude turned away from the look of outrage that Claud directed at him. 'The injuries were very recent. When you found the body it can't have been long since he was attacked. If we can pin down exactly what time you found him, then that narrows the window for the time of the murder. That's all.'

'Oh, of course. I won't have to give you the tracker, though? I'm a bit obsessive about it.' Her wide, pale eyes regarded him with a touch of concern. 'It's my anxiety. I like routine.'

'We can get you another tracker, sweetheart.' Claud's tone oozed endless patience

'But Claud, then I wouldn't be able to tally up and—'

'You can download the data, I imagine?' In fascination, Jude observed the signs of Natalie's

28

anxiety, watched her fingers tapping relentlessly on the black rubber strap, the wrinkling of her brow, the snatched glances at Claud as if to reassure herself that he'd help her.

'Yes.' The news delighted her, and she relaxed. 'It'll tell you where I was and when. It'll tell you how long I stopped for, and where. You'll know everything, won't you? That'll help.'

'Yes, that's a great help.' Aware that he had a dozen other things to deal with before the opening phase of the investigation was complete, Jude set his half-finished cup of coffee down on the table, closed his notebook and clipped his pen into the inside pocket of his jacket. 'Thanks again for your time. I know how distressing it must have been. I'll get this typed up and send someone back with it for you to sign.'

'Thank you.' Natalie stood, with what seemed to be characteristic poise, and Claud bounced to his feet in an altogether more pugnacious manner.

'Will you be all right?' Jude shot a look out through the window. It was impossible to miss the frantic activity that was taking place in the lane.

'It's fine.' Claud guided him out of the door. 'Nat, why don't you run off and have a lie down, now. You'll feel better after that.' Then he leaned in towards Jude, sharing a confidence. 'She can get a bit frail sometimes, but it's nothing serious. Just highly strung. But nothing I can't handle.'

29

'If you think of anything else, let me know.' Jude had intended to address himself to Natalie, but she'd already ghosted her way off through the house so he was left to deal with Claud, who seemed accustomed to dealing as his wife's gatekeeper. 'Here's my card. You can call me at any time.'

Claud took the card, looked at it, turned it over in his fingers and laid it on the hall table. 'Yes, of course. Thanks for being so understanding with Nat. And good luck with your search.'

As if he was looking for a long-lost relative, Jude thought as he stepped out into the lane, not a vicious killer who'd almost certainly disappeared into the anonymous traffic of the A66 and could by now have made it south to the spaghetti of the urban motorway network or east to the M1. He took a long look at the line of cars and lorries building up along the main road.

Or the the killer could have gone as little as a few hundred yards, to hide in plain sight.

Chapter 2

Monday morning. Anything but fresh from a holiday that had overrun into a cancelled flight, a sleepless night at the airport in Dubai and an eventual arrival at Manchester airport in the small hours of the morning, Ashleigh O'Halloran staggered into the police headquarters in Penrith on the back of a monumental misjudgement. Jet lag was a brute at the best of times, bestowing all the privations of a hangover with none of the fun that might have preceded it. She should have called in with an explanation and come in after lunch, with a few hours' sleep to see her through. She could have made up the time later and Jude would have understood.

He'd have understood; but because he was her partner she daren't put him in that position. Another boss might reasonably have been less sympathetic than Jude always was but she couldn't afford any accusations that he might be treating her favourably. They'd be unjust, because his attitude to her in the workplace was so strait-laced compared to the way he behaved outside it that it was almost schizophrenic, but so it was.

She yawned as she signed in at reception. Ten minutes early, just enough time to track down the strongest shot of caffeine in the building. Turning towards the canteen where she normally turned straight to the office, she ran straight into her past and her present lovers, deep in conversation outside it.

'Jesus!' It was an uncharacteristic loss of composure. Both surprised and amused Jude lifted an eyebrow at her, and Detective Superintendent Faye Scanlon, who she'd last seen in her previous job in another force, stopped in the middle of what she'd been saying and lasered her former girlfriend with a look that would have shrivelled a daisy.

'Ashleigh.' Utterly unaware of the complicated relationship in which he was, by default, now involved, Jude stepped aside to let her join the conversation. 'Did you have a good holiday?'

The confusion over flights had been so all-consuming she hadn't texted him with every twist and turn in her convoluted journey. Despite her confusion, she struggled to keep back a smile. He could seem stiff and austere to the outsider but those close to him knew better — and these days no-one was closer to Jude than Ashleigh herself. 'The holiday was fine. It was the travelling that was grim. Sorry I didn't call in. I've only just got back from the airport, and I haven't slept for two days, but I made it.'

'Your dedication does you credit.' Faye, her look designed to chill in bottle-green skirt suit, crisp mint-coloured shirt and with a necklace of beaten copper solid as a breastplate, scowled at her, took off her glasses and turned them over in her fingers. Gimlet-sharp grey eyes, the same colour as Jude's but fifteen degrees colder, looked Ashleigh up and down and denied any acquaintance, but Ashleigh could read the message in her eyes. *What the hell are you doing here?* 'Nevertheless, I can't help thinking you might have been better off staying at home and making sure you were fit to work.'

It had been a mistake ever getting into bed with Faye Scanlon. Sufficiently self-aware to understand that for her it had been an act of self-destruction committed in the death throes of her marriage, Ashleigh had no idea what had possessed Faye. The older woman's marriage and career had been outwardly stable and yet she'd risked — and quickly regretted — an adulterous office affair.

And now here she was, a new arrival on Ashleigh's turf, looking as confident as if she'd been there for years. Too tired to grasp the implications, Ashleigh took the cowardly option and turned instead to Jude. 'I knew you'd be busy so I thought I'd better get in.'

'We can certainly use you today.' He softened his usual sardonic expression with a smile that she had to fight not to return. The last thing she needed was Faye Scanlon jumping to conclusions, worst of all the right ones.

To avoid temptation, she looked beyond the sharp edge of his jaw to a health and safety notice on the wall behind him. 'Has something happened?'

'You don't watch the local news?' Faye carped at her from the side lines.

'Of course, but I haven't had a chance.'

'There was a particularly nasty homicide in Temple Sowerby yesterday,' Jude said, soothing her as if she were a probationer. 'We'll get to that soon enough. In the meantime, let me introduce you. This is our new Super, Faye Scanlon. Faye, this is DS Ashleigh O'Halloran.'

Ashleigh waited for Faye to acknowledge that they knew one another but Faye, still twirling her glasses in irritation, passed up the opportunity for a second time in a minute, allowing her nothing more than the briefest of nods before flicking Ashleigh's questioning look aside it the briefest shake of her chestnut head.

So that was how it was going to be. 'Lovely to meet you, Ma'am.' Shuffling backwards, Ashleigh tried to cover her confusion but Jude would have spotted there was something amiss. If he asked her in public she'd blame it on jet lag and explain later. Faye needn't think she had any control over Ashleigh's past, no matter how strongly she might choose to exert it over her own.

'It's a pleasure, Ashleigh.' A fractional pause. 'You'd better call me Faye. I don't think we need to follow any unnecessary formalities in the office.'

At least familiarity wouldn't trip her up. Ashleigh nodded in reply, planning her getaway. 'Jude.

I'll just get a coffee and head up to the office. Fill myself in on the details. Okay?'

'I'll come along with you. I was heading that way myself.'

'I'll see you later. Good to meet you.' Faye's voice was already drifting from down the corridor.

Ashleigh's jet lag headache intensified. A boiling, bubbling tension reared up inside her, stretching her composure, already worn thin by her travels, to its limits. She flung open the door to the canteen more sharply than she'd intended, and allowed Jude in first. She'd have to tell him, but this was neither the time nor the place, and in any case discretion won out. By whatever twist of fate Faye was now Jude's boss as well as hers. 'Nobody told me we were getting a new Superintendent.'

'There was an announcement about it just after you went off. Thought you might have come across her, but no?'

She avoided the question. 'And she was in post in three weeks? That's pretty sharp.'

'If she's the right person and was available to start immediately, why not? The post had to be filled.' He led the way up to the counter. 'Two coffees,' he said to the girl on duty. 'You'd better make it a triple espresso for Ashleigh. She's had a rough weekend.'

'You're mighty cheerful today,' the girl said, busying herself with the machine. 'You've lost that sultry snarl. Shame. Oh, I probably shouldn't say that, should I, or someone will have me for harassment? That would never do. Or maybe it would — early retirement and two months' gardening leave on full pay. Can I harass you a bit more?'

'Harass away.' Cheerfully, Jude pushed one of the coffees to Ashleigh and settled up. 'It doesn't bother me.'

He and the girl behind the counter might think it was funny, and Ashleigh herself had joked about the Faye's predecessor and his unfortunate and ultimately career-ending attitude to his younger female staff, but that was before she'd realised who his replacement was. She stole a sip at the coffee while Jude gathered up his change, waiting for the buzz of caffeine to jolt her back into the real world. There would be plenty of time later to formulate a strategy to deal with Faye, and in the meantime the best tactic was silence. 'Okay. Let's get to work.'

'Did you enjoy Sri Lanka?' He held the door open for her and fell into step beside her as they made their way back along the corridor.

'Apart from that nightmare of a journey, yes.'

He looked at her. 'The new Super might be right. Maybe you should go home and catch up on some sleep.'

'I'm not going to lie. I'm knackered. But if we're busy—'

'I did a full briefing first thing and everyone's off doing their stuff. Shame you missed that, but I'm about to sit down with Doddsy and Chris. I'd like you there too. Sit in on that, then go home and get some sleep. I'd planned on having you out supervising the house-to-house inquiries, but you can pick that up tomorrow.'

'Maybe I will.' Aircraft cabins sucked you dry, aircraft seats cramped your limbs, airport lounges denied you your last hope of sleep. 'I'm feeling rough.'

'You're looking great.' He lowered his voice, in case anyone should overhear the compliment. 'I've missed you.'

'You, too.'

'Next time you go away for three weeks, take me with you.' He stepped ahead of her, opened a door. 'We're in here. Morning everyone. Look who I found wandering about in the corridor.'

Three faces looked up at her — Doddsy with his usual thoughtful nod, the newly-promoted sergeant Chris Marshall, and Tammy Garner, the CSI. Tammy was normally the most placid, but today her greeting was cursory and she sat turned half away from the table.

'The sun suits you, Ash.' Chris Marshall gave her an enthusiastic thumbs up. 'You're looking great. Here. Have a seat.'

She pulled up a chair next to him. The table sat beneath a whiteboard adorned with the grim collage of information that accumulated in the wake of a homicide, and she gave it a quick look. A nasty one. Great. Opposite her, Tammy scowled when Jude sat down, then remembered herself and uncapped her pen, scrawling her name and the date on a sheet of paper. 'Sri Lanka, did someone say you were? It's on my bucket list.'

'Yes. We were there for three weeks. Amazing place.'

'That's enough chat.' Jude set his coffee down on the table and stood up again in front of the whiteboard. 'I'll just run over the background to bring Ashleigh up to speed.'

'If you don't mind, Jude, I'll say my piece first. I've a dozen other things to do and I don't have the time to go over old ground. It's not as if we didn't cover this in the 7.30 briefing.' Tammy drew a savage line under the heading *Second Team Meeting*.

Ashleigh, who noticed everything even though today she was too exhausted to pick up on its significance, saw Jude lift an eyebrow and direct the swiftest, most discreet glance towards Doddsy before passing on. Small group sessions with his smartest, most complementary thinkers were his favoured method of focussing on an issue once an investigation was in full swing. Tammy knew that. 'Yes. Of course. But I'd like to bring Ashleigh up to speed first.'

Tammy was displeased, or so Ashleigh thought, but Jude ignored her, rattling off the briefest outline of what had happened the previous day. As he spoke,

Ashleigh jotted down the details of Len Pierce and Natalie Blackwell's macabre encounter in the bright March afternoon.

'So,' Doddsy said, with a suppressed sigh as Jude concluded his summary and sat down, as if he knew he'd get no joy from the question he was about to ask. 'What did you make of it, Tammy?'

She ignored both him and Jude, turning her attention to Ashleigh instead. 'You probably don't know the place. It's a farm track off the A66, on the right hand side, just after the turnoff for Temple Sowerby.' She roughed out a rapid pencil sketch of the scene. 'It's a dead end. It goes down to some ruined farm buildings and there's a riverside footpath cutting across the end of it, which cuts through a field to the Blackwells' cottage. That's where Natalie was running. You'd expect there to be very little traffic other than the occasional farm vehicle, but that doesn't seem to be the case. There are plenty of tyre tracks there.'

'People turn their cars there if there's a queue on the road.' Jude looked up at the map on the board. 'I've done that myself before now. But I've never gone all the way to the end of the lane.'

Doddsy rubbed his chin. 'It's well known locally as a bit of a lover's lane. But more for…shall we say casual encounters.'

'Dogging?' Chris had none of Doddsy's slightly old-fashioned restraint.

'That would explain a lot.' Tammy sniffed. 'I did wonder. There are plenty of tracks, and we got some good readings. I'll send you a list of everything we retrieved but the best ones are for what look like the two most likely. They're the only fresh ones. One belongs to the Volkswagen car recovered at the scene.'

'Owned by Len Pierce.' Jude nodded towards Ashleigh.

'I've had someone run the second through the databases. The best match I can come up with suggests a passenger vehicle that arrived after the VW and parked ahead of it in the lane. There was no room for the two to pass. You might speculate about whether this was done to prevent the VW driving away.' She didn't look towards Jude as she spoke, keeping her head down, pushing her glasses up her nose as she stared at her notes. 'The tyres were worn more on the left than on the right.' She withdrew some printed images from a folder and spread them out in front of her on the table, highlighting particular points as she spoke. Succumbing to a sudden wave of tiredness, Ashleigh lost concentration as she rattled though them.

'We'll have someone for something when we trace the car.' Chris picked up one of them and scrutinised it carefully. He was the only one of the team not in some way subdued, but he never was. There was something in his puppyish enthusiasm that reminded her of her ex-husband, both appealing and a warning. 'Those nearside tyres are illegal. I've picked up enough people for that in my time.'

'This is murder,' said Tammy, with unusual irritation in her voice, 'not a traffic cops' tea party.'

'Yeah, but you know what happened with Al Capone. It's the little things that get these guys.'

'The rear tyre tracks were more heavily imprinted than the front ones.' Tammy shook off his good-humoured enthusiasm and carried on.

'As if someone had sat in the back while it was stationary?' Still a relative newcomer to the Eden Valley, Ashleigh was unfamiliar with the location. Staring at the annotated Ordnance Survey map Chris had pinned up on the whiteboard, she tried to envisage the scene, matching the map to the photographs, the distant houses to the village. If she'd read the map right it was a clever place for a murder, with no clear line of sight to any dwelling save the bungalow the Blackwells occupied, on the edge of the village.

'Yes. I can't put a time to it. The ground was muddy. I imagine when you get the results of the PM it'll tell you how long the man took to die and when he might have been attacked. And there are footprints. Man's size ten, brogues by the look of it.' Today, she was spectacularly brisk.

'The sort that Len was wearing?' Ashleigh nodded down to one of the photographs in which Len's smartly-shod foot was clearly visible.

'Yes. Slightly worn at the heel. I'll email pictures and full details to you.'

'That's a good start.' Jude rattled his pen on the desk. 'Thanks, Tammy. Good stuff.'

'Please don't patronise me, Jude. I'm doing my job as best I can.'

There was a short silence, in which Doddsy suppressed yet another sigh and Chris looked startled. Ashleigh, who knew and liked Tammy, tested her bad temper with a smile but the investigator's dogged determination not to respond was too much for her.

'I'm sorry,' Jude said, in a tone of complete neutrality. 'Carry on.'

'There was a cigarette end on the ground near the car. There was blood beside the car, and on the grass. Someone had knelt down beside the body, then run onto the lane. The footsteps petered out towards the track.'

'That would be Natalie Blackwell. She told us she held him when he died and then ran home.'

'That follows. I take it you've sent her clothes off for analysis?'

'No.' Jude set his pen down again. 'By the time I went to speak to her she'd already showered and changed and her clothes were in the washing machine.'

'No-one thought to tell her about that?' Tammy finally looked at Jude, her frustration apparent. 'No-one thought to tell her that it might be evidence? Surely you know how important—'

'Thank you, Tammy.' There was an edge to Jude's tone. 'I think I know how to do my job, too.'

'Of course she'd want to get out of her clothes if they were covered in blood.' Ashleigh frowned, trying to imagine what Natalie Blackwell must have thought, how she must have felt. 'But you'd think they'd have known we'd need any evidence from the crime scene. And she should have been told.'

'The PC must have made a mistake.' Chris rushed in to try and help. 'Jesus, but that's pretty basic.'

'There was no mistake. The Blackwells were told,' said Jude. 'But Mrs B was in a state of shock.'

It was normal enough, maybe, if someone didn't understand the significance, but Ashleigh could see that Jude had marked an asterisk beside the word *clothing* on his pad. 'Don't you think that's a bit odd?'

'She suffers from OCD and anxiety.' He'd folded his lips together as if he was reluctant to criticise. 'She'd taken some kind of medication by the time I spoke to her. I think we can conclude her actions weren't entirely rational.'

'Hers, maybe. But what about her husband? If she went for a shower he could surely have taken them.'

'Indeed.' Jude wrote *CB* next to the word *clothing* and underlined it.

'Never mind. We don't have them. We can't learn anything from them.' Tammy resumed her narrative. 'The murder weapon wasn't at the scene and your people still haven't found it.'

'They're still looking.' Jude's patience with Tammy's briskness was clearly running thin and Ashleigh couldn't blame him. He shouldn't have to defend what was normal procedure to someone who was looking to pick a fight. 'It's possible the killer, whoever he or she was, took it with them.'

'Right. The car's currently in the garage being checked over but I didn't see anything unusual about it. And that's really about as much as I can tell you.' Tammy was already pushing her chair back. 'If there's anything more you need, you can ask one of the team. I'm out and about today so I won't be answering the phone. I'll have someone get back to you once we've got the results from the garage and the lab.' She stood up, scowled at the whiteboard, and stalked out, leaving the door to bang shut behind her.

'Not answering the phone?' Chris stared after her in puzzlement. 'Was it something we said?'

'Who knows?' Jude picked up the photos Tammy had left and pinned them up on the board next to those already there. Yellow markers showed the position of blood, the body, the cigarette end.

'Let's pull together a bit more information. Chris. What do we know about Len Pierce?'

While Chris opened up a document on his iPad, Ashleigh took another long swig of her coffee. It might be enough to get her through the meeting but Jude — and Faye — was right. Coming to the office was a misjudgement which clearly proved the point: she shouldn't be at work. Her eyelids drooped. Stifling a yawn, she tried to catch up with what Chris was telling them.

'…well-known locally,' he was saying. 'He part-owns a cafe on Boroughgate in Appleby. The Cosy Cupcake Cafe. It's been there for twenty years, apparently. Anyone know it?'

'I do. It's a bit kitsch for my taste. Too much chintz and pink knitted tea cosies. But it does a decent chocolate brownie, if you're ever out that way.' Doddsy licked his lips.

'I've been in it a few times, but I don't recognise him.' Jude was staring at the picture, in perplexity. Not knowing things hurt him, almost as much as a personal affront, and Ashleigh, who had been dating him long enough to understand the way his mind went, had to struggle to hide her amusement. 'I've never seen him in the shop. There's always a woman behind the counter.'

'That'll be his sister. Maisie Skinner. She owns it with him. She runs the shop. He does the baking — did, I should say.' Chris flicked up a piece of paper. 'I went to break the news to her yesterday evening and took her to Carlisle to do the formal ID. She's devastated, of course, and didn't really want to talk about it. But from what she did say – and what she didn't – I thought she wasn't really surprised.'

'Oh?' Jude raised an eyebrow.

'Yes. Lenny was openly gay and it's pretty clear she disapproved of him. She said he'd never had a steady partner but tended to go in for more casual liaisons.'

'Did he tell her about them?' Ashleigh yawned. 'Or is she just assuming things?'

'No, she said he never shared his business with anyone. She said she'd warned him off what she called *that kind of behaviour* but he just laughed.'

'I think I'll go down and have a chat with her myself,' Jude said. 'When we get the results back from the lab we might have a clue who he was meeting or why. But it sounds to me as though she'll have a view.'

A lover or a would-be lover, even a spurned lover. A business associate, a stranger or a friend. Len Pierce could have arranged to meet anyone on that lane. His sexuality was only the starting point for the investigation. 'No leads?'

'Not yet. He had a Facebook account but he didn't post very much.'

'Only pictures of cake, as far as I can see.' Jude licked his lips as though the thought made him hungry.

'He wasn't on any other social media,' Chris continued. 'At least, not under his own name. He may have had other accounts. We've got his laptop and his phone and the tech guys are going to have a look at those. It'll be interesting to see what comes up. His sister certainly wasn't aware that he was involved in the local gay community.'

'There's no need for stereotyping. Loads of gay people don't play a part in the gay community.' Doddsy's normal sweet nature showed the slightest signs of strain. 'Most of us are happy to be part of the same community as everyone else.'

'We can't assume he was promiscuous just because he was gay.' Ashleigh turned a reproachful eye on Chris, why ought to know better.

'I'm not, but his sister does, and that's our starting point. That bit about the gay community was her phrase, not mine.' Chris's perpetual smile turned away any dissonance. 'She's the certain generation — his older sister, I'd say by a good ten years, and probably not far off retirement age. Anyway, before she dissolved into tears and couldn't tell me any more she did say she'd always told him that kind of thing — her phrase again, Doddsy, not mine — would get him into trouble.'

For no real reason Ashleigh thought of Faye, and the affair of which they'd both been ashamed and tried to conceal. She had no idea of Faye's motivations but her own had been rooted in a fear of her own vulnerability. There were many reasons for being furtive. 'It does look as if he was meeting someone. Suit. Neatly ironed shirt. Shiny shoes.' The photographs of Len Pierce, sprawled in the mud, were distressing in their sense of optimism. 'Dressed to impress, I'd say.'

'Yes.' Jude scribbled a frowning face and a question mark side by side on his pad. 'It's possible. Meeting up with someone seems the obvious reason for him to be where he was, but it doesn't necessarily give us a motive. And it doesn't follow that his killer was the person he met.'

'Could it have been robbery?' Ashleigh asked.

'No. His wallet was in his jacket pocket. Cards and cash.'

'And what do we know about the woman who found him?' Ashleigh looked down at the notes she'd been making as the conversation continued. The clue to Len's murder would be in his personal life. It always was.

'Natalie Blackwell. She lives in the cottage on the other side of the field.' Briefly, Jude ran through a description of the circumstances in which Len Pierce had been found. 'She claims to have seen nothing and nobody. The CSI team haven't turned up any evidence that anyone had tried the riverside path. It collapsed into the river a few weeks back, and it's closed. We know from the information on Mrs Blackwell's fitness tracker that she did go on a run, and we know where it was and when. All as she said.'

Ashleigh looked at the whiteboard. Someone had already marked up Natalie's route, with its times, on an OS map, a winding line looping back on itself and marked with crosses near either end where she'd stopped to stretch off.

'What do you make of her?' Doddsy twirled his pen between his fingers and addressed himself to Jude. 'And her husband, of course.'

'Did you say you knew him?'

'I know of him. He's a diversity campaigner. He's been touting an idea for a Rainbow Festival around the local churches. We're to get together and encourage LGBTQI folk to join in and feel welcome. Us Christian folk being all so straight and narrow-minded.' He rolled his eyes.

Ashleigh struggled not to laugh. Doddsy, ploughing his own quiet furrow, quietly minding his own business and never looking for attention, was the obvious candidate for a congregation to put forward as representative of their tolerance. She could see from the twist of his lips that whatever he thought of the concept, he'd want to keep clear of the execution.

She could sympathise with that. The main thing she'd learned from her adventure with Faye Scanlon wasn't the obvious, that attraction to the same sex was as normal and natural as it was to the opposite one. It was your own insecurities that were damaging. 'How did it go?'

'As you'd expect. Half of the congregation jumping on the rainbow bandwagon and the other half quoting Leviticus.'

'And which side did you come down on?' Jude joked.

'I've never been one for hellfire and damnation. And I'm not sure about Blackwell. He means well enough, but I don't think he understands his audience.'

'He's a natural campaigner. Has been all his life.' Jude checked his notes. 'For just about any cause under the sun. Anti-Zionism when he was a student, then worked for a disability rights charity, then moved into gay rights. I presume that's why they've renamed the house. It used to be called Neville Cottage.' He frowned a little, at a puzzle he couldn't quite unravel.

'He runs his own company taking equality training into the workplace.' Chris tossed a leaflet onto the table and Ashleigh picked it up and skimmed it. *Refreshing your knowledge of current legislation…exceeding legal requirements to promote positive viewpoints and a productive and healthy workforce.* 'He's done some work for the NHS and the Council, among others, and he's in advanced talks to do the same for us. So we can look forward to seeing how he reads his audience first hand.'

Ashleigh thought of Faye's predecessor, the unlamented Detective Superintendent Groves, and her lips twitched. 'This would never have happened three months ago.'

'No harm to them.' Doddsy said, shaking his head, 'but if I tell them I'm gay do you think I can be excused and just get on with my work in peace?'

Jude waved the general laughter aside. 'Let's move on. There's something unconventional about the Blackwells. Of the two of them, she interests me more. She's had half a dozen different careers, I'm told, and hasn't stuck to any one of them. Classically unsatisfiable, I'd say.'

'Didn't you say she has anxiety issues?' Ashleigh sighed. 'No wonder she can't settle to anything. Poor woman. Finding Len must have been a hell of a shock.'

'The PC who was first on the scene was genuinely worried about her, but by the time I got to her she was totally composed. I thought she must have taken some kind of medication. Her husband was looking after her and she seemed to have complete trust in him. Nearly had a meltdown when he tried to leave the room. She was looking to him after every question I asked.'

'I think I'd find that rather freaky.' Bitter experience, learned in a failed marriage to a charming but controlling man, had taught Ashleigh that devotion too often worked only one way.

'I didn't think so. It wasn't as if she was looking to him for the answers. More as if to make sure he was still there.' Jude sighed and sat back, glancing down at his empty coffee cup. 'Next steps. We'll get the PM results in later on today with luck, and we'll put out an appeal for witnesses. Chris, as usual I'd like you to get digging. I want to know everything there is to know about Len Pierce and his friends and acquaintances. I need more background checks on the Blackwells. We'll reconvene tomorrow after the early briefing and you can talk me through what you've got.'

The meeting dissolved. Ashleigh shuffled her notes into some sort of order and failed to stifle a yawn. Chris and Doddsy had gone. 'Are you sure you don't need me to do anything?'

'Yes, but I need you to do it when you're awake. I've got someone else on the door-to-door inquiries for today. You can pick that up tomorrow.' Jude checked his watch. 'I need to pop up and have a chat with the new boss just now, but I'll get down to Appleby afterwards.' He hesitated. 'If you've caught up on your sleep by this evening, why not pop round to my place? I can rustle you up a curry. It won't be as hot as your average Sri Lankan one, but it'll be edible.'

She smiled at him, reached out and touched his sleeve. 'I'll see you this evening then.' And she picked up her coat and slipped it on, wondering just how she'd manage to square the circle of working with a boss who was her lover and whose boss, in turn, was her former lover, and how long it would be before each of them found out about the other.

Chapter 3

Watching Ashleigh disappear down the corridor, Jude allowed himself a moment of appreciation and a smile to go with it. It was more than three years since the woman he'd been so sure he'd marry had got tired of coming second to his job and picked out an excuse to throw him over, and it had taken him longer than he'd expected to get over her. Even now his feelings for Becca Reid lingered, because the blunt truth was that she still attracted him, and her slavish devotion to everyone else's goodwill and her redoubtable community spirit conspired to throw her in his path. With Ashleigh out of the way for three weeks, he'd run out of excuses not to go down to the village where Becca lived in the cottage opposite his mother. Whenever he came or went he'd risked running across his former lover's scathing, scornful stare.

In those three weeks he'd missed Ashleigh, and it unsettled him. Caring too much for other people inevitably brought more pain than caring too little. Caring about his younger brother, Mikey, had brought about the final split with Becca when she disagreed with how he'd dealt with Mikey's teenage experimentation with drugs. He had no regrets over that, he reminded himself as optimism asserted itself. Caring was positive, too. The very reason he was in the police was that he cared.

He allowed himself a wry smile. Becca cared about Mikey, too, recognising the pressure that David Satterthwaite's absence had placed upon Jude himself to be a substitute father, and this fundamental difference of opinion about how he handled it had been symptomatic of deeper problems in their relationship. When he thought of Becca it still hurt, but he'd learned the lesson. It was too late to go back and try again even if he wasn't too proud to do so, and it was the right time to learn from the experience, build a new relationship and get the balance right. With that thought, he consigned his personal life to the back of his mind and set off to begin building a relationship of an entirely different kind — a professional relationship with his new boss.

Faye Scanlon had left the door to her office wedged open. That looked like a statement of intent, a notice of accessibility. For form's sake he tapped on it, but she was already looking up from where she sat behind her desk and motioning him in. 'Come on in, Jude, and have a seat. Shut the door behind you, would you?'

He did so, trying to judge how deep her apparent friendliness ran, how much it was a mask for something else. It hadn't escaped him that she'd been mightily put out when Ashleigh had appeared in the canteen that morning.

'Obviously you're busy with the Pierce case, but it's important that we talk. I'm making a point of having a chat with all of my inspectors and chief inspectors. I want to be sure we understand one another.'

He nodded. Faye's predecessor had been stiffly formal with colleagues he didn't like but erred too far on the side of unwelcome informality with some — mainly younger and exclusively female. It was only to be expected that there would be some sort of correction. Sitting behind her desk, with ringless fingers clasped in front of her as she matched his quizzical gaze, Faye showed every sign of being the antidote to the recent past.

'I didn't know Detective Superintendent Groves,' she went on, taking off her glasses and twirling them between her fingers as he pulled up a chair, 'although I understand that, on his own admission, he was…shall we say… of a different generation.'

'I know what you mean.' It wasn't just generational sexism. Groves had always had favourites, and anyone who didn't fit his profile of the right sort of policeman struggled to achieve promotion. His disapproval had held them back, the grit in the machinery of advancement that should otherwise have run smoothly. To be a favourite you didn't have to like him, or be liked by him – merely to have a face that fitted. Young women of childbearing age somehow never won promotion under Groves and Doddsy had remained at his level for 15 years, during which Jude had made a meteoric rise to outrank him.

'I might as well be blunt with you, Jude.' In an over-deliberate pause, she looked out of the window behind him towards the town. 'There are a number of officers here who've been promoted because of what they were rather than on the basis of their skills and capabilities. While we can't undo those mistakes, we won't repeat them. When I was appointed, it was on the basis that my job would involve a clear focus on redressing the imbalance which has built up within this force. It's a strategic decision taken at a very senior level and I'm playing a small part in the process. Things are going to change.'

She looked at him as if she was expecting a reply, but when he opened his mouth to speak she cut straight across him. 'One of the proposals I put forward at my interview to correct this issue was to introduce a series of workshops on equality and diversity for all officers, as a matter of urgency. I'm glad to say the idea was well received and implementation began even before I arrived. Those workshops will begin this week.'

'An excellent idea.' A smile flitted across his lips as he thought of Doddsy's pained tolerance of the Rainbow Festival.

'Thank you.' His smile must have irritated her. She scowled in response. 'I can speak frankly to you. You're young to be a DCI.' An upheld hand stopped his reply. 'I'm not questioning your competence. Merely saying that some of your junior colleagues might be equally competent and vastly more experienced.'

She meant Doddsy. Jude stayed silent.

'I want you to be aware that the system has previously worked in your favour and won't do so in the future. I'll be honest with you. I've heard that you can be quite a disruptive figure, and I'm assuming I'll get your full and unquestioning support.'

'Of course.' Rapidly, Jude reviewed his own behaviour and found himself not guilty of any irregularity. He'd divided his friends and family throughout his time in the police, and if he was honest with himself he was probably enough of a control freak within his job to alienate people who didn't like to work the way he did. It was why he relied so closely on a small group of officers and broke the traditional roles of rank where he felt it was beneficial. But disruptive?

It was a debate for the future. Rather than pursue it and make an immediate enemy of his new boss, he changed tack. 'And the workshops?'

'There will be a range of them, beginning this week. We'll be using a local provider who tailors courses for public and private bodies.'

'Right.'

Faye's gaze, already keen, perceptibly sharpened. 'You seem uncomfortable with that.'

If she thought she'd picked up some resentment in his attitude she was right. He couldn't challenge her over the fact that he'd benefited disproportionately from being the right sort of person in Groves' eyes, but his irritation was more akin to Doddsy's. No matter how worthy, desirable or even necessary the workshops might be, he could ill afford a day or a half day, or even a couple of hours, out of his busy schedule in order to learn how to treat his colleagues with the respect he already accorded them. And there was something else. 'Would this local provider be Claud Blackwell?'

'Do you have a problem with him? He's locally very well known and highly regarded.'

'No. But it's interesting his name has come up. It was his wife who found the body off the A66 yesterday afternoon.'

Faye's eyes narrowed, and she picked at her necklace. 'Is he a suspect?'

No,' said Jude, after a moment's consideration. 'We haven't ruled him out yet, but the investigation isn't even a day old. He was at home when his wife found the man, still alive. I've no reason at all to think it might be him.'

'Then there's no reason to change our plans.' She nodded towards him, graciously. 'That's all just now. But I'll be very hands on, so you can expect me to be very much around and about.'

*

'Gracie, Gracie, Gracie,' breathed Giles's voice into the phone. 'What the hell am I going to do?'

Out in the car park of the Penrith Hospital, Gracie Pepper turned her back on the colleague who was waving in her direction, pretending she hadn't seen. 'Giles.'

'But what am I going to do?' he wailed.

She crammed the phone between her shoulder and her ear and scrabbled in her bag for cigarettes and a lighter. The spring wind played up, trailing a strand of long copper-coloured hair across her mouth as she tried to take a drag of the first cigarette. 'Giles.' She fought the wind and won, got a lungful of nicotine and retrieved the phone before she could drop it. 'Do you need to talk?'

'Of course I want to talk. We're talking now, aren't we?'

'I can't talk for long. Fag break.'

'You should give up.'

'I didn't want this one, but I saw your message. It was the only way of grabbing a moment's peace to call you.'

The panic she'd sensed in his voice broke into a chuckle. 'I appreciate it. Sorry. I know you're busy. And I know I ought really to talk to Janice because–'

He couldn't possibly talk to Janice. Not about this. Gracie smiled and held the cigarette away from her. 'It's not a problem for me, darling. I'm all yours. Just let me know when.'

'I'll need to check my diary. And I don't want it to look too obvious.'

For such a capable, successful man, Giles was given to surprising bouts of inadequacy. 'Find a time to come and visit your Dad. Meet me at the hospital. And don't get into a state, right? You don't want anyone asking questions.'

'Especially not Janice,' he said, rather mournfully.

She shook her head in amusement. The tip of the cigarette glowed in the wind. 'Whenever suits you. You know I don't have any commitments other than work.'

A pause, in which she almost heard him pull himself together. 'You need to get yourself a man, Gracie my girl.'

'Oh, Giles!' she said, one last time, this time with more than the usual measure of affection. 'Just let me know, okay?'

CHAPTER 4

Very hands on was an ominous phrase, Jude concluded as he drove along the A66 towards Appleby; a veiled threat to him to behave. Whether it was personal, or whether it was a weapon Faye Scanlon was carefully deploying in an attempt to set up her position with regard to her junior officers, remained to be established, something he could easily determine by checking with Doddsy. On the whole he thought not, recognising in Faye someone who was fighting against some insecurity he couldn't identify and she wouldn't reveal.

Taking on a new job was difficult enough. Replacing someone who'd left more than a whiff of scandal behind, armed with a remit to right all the actual and perceived wrongs they had committed or allowed others to commit, was even harder. On that basis, he was inclined to give Faye the benefit of the doubt.

Maisie Skinner, Lenny's older sister, lived in a cottage just below the viaduct, but she must be a woman who believed that life must go on and had insisted on meeting Jude in The Cosy Cupcake Cafe in the village centre. On another occasion Jude might have interpreted that as indicative of lack of regret at a loss and given her motives a second look, but he hadn't got the impression from Chris's account that Maisie and her brother were that close, and plenty of people preferred the protection of routine.

Appleby was going about its Monday business as usual, the idyllic English county town apparently unmoved by the loss of one of its own. He parked on Boroughgate, slipped the parking disc onto the dashboard and got out of the car. The flag of St George fluttered from the church tower and a traffic warden moved from car to car outside the market hall, from which two rows of sandstone buildings scaled the hill like a stairway to heaven.

The Cosy Cupcake Cafe was on the square and he paused outside it to contemplate the menu (*all dishes home-made*). A card in the steamed-up window announced that it was business as usual and inside every seat was full.

The smell of good coffee was first to greet him when he pushed open the door, with the fragrance of an all-day breakfast hot on its heels and a meaty scent — lasagne? — trailing in their wake, ushering him in from the chilly afternoon. Inside the cafe a knot of interested customers clustered around the counter.

Appleby's citizens, seated and standing, turned and froze as one as he came in, as if he'd walked into the wrong Glasgow pub, expecting him. Used to that kind of reaction, frequently in more threatening situations, Jude offered the general population an iron-clad smile and sidled up to the counter. Doddsy had been right about the chintz and the tea cosies, but the wholesome smells of the place made his mouth water and gave him a moment of regret for the petrol-station sandwich he'd snatched on the go as an excuse for lunch. If the home cooking was Len's it must be a fine tribute to him but the cakes on display had a distinctly mass-produced look, a sad stop-gap for something authentic. 'I'm looking for Mrs Skinner.'

The knot of humanity unravelled to reveal a short, solid woman behind the counter, and she emerged to meet him. She was clad in an appropriate amount of black, her mourning leavened by the pinny imprinted with comic ginger cats that was unravelling from around her waist. He put her in her mid fifties, a twinkling and active woman, quick on her feet. Her face had the same shape as her brother's, the same mouth, the same square forehead and something in her eyes — life — gave him a clue as to what Len Pierce might have looked like had he lived beyond Sunday afternoon. 'I'm Maisie Skinner. You're Detective Satterthwaite?'

He flashed his warrant card in confirmation and she looked from it to him and back again as if she mistrusted it until, seeming satisfied, she stepped back. 'Come through the back.' She turned back to her customers. 'You lot can look after yourselves. But make sure you leave the cash on the counter for me. And behave. We've got the law in here.'

Under the keen stares of the onlookers, Jude followed her into the back of the the cafe, through a small area where the paraphernalia of sandwich-making littered a steel-topped unit, and into a tiny office. She closed the door behind him and motioned him towards the only chair. For herself, she pulled a stool from under the desk, removing a sheaf of invoices from it and dropping them on the floor. A shaft of light filtered through a dirty window and onto a desk covered with box files whose labels showed ten years' worth of paperwork. Maisie Skinner's loss looked as if it might be financial as well as personal.

'You want to talk to me about Lenny.' She settled her broad backside precariously on the narrow stool.

'Yes. I imagine you're very upset by the whole business—'

'But you need to talk to me to find whoever killed him. Yes.' Her bottom lip trembled and she folded her hands on the desk like a schoolteacher. 'Poor Lenny. He was such a lovely man. But I did warn him. If you mess with the kind of people he mixed with, this sort of thing is always going to happen. It's like consorting with prostitutes.'

Maisie Skinner was, Jude recognised, one of those people with an old-fashioned view of sexual morality and a clear idea that virtue was the only guaranteed protector. 'I'm not looking for moral judgements, Mrs Skinner.'

'No, you're right.' She surprised him by laughing. 'I might as well be honest with you.

Someone else will tell you what I think if I'm not. I didn't approve of his lifestyle. Not at all. But that didn't mean we didn't get on. We did. Just because he made the wrong choices didn't mean I didn't care.'

Wrong was relative, and Jude didn't bother to challenge her because he was policing to the law not to someone else's prejudices. Anyway, he knew exactly what she meant because he'd come across the exact situation with Mikey, whose idea of harmless fun had nearly led him into very serious trouble. Jude disapproved of his young brother's approach to life just as Maisie Skinner had disapproved of hers, though in a different context. 'When did you last see him?'

'Saturday evening. He came to cash up and take the takings away. We never leave money in here overnight, even in an honest place like this.'

'You own the business jointly?'

'Yes.' She waved a hand at the paperwork and her face creased in perplexity. 'God knows what happens now. It's not the sort of thing you plan for, though maybe we should have.'

'And the shop?'

'It's rented. The business just about washes its face but it'll struggle without our Lenny's baking.' She shook her head. 'Him and me have been in this business nearly thirty years. Now look at it.' She pulled a paper tissue from a box on the desk and dabbed at her eyes. 'Nothing left of him but a freezer full of beef stroganoff and a double chocolate cake that never got finished on Saturday. I don't know how I'll bear to throw it out. We joked about that cake when he came in Saturday to pick up the cash.'

'Was there much? Cash, not cake.'

'Not a huge amount. Three hundred pounds, maybe. So many folk pay contactless these days. When I heard he was dead I did wonder if someone had hit him over the head for it, but your constable said it was all there.'

Len's flat hadn't been broken in to and the cash had been in a brown envelope on the mantelpiece when Chris had gone along to take possession of his laptop. He made a note to check the will. Three hundred pounds in cash wasn't all that Lenny had left and people had been killed for less than a two-bedroomed flat in Appleby. 'Tell me about him. What was he like?'

A pensive expression crossed her face. 'I don't know what I can tell you that'll help. He was just our Lenny. He cooked and baked. It was his hobby as well as his job. He liked a smoke. He had a dog but when the dog died he never replaced it. Devoted to old Fly, he was. But that's all, really.'

'Mr Pierce was gay, is that right?'

She gave him an injured look, as though they were already into terminology she preferred not to use. He could imagine her whispering to her friends that Len was a confirmed bachelor. 'Yes. Always was.

He never told anyone about it, as such, never mentioned it. After our parents passed away he stopped even pretending.'

'So he'd been openly gay for how long?'

'Five years. But you say openly… really. Folk around here know him. They either don't care or don't talk about it. I'm not judging him. It was his life and he knew the risks.'

'The risks?'

'Yes. It's not like he ever settled into a proper relationship. Maybe he was just happy living on his own. I don't know. He never told me he was meeting people, but I guessed he was. People like that always do.'

Jude thought of Doddsy and how he might have rolled his eyes extravagantly at the phrase *people like that*. No doubt Faye Scanlon, with her determination to bring the police into the forefront of the twenty first century, would have pulled Maisie up on it and ended by alienating her. What mattered to him was what Maisie had to tell him and even her prejudices, tinged with affection though they might be, were of interest. 'People like…?'

'You know.' She pursed her lips.

'Did you know for certain he was meeting people?'

'Everybody knew.'

'But not for certain?'

'Not for certain, no. But he'd often get dressed up to go off in his car on a Sunday afternoon. Why do that if you aren't making an effort for someone? And one time last year one of my customers said they saw his car parked up beyond Temple Sowerby, right where they found him. So it stands to reason. Meeting people on line. Nasty, sordid business.'

Speculation. All speculation. 'One time last year? Do you know when?'

She shook her head.

Jude spared a thought for Len, dressing up in his Sunday best and setting off on a sunny day, to meet his fate. 'Did he have many friends?'

'I'd say none, not what I'd call friends. Not people he'd tell his secrets to. Oh, he'd stop and chat as long as you wanted about the weather and the like, always give you the time of day, but never anything about himself. Some'd call him a loner. Even when he was a kid. He was civil enough, and everyone knew who he was, but he never went out. He never went to the pub. He'd always come to us for Christmas and family occasions — the kids' big birthdays and so on — but even then he never said much about himself. I wouldn't say he was a listener, either. Sat in the corner with the telly on.'

'Was he happy enough in general?'

'I'd have said so, sitting there with his own thoughts for company, but I could be wrong. And that's what happens, isn't it, if you go meeting up with strangers on line and not knowing who they are? I warned my daughters about strangers long before the age of the internet, and it applies just as much to a grown man. Sometimes I'd say something, in a roundabout way. But he thought he could look after himself. Turned out he was wrong.'

It was hardly surprising Len hadn't confided in his sister, with her narrow judgement and her insistence on lecturing him for his own good, but there was every chance her guess about what had happened was correct. The post mortem would tell them whether Len had put up a fight, but Jude's assessment of the scene had suggested not. There had been no marks on his hands, as if the first blow had caught him so completely he hadn't been able to respond. 'Did he make a will?'

A shadow passed over her face. 'I don't know. He never thought about death, or if he did he never talked about it.' She shrugged. 'I'll just keep carrying on until someone tells me I have to stop. As long as I can find someone to do the baking now he's gone.'

'Six days a week,' said Jude, remembering the opening hours pinned on the café door. 'But the shop's closed on Sunday?'

'Aye. It's the only day off I get. Tony – my son – was back from college yesterday and we went up to Ullswater for lunch.' She brushed a wisp of grey hair back from her face, tiring of him. 'Check if you want.

They have a note of the booking. Four of us, at the Sun at Pooley Bridge.'

The bell in the shop clanged, and she shot a look towards the door. Accepting that Maisie had told him all she could, Jude allowed her to bring the interview to an end, folding the cover of his notebook down and disentangling his long legs from the cramped space beneath the desk. 'Thanks, Mrs Skinner. That was very helpful.'

'Aye, that'll be right,' she said with scorn. 'I can't tell you what he didn't tell me. Just find out who did it.'

'I'll do my best.'

He followed her into the shop, nodded at the customers and went out into the street.

Chapter 5

'Nat! Where the hell are you?'

Natalie had stopped in the darkness of the underpass, on the riverside path. At the sound of Claud's voice she turned, and the light from her head torch bounced off the concrete and sent the shadows stretching and contorted around her. The rumbling of lorries on the A66 overhead throbbed like a pulse in a mother's womb.

She shivered, aware of her weaknesses and her strengths. She was anxious about everything, afraid of most things, but as long as she was running she wasn't afraid of the dark. Now Claud had appeared to throw her routine out of kilter and with it her moment of calm.

She checked her tracker. A minute to go of the ten she made herself spend on stretches. Bracing her hands against the wall she stretched her left leg out behind her. *Go away, Claud. Let me be calm. Just for a minute.*

'Nat.' The beam of his torch came ahead of him round the bend, spearing through the new growth of the bramble bushes, raising ripples from the river. With another light, the fusion of light and dark became even more frenzied. Fascinated, Natalie watched her own shadow appear, leaner than reality and twisted like a skeleton on the wall in front of her. 'Why the hell did you go out?'

'I told you. I needed a run. To calm me down.'
'I didn't hear you.'

'But I always run.' She stretched the other calf. The minute ticked away and the stretching was complete, but with Claud present she wouldn't be able to jog along the final stretch alone. She shook her head in frustration.

'Yes, but I didn't think you'd want to—' A shrug. 'For Christ's sake, Nat. It's barely twenty-four hours. The police are only just out of the place.'

But you couldn't let fear dominate you. The memory of the dead man's face was vague like a fading bad dream. Sometimes it surged back at her, sometimes she couldn't even bear to look out of the window towards the scene of his death, but if she was going to run she had to do it straight away. Claud wouldn't understand. Even as she thought it, the fear came back to her. After all it was a good thing that he'd come to find her and she wouldn't have to run past the end of the lane alone so soon after the man's death. 'It's fine. Really. I'm fine.'

'For God's sake.' Claud was an impatient man, though not normally with her. Today the mask had slipped a little. 'Are you mad? There's a knifeman running around out there somewhere. He could kill anybody.'

'Yes, but in the village they're saying the poor man was gay and I'm not. So whoever killed him isn't going to kill me.'

Even in the darkness Claud twitched, as though this statement of the obvious had offended him. 'We don't know that was why he was killed. It may have been nothing to do with his sexuality. Robbery, maybe. A madman.'

Oh God, Claud. No. Think before you say things like that. 'The police haven't said but that doesn't mean it wasn't the reason.' She finished her stretching, checked her fitness tracker as the backlit figures glowed in the dark. Forty thousand steps. It was her second long run of the day. The numbers, representing the security of achievement, comforted her. Her breathing was calm and controlled. Tomorrow, she'd do more.

'It could be for any reason.' He came forward into the pool of light from her torch and smiled at her. 'Come on. Let's get back. I don't like being out here any more than you do.'

'I don't mind,' she said, and as they emerged from the tunnel onto the muddy path the sleet chilled her. 'Shall I run on ahead?'

'I think we'd better stick together, don't you?'

If you want, Claud. If you want. 'Yes.' And she slipped her hand in his like a trusting child.

CHAPTER 6

'I've brought you a present.' Curling her feet up underneath her on the sofa, Ashleigh watched through the open door to the kitchen as Jude slid the used plates into the dishwasher and turned his attention to opening a bottle of wine.

'Oh?' He turned his head towards her, initially with a quizzical expression, but he caught her eye and the raised eyebrow gave way to a smile.

In the three weeks they'd been apart she'd experienced a niggling sense of incompleteness, something she hadn't expected. Nor was she entirely sure she welcomed it. But what the hell? It was easier to live in the moment.

'You'll laugh.' She uncurled her legs again and reached for her bag, stirring among the debris of an intercontinental flight — passport, boarding pass, flight socks, an empty packet of paracetamol. The brown paper bag she'd nurtured across continents smelt faintly of incense.

'I never laugh at you.' He slid onto the sofa beside her and placed a glass in her hand. 'Here. I know it's a work night, but you probably need it after all the traumas of the last couple of days.'

She curled her hand around the chilled bowl of her glass, turning it round, considering how the rest of the evening might go and finding the answer acceptable. 'If I drink it I won't be able to drive home.'

'Damn.' He brushed aside her fake protest, raising his glass in salute to a mutually satisfying solution. 'Then you'll have to stay. I can't be bothered to make up the bed in the spare room, though. You'll have to share mine.'

They clinked glasses, and she settled back down on the sofa, close to him. On principle, she didn't, wouldn't, love him and she knew that on the same basis he didn't love her, but sometimes a devil at her shoulder tempted her to whisper that little lie. Only the fear of the consequences stopped her.

Discretion – and experience – triumphed. One day she'd have to tell him about her affair with Faye but tonight wasn't the night for confessions.

Setting her glass down on the side table, she clasped her hand round the packet, reached for Jude's hand and closed his long fingers around it. 'You can deduce what it is before you open it.'

'Jeez, Ashleigh. I'm not at work now.' But he laughed as he moved the packet from one hand to the other to feel its shape and weight, lifting it to sniff at it. Everyone knew his heart was never off duty. 'Soap.'

'Not even close.'

'Chocolate.'

'You think I'd get a bar of chocolate all the way from Sri Lanka without eating it?'

'Fair point. Then it must be a door stop.'

'Now you're being ridiculous. You know perfectly well what it is, don't you?'

'Indeed, Moriarty. I hypothesise that you're trying to drag me into your web with a pack of tarot cards.' He delved into the bag and drew out a cardboard box, a little thicker than a standard pack of playing cards, which he turned over and over in his hands, examining the abstract pattern on the back, lifted it to sniff at that teasing scent of patchouli and sandalwood. 'Where did you got them? A temple?'

'I found them in a little shop in Kandy. It was full of all sorts of stuff and I was just browsing, but as soon as I looked at the cards I thought of you. You'll see why.'

He opened the box and fanned the cards out, and then he laughed. The cards were cheap and gaudy with stylised images of gods and goddesses, and in the bottom corner of each one a tiny, smoke-grey cat stretched or slept or yawned. 'Well, well.'

Too late, she realised that it might have been a mistake. When she'd seen the cards in the shop she'd remembered a moment when she'd seen him with a grey cat just like that one, reaching his hand down to fuss it, and the cat had entwined itself around his hand in utter ecstasy. But Holmes wasn't his. The cat belonged to his former girlfriend. 'It was just a bit of fun.'

'Thank you. But I know the real reason you bought them.'

'You do?'

'Yes. Because now I've got a set of tarot cards my credibility will be completely ruined as a detective if anyone finds out.' He cut the cards, shuffled them, grinned at her. 'And so I daren't risk telling anyone that you read the bloody things seriously. You've stitched me up completely, Madame Vera. But don't worry. Your secret is safe with me.'

She relaxed. 'It's okay. I'm not going not lead you any further astray.'

'That's a shame.'

'Not with the cards, at least.' She sipped her wine. Reading the cards was an unconventional hobby, one she kept secret from her workmates. Once he'd found out about it Jude had teased her mercilessly, but she thought he was beginning, at last, to understand that it wasn't the psychobabble he though it was. Thoughtful consideration of the cards had led her towards the solution to many a personal problem, not least of them the decision to end her toxic marriage.

If only she'd found a moment before she came out to quiz them over the problem of Faye Scanlon.

'Why don't you have a go at reading them?'

'Because I'm a sceptic. I give off all the wrong vibes.' But he looked at them with interest, shuffling them face up as if he were born to it. 'And it's all nonsense.'

The fortune telling side of it was nonsense, and there were plenty of charlatans who'd used it to take advantage of others, but today Ashleigh was in the mood to push it. It mattered that he understood her, why it was important. 'I've told you endlessly. It's about making you think. One card in isolation tells you very little, but a proper spread can lead you in the right direction.'

'Not unlike your average criminal investigation,' he said, in a tone that suggested he was humouring her. 'Take all the bits of evidence, look at them in context, and see the answer.'

'Just like that.' She took the pack from him, carried on shuffling and then held them out. 'Of course, each card can be read in isolation. I sometimes choose one just to give me food for thought.'

'Like a thought for the day,' he said, distracted from the cards and running a finger through the curling end of her pony tail.

'Yes.' She shook him off. There would be plenty of time for that later. 'It's probably a good place for a beginner to start. Go on. Take one.'

'You're secretly filming this, aren't you? You're going to show it to the team and I'll be buying cakes till kingdom come on the back of it to shut them up.' But he took a card from the pack and held it out to her. 'What's this?'

'That's the Queen of Wands. Look at it and tell me what you think of it.'

'I don't suppose it does any harm to get into the mind set of you spiritual people.'

'There are more of us than you think. You might learn something about human nature.' If you wanted to you could rationalise anything, and it amused her to see Jude peering down at the card with the intense concentration he applied to any other problem. 'What's your verdict?'

He laid the card down on the arm of the chair and took a quick check at the rest of the pack. 'This card has two cats. The others have one.'

'Yes.' The black cat that was the characteristic companion of the Queen of Wands was, indeed, squaring up to the grey one that had drawn her to the deck, the two of them with their backs arched, their tails bushed out, their ears back. 'The black cat signals domestication. That's one interpretation for the card.'

In front of her, the card offered the most oblique of warnings. There were many tarot decks and this one was so different to any other that she'd seen that it almost made interpretation impossible. The usually-benevolent depiction of the Queen had no place here. Her narrowed eyes made her aggressive, thorns studded the stems of the flowers she held in her left hand, and she tilted the staff she gripped in her right towards the battling cats like a weapon.

'Domestic discord,' he said, reviewing the card again, this time sitting back for a different perspective. 'A very strong woman.'

Had he seen what she'd seen? 'Yes. It's usually a card associated with benevolence, but this particular depiction doesn't look very benevolent to me.'

'And what should I learn from that?'

'Nothing. It's a thought to hold. Something for you to turn over in your head and come back to when you have an issue.'

'Come back to when I have an issue. Right.' He laughed. 'Is it me, or does she look like our new Super?'

'I thought that, too.' So he had seen it. Now, then, was the moment to confess, offered to her on a plate by a cheap pack of cards, bought at random in a junk shop. All she needed to do was find the right form of words. She picked up the card and looked at it, at the narrowed eyes that so clearly represented Faye's expression when they'd met outside the canteen, at the confrontational body language, even at the short dark hair and the unrelenting scowl. 'And do you know the funny thing about Faye?'

She said it quietly so that it was a whisper and she'd turned away from him as she spoke. He didn't hear, and perhaps she hadn't really wanted him to.

'I'll take that as a warning to mind my Ps and Qs,' he said, still looking at the card. 'Or I should say, a reinforcement of the warning she's already given me.'

For all her authority and confidence, Faye was insecure. That might be the reason she'd rushed into a same-sex relationship with a junior officer. From a position of power, she could pretend they were equal partners and yet exert a measure of unspoken control. There was a hint of insecurity behind the Queen's scowl, too, a woman who would choose a pre-emptive strike rather than wait for the past to catch up with her. 'What warning?' Did Faye know about her and Jude? Was the warning to her as well?

'She's concluded I'm over-promoted and the beneficiary of privilege. As such, she doesn't need my entitled presence getting in the way of her new order.'

'It's just what she's like.'

'We don't know what she's like. She's only been in post for one day. That's my point. She doesn't know what we're like, either. I've no issues at all with anything she said, in principle, but the woman could at least have given me a chance to prove I'm in the job on merit.'

He was young for the job and his rapid rise through the ranks had almost certainly been facilitated by a preference for the traditional, but he delivered. Maybe there were others who could perform equally well, but you couldn't argue that he wasn't capable. 'She's a bit sensitive about her position. That's all.'

'She's no need to be.' He looked down at the card and his scowl turned to a smile, most probably at the sight of that feisty grey cat. 'Let's put her back in the pack. I don't want to talk about her just now.' He shuffled Faye Scanlon, Queen of Wands, back into the deck, replaced it on the bag and dropped it on the floor beside the sofa.

She should tell him about Faye now, while the subject was up, but her courage failed her. Instead she put a hand on his forearm to tease him. 'What have you been up to while I'm away? Chatting up all the chicks?'

He slid his arm around her. 'I was thinking while you were away. It's maybe time I took you along to meet my mum.'

'You think?' It was a curse to be born sensuous, to love smell and touch and colour. She closed her eyes and pressed her face against his chest. They'd been together for four months and if it had begun as a fling, an affair for each of them to get an obsession out of their system, it was taking a long time to clear.

'Yes. It's Mikey's twenty-first in a few weeks and I'm going to have to show up. I thought I might take you along for some moral support.'

Jude's relationship with his brother was rocky at best, but she suspected that wasn't why he'd want her with him. The real source of his annoyance was the ex-girlfriend, who was bound to be there. He wouldn't be human if the Queen of Wands, with her hints of at jealousy, hadn't made him think of her, just as every card Ashleigh turned up when she carried out a reading for herself always hinted at the loss of Scott, her only love. 'Will Becca be there?'

He pulled her closer. 'Yes. But she doesn't bite.'

Becca Reid didn't bark, either. She was the mildest-mannered pillar of her community. There was nothing to fear from her. 'Then it sounds like a plan.'

'Good. Maybe we'll pop in and catch Mum some time before then, if we're passing.' And his lips touched the top of her hair, an offer she wouldn't refuse.

CHAPTER 7

The search for Len Pierce's killer moved with infuriating slowness. Whoever had murdered him must have taken advantage of Sunday afternoon traffic, perhaps even counted on it in a carefully-worked plan, and slipped easily from the side road on to the main arterial route to make their escape. Work on the case had slowed to a mosaic of shaken heads and blind alleys, of apparently random intervention by Faye Scanlon and a run of unrelated activity elsewhere in the county which had to be dealt with immediately.

In his office Jude checked his watch as an email pinged into his inbox. Half five. He scanned the email, hit the print button and got up to collect the sheet from the printer before heading into the corridor.

Faye was walking along towards him. In a week she'd established the habit of being visible, one that attracted irritation from others apart from him. She slowed as she reached him and he, perforce, had to stop. 'Jude. I've observed from my past experience that walking about carrying a piece of paper is a useful screen for doing nothing on a Friday afternoon. But of course that's not the case with you.'

It had to be a joke, or he thought it did, but it annoyed him nonetheless, as though there was something about him that brought out the most waspish side of her character. 'It's an email from the Intelligence Unit, about the Pierce case. I was taking it down to talk it through with the team before we finish. Routine and almost certainly futile, but I like to make sure I know everything that's new before I go off.'

'A good idea. Regular briefing meetings help keep us all fresh, don't they?' As if he was a probationer in need of constant supervision. 'I saw you did the TV appeal. Any joy from that?'

'Not so far.' He checked his watch again, so that she saw it, but she wasn't a woman to take that kind of a hint when she could assert her professional superiority over him. Instead she stood there looking at him, nodding. In her gaze Jude, who was attracted to confident women, recognised a suppressed sexuality without falling victim to it. When she didn't reply, he nudged a little further. 'They'll be waiting for me.'

'Who's your meeting with?'

As he named Ashleigh, Doddsy and Chris he sensed a shift in her expression, as though she'd changed her mind. 'I wondered if I should sit in, but perhaps not this time. It's been a long week. You'll all want to get home as soon as you can.'

Occasionally on a Friday the late afternoon team meetings led on to a drink or two in the pub with some other strays from the office. Today was one of those days and if it had been someone other than Faye he might have invited her along, but he wasn't in the mood for her judgemental presence. If he mentioned it without an invitation, she'd probably commend him for his team-building and he didn't need her approval for the way he worked. 'We'll stay until the work's done.'

'In which case, none of us will get away. Don't work yourself into the ground.' Still she lingered. 'You'll have seen my email about the diversity workshops.'

'I saw it.'

'It's a matter of priority. Of course I wouldn't suggest that anyone here is guilty of any conscious level of discrimination but it's the unconscious bias we need to work at. And from a public perspective it's very important that these processes are visible. You're reasonably high-profile it seems to me, so it's important to me to have you on board.'

'Obviously I'm on board.' Would the woman never stop talking and let him get on? 'I've cleared Monday morning.'

'Good. I'll see you there. No excuses.'

At last she moved on, the click-click of her low heels fading away behind him as he headed down to the incident room. She'd made him late. The place was all but deserted except for the last of the detective constables working away at the background of the case, and even they were packing up their bags and putting on their coats. Around the table under the whiteboard, Doddsy, Ashleigh and Chris were waiting for him.

'Sorry.' He slid into his seat and laid the printed email down in front of him. 'I bumped into Faye and she wanted to go over things.'

'There's not a lot to go over.' Doddsy gave a petulant, Friday-afternoon sigh as Jude pulled up a chair in front of the white board. 'Whoever he is, he's vanished. Into thin air. I haven't any leads.'

'I might have something to add. I've been on at the guys in intelligence about Len Pierce's computer all week, but they've waited until five o'clock on a Friday to get back to me.'

'That's quick for them.' Doddsy sniggered. Jude wasn't the only detective to have trouble extracting information from the Intelligence Unit.

'They must have been bored. I haven't had time to look at it in detail. Talk us through what we've learned this week, would you, and I'll see what information they've got for us. If anything. The sooner we can all get down to the pub, the better.' He dared to flash a smile across the room at Ashleigh in a way he wouldn't have done if Faye had been present.

'There's the post-mortem results. They don't show us anything that we couldn't have guessed from the body, other than that we know Len had had sex, with an unknown man, shortly before his death.'

'And didn't resist his killer.' Other than the single knife wound that had ripped into his heart the body bore no signs of violence, and all the evidence from the post-mortem suggested that whoever had killed Len Pierce had surprised him so completely that he couldn't have seen the death blow coming even though it had been struck from in front of him, a sharp, right-handed thrust to just below the heart. 'And there's no match for the DNA, either, so the other man obviously has no criminal record.' Irritating. The cigarette had been Len's, too.

'None. So, to the car.' Doddsy ran down his list like the expert meeting-manager he was, one eye on the agenda, one on the clock and a good chunk of his concentration almost certainly already in the pub. 'Chris, what can you tell us about it?'

'Just about everything except its colour, reg and chassis number.' Chris shook his head. What he had wouldn't help to trace the vehicle, only to confirm it had been on the scene once they'd finally found it — if they ever did. 'A Toyota Rav, probably heavily loaded, left rear tyre more worn than the right. The left tyre was illegal. Tammy's reasonably confident she's identified a trace of very similar tyres elsewhere on the verge, which suggests that this wasn't the first time that person had been there. There were indications from tyre tracks — degraded but just about usable — that Len Pierce's car had been there before. The only other tracks at that end of the lane were from a tractor, and they've been matched to the one at the farm. The farmer had been along the lane on the Saturday morning.'

Jude nodded and took a moment to scan the email a second time. 'That implies a regular meeting place, and it ties in with Maisie Skinner's claims that Len met men online. But she didn't offer any evidence for it and according to this,' he tapped the printed email, 'there isn't any suggestion of that on his laptop, either.'

'What about the dark web?' Chris would do well in the tech team, if he ever wanted to go there. 'Have they looked a bit deeper?'

'I imagine they have.'

'Yes, but if he's meeting—'

'We don't know that he is.' Ashleigh joined in. 'Just because Maisie falls into the trap of thinking being gay makes you dangerous and promiscuous, there's no reason why we should. The opposite, I'd say.'

'We can't let political correctness obscure the possibility, either. Everything suggests he was meeting someone in secret.'

'It's a public place. Hardly secret.' Ashleigh glared.

'Okay.' Jude lifted a warning hand. 'Chris. You have a good point. The tech team haven't finished. They may find something else.'

'What about his phone?'

'Not that we've been able to access. There are a couple of cryptically named WhatsApp groups but they could have been group conversations, or just

Lenny and a mate. He didn't bother to encrypt any messages to his sister. They're straightforward texts, and there's nothing in there that goes beyond the mundane.' Jude consulted the next paragraph of the email. 'They'll keep digging.' The slenderness of information in the email disappointed him, but it was hardly unexpected. He turned to Ashleigh. 'I imagine if the door-to-door inquiries had come up with anything I'd have heard, but at least you can run me through what we don't know.'

'You're right, I'm afraid. We did extensive door-to-doors in Appleby, but none of Len's neighbours could tell us anything, other than the fact that he was quiet, pleasant, a bit of a loner, and most of them either knew or suspected that he was gay. And we've knocked every door in Temple Sowerby, except Doddsy's.'

'Okay. And can you give me a quick sketch of Len Pierce?'

'I can. His neighbours liked him. He was friendly and helpful. Watered their gardens when they were away, delivered surplus baking to them. Nobody but his sister seemed to think he was at all promiscuous and nobody cared, except for a couple of slightly prim folk, and even they liked him. He loved animals. He worked hard, but he loved his job.'

'Okay. And no-one saw anything on the A66?'

'Not that we've been able to confirm. We stopped traffic on there on Monday and Tuesday.

You can image how popular that made us with the public, but it couldn't be helped. I'm planning to repeat that on Sunday afternoon, at the time Len was killed and for an hour before and after, to catch anyone who makes a regular trip and see if it jogs any memories.'

'You'll be supervising that?'

'Yes. Theoretically, I'm not working then but I took most of Monday so I need to make it up.'

He nodded. 'And I don't suppose there have been any responses to my TV appeal?'

Chris smothered a laugh. Everyone knew how much Jude hated having to appeal to the public, and whenever he could he'd pass the job on to someone else, but this time Doddsy had been out of the office and he'd had to take the job on himself. 'Apart from the usual half-dozen elderly ladies asking if you could come round and interview them? You seem to appeal to a particular demographic.'

Jude rolled his eyes. 'It was a waste of time and effort, then. But it had to be done.' He checked his watch. 'One more thing before we go. The will.'

'I checked that.' Chris swiped across the screen of his iPad and offered a scanned document for them all to see. 'Simple as you like. His sister inherits.'

It would have been interesting to see what Len had thought of Maisie, given her view of him seemed so different to everyone else's. Or maybe she was the only person brave enough to express her reservations to the police. 'She said she didn't know if he'd made a will.'

'She must have guessed she'll be richer by a six figure sum when probate goes through.' Chris, of course, had Googled the value of the property.

Jude sat back and thought about it for a moment. Was it possible that Maisie had killed him and her hostility was intended to point the blame elsewhere? 'It might be worth checking where she was on Sunday. She said she was at the Sun at Pooley Bridge.' He laid down his pen. 'That's easily confirmed.'

'It would be good if it was her,' Chris said, adding that to his list. 'Because that would make it neat and tidy. One person killing one other person for a particular reason. Much less messy than dealing with some nutter who's going to start bumping off anyone who looks a bit camp.'

Beside him, Ashleigh drew in an outraged breath and Doddsy allowed himself a cough but Chris, unaware, merely drew a line underneath the list and smiled at them.

Jude shook his head in irritation. Faye's workshops would give Chris something to think about in terms of unconscious bias. 'So that's where we are. I don't know if there's anything more we can do until we hear back from the tech guys and see if they come up with anything. But I really want to find the man Len met on Sunday lunchtime. I'll let you all get off. And some housekeeping. I'll be at a diversity session on Monday morning.' And he smiled at Chris, the reminder he shouldn't have needed. 'I think we're all scheduled to attend at some point.'

They drifted off, leaving him with only Ashleigh in the half-lit incident room. It had been a tough week, and he welcomed the chance of sitting down and talking about something other than work, knowing that if he was at home he'd be worrying on about it late into the night when there was nothing he could realistically hope to achieve.

'Are you coming to the pub?' Ashleigh picked up her jacket.

'I've something to finish. Tammy wanted a word. She's going to pop down here at the back of six. But I don't imagine I'll be very long after that.'

No-one who worked in the office could possibly be unaware of the mood that Tammy had been in recently, and Jude probably wasn't the only one with a sneaking suspicion what it was about, but if he was right it was nothing to do with him. Quite what Tammy wanted, then, was a mystery.

'Intriguing.' Ashleigh picked up her coat. 'Do you think Chris is on to something? About Maisie? Or rather, about not Maisie?'

'He's certainly right that it'll be a lot easier to solve if it's her.' But they could rule nothing in and nothing out on the available evidence. 'Time will tell. We'll keep working on it.'

'Text me when you're done. Or I'll see you there.'

When she'd gone, he went back up to his office, turning away from Len Pierce's death to one of the many other matters that strove for his time and attention, ticking off the ten minutes it took for Tammy to turn up. 'Jude.' She hovered in the doorway.

'Hi, Tammy.' Neither her voice nor her attitude was any friendlier than it had been earlier on, but he knew how she worked. She was dedicated and sensible and she didn't respond well to confrontation, so it would be interesting if she chose to provoke it. 'How are things?'

'Things are very difficult just now.' She came in, closing the door behind her and stopping just inside it, as if reluctant to commit herself to a seat. She had her coat on, a clear message to him that the meeting was to be short and to the point and that she was on her way elsewhere.

If that meant the interview was over sooner rather than later, that suited him. 'Sorry to hear that. Anything I can help you with?'

'Yes. It's Doddsy.'

'What's he done?' As if he couldn't guess.

She looked at him with the exasperation of a mother towards an unresponsive teenager. 'You know exactly what he's done. He's carrying on with my boy.'

'Okay.' Tyrone Garner, Tammy's son, was a grown adult and a fully-fledged police constable more than capable of looking after himself. Steeling himself, Jude set out to deal with Tammy's prejudices. 'Just before we go any further. You might want to choose your words carefully.'

'I've been careful what I've said and careful what I've thought. I'm not homophobic in any way. You should know that.' Her lip wobbled in injured innocence, but emotion got the better of her and she didn't stop. 'I knew Tyrone was gay before he knew it himself and it doesn't bother me one bit. Don't you dare suggest otherwise.'

'Then that's fine.' If he'd had any sense, he'd have trusted his instincts and told her he was too busy to see her. He wasn't her line manager and he didn't want to be involved. 'Is that all?'

'It isn't fine at all. Doddsy—'

'Stop right there.' He held up a hand, and either that or the sudden recollection of a disparity in rank brought her to a standstill. 'This isn't a workplace issue. What my staff get up to, or what my staff's families get up to, in their own time isn't any of my business as long as it's legal. And you aren't suggesting anything illegal, are you?'

'No, of course not.' She got control of herself with three, quick deep breaths. 'It's like I said. It's not because Doddsy's gay, Jude.'

'I should hope not.'

'Dammit. It's coming out wrong. It's the age gap. I'd be the same if he was a woman, or if Tyrone was.' She folded her fingers in front of her, agonised. 'He's more than twice Tyrone's age. That's what worries me.'

He regarded her, thoughtfully. Tyrone was just twenty-one and Doddsy the wrong side of forty-five. If he was in her position, would he have been bothered? 'The point stands. I understand why you're uncomfortable about it, but it's nothing to do with anyone but the two of them.'

'I thought you'd say that.' She frowned at him, in discontent. 'I had to ask, though. I told Phil I would.'

He spread his hands wide, an attempt at sympathy the only thing he could offer her. 'I'm not saying I don't see where you're coming from. But even if I had a view on it, there's nothing I could do.'

'You could talk to Doddsy about it.'

'And say what?' Doddsy was Jude's close friend as well as his colleague, but the inspector was a man who kept his life partitioned, and it was only after he'd met the dangerously attractive Tyrone Garner that there had been any crossover at all. Their friendship was built on an implicit understanding of that, and it wasn't something Jude was prepared to compromise. 'No, I'm sorry Tammy. Impossible, as well as inappropriate.'

'Perhaps I should take it up with Detective Superintendent Scanlon.'

It had taken a week of Faye's hands-on management to show that her crusade for equality wouldn't stand for that kind of challenge. 'I wouldn't advise it. She's very politically correct.' He paused, looking down at the note he'd written for himself about Faye's equality workshop. *No excuses*, she'd said. 'Rightly so.'

Tammy had turned scarlet. 'Yes. But it's not about that, is it? It's about age-appropriate behaviour. That's what bothers me and Phil. Tyrone's our son. We care.' But she was backing away towards the door as if she regretted approaching him.

'Of course you do. But they're both old enough to know their own minds. Tyrone's hardly a vulnerable adult.'

'Try telling Phil that.' She shuffled out of the door and snapped it shut behind her.

Left behind in after-hours silence, Jude sighed, shut down his computer and turned his thoughts to Ashleigh and the pub.

CHAPTER 8

In one of those accidents of timing that can only be the fortunate intervention of the fates, Doddsy arrived at the pub just a few seconds after Becca Reid. It was a cold night and the spring rain had turned briefly to sleet, so that he hadn't recognised the figure he'd followed down the street and into the bar until she flipped down her hood and paused on the mat to shake off the rain.

Caught in the spray of raindrops, he stepped aside and she, noticing, spun round, already well into an apology. 'I'm so sorry. I didn't see you there. Oh. Hi, Doddsy.'

Her almost-permanent smile had faded to a shadow when she saw him, but he wasn't so self-centred as to think it was anything to do with him. He liked Becca and was reasonably certain she'd say the same about him, but he was Jude's best friend. Hardening his heart towards her, as he had done from the moment she'd instigated the split and he'd aligned himself, instantly and unequivocally, beside his friend, Doddsy nevertheless found it in himself to smile. 'Hi, Becca. We don't see you about much in here these days.'

'No, it's not usually my sort of pub. I—' She looked over his shoulder with a nervous flick of her hair, then back at him and relaxed. Chris's laugh, carrying across the bar from round a corner, indicated that most of the group going out for Friday drinks were in situ, but Becca's lack of panic suggested that Jude wasn't yet among them.

A quick peek showed Ashleigh, laughing at whatever had amused Chris, a couple of the other detectives from the team, and — an unexpected pleasure —Tyrone. 'You're well?'

'Oh, I'm fine.' Still she hovered just inside the doorway, neither forging forwards nor beating the retreat. 'What about you? I heard on the grapevine that you'd had an accident. Are you okay?'

A chill ran down the back of Doddsy's neck .The last murder case he'd dealt with had nearly taken him with it. Not liking to think of how close he'd come to becoming a homicide statistic, he waved aside a brush with death as easily as if he were on point duty somewhere in town, blessing the local gossip network that would make sure everyone knew everything and he didn't need to explain himself. 'Right as—' He glanced through the door as someone else came in and was relieved to see that it wasn't Jude. 'Rain.'

She giggled. You couldn't keep Becca's sense of humour down, and even the bad temper that always seemed to surface when Jude was around held a witty, waspish sharpness if you cared to listen for it. 'Glad to hear it.' A pause as she looked around to see if there was anyone else there she knew. 'Meeting anyone?'

He read the subtext there, too. 'Yes. A few of us are coming down from work.'

'Oh.' She looked over his shoulder again, felt in her pocket for her phone, a decision made. 'I'm supposed to be meeting Adam here. Maybe we should go somewhere else. It's been lovely to see you, though, Doddsy. Stay safe.' And she shuffled off towards the exit.

She was too late. As she reached the door it opened and Jude appeared, striding in with purpose. He ground to a halt and the two of them did a little shuffle as he shifted aside to let her past. 'Hi Becca.'

'Hi Jude.'

'All fine?'

'Yes. I was just leaving.'

'See you around then.'

'See you.' Dodging past him, she almost ran out into the rain. Turning to see the conclusion of the scene, Doddsy stared through the window in time to see her intercept the man approaching the door, tuck her arm through his and turn him in one fluid movement so that they were heading across the road and into a different pub.

That was a relief. Turning back again, Doddsy watched the way that Jude chose to play out the ending — by crossing to the table full of his workmates and kissing Ashleigh as if Becca was still in the room to see it, a clear declaration that the past was the past and needn't trouble him.

It did, of course. Being let down by someone who cared about you always hurt and the only thing to be thankful for was that Becca's sharp exit had spared them the arrival of Adam Fleetwood, local charmer, ex-jailbird and Jude's former friend. Satisfied that the drama was over for the evening, Doddsy crossed to join the group where Jude was already taking the order for a round of drinks.

'Mine's a St Clements.' He caught Tyrone's eye and a smile flared up on his lips unbidden, just as Becca's smile had died at the prospect of meeting Jude. Love made the world go round for some and slowed it to a crawl for others. 'Want me to come and help carry them?'

Jude's nod was fleeting but clear, and so Doddsy followed him across to the bar. 'It's just as well Becca was just leaving,' he said, a conversational opening that Jude could take or leave.

'She had rain on her coat. It looked to me as if she'd only just arrived.'

'Maybe she changed her mind.'

'Or knew I was coming and ducked out. I've used that trick myself. I don't blame her, if she thinks she'd be uncomfortable.' Jude had written the orders on the back of his hand and reeled them off to the barman. 'At least it spares me.'

Across the room, Ashleigh had broken off from her conversation long enough to watch them as they stood by the bar, but when she saw Doddsy looking at her she looked away again. 'What do you need to be spared? You've found what looks to me like a high class replacement.'

'I know.' Jude grinned. 'She's far too good for the likes of me. It's pride, I suppose. No-one likes rejection. And I don't want to sit and watch my old mate Adam flirting with Becca to get back at me.'

Adam Fleetwood was a braggart and a troublemaker, a man who might deem it worth coming off worse in a fight with Jude in the knowledge that his enemy would have a professional misconduct charge to answer if he succumbed to temptation and took a swing at him. In the face of such flagrant provocation, Jude maintained superhuman patience. Self-discipline had always been both his strength and his weakness.

'You think that's it?'

'I've known the two of them all my life. They're incompatible and he doesn't know the meaning of forgiveness. It won't last, and she'll get hurt when he realises he can't get to me and he dumps her. Hopefully by then I'll be past caring.'

There was bitterness in his voice. Doddsy, who knew him well, wasn't surprised but it wasn't like Jude to let these things show. Nor was that public display of affection something he'd normally have allowed himself. 'Let's hope so.'

'And what about you? Setting out on the dating game, are you?' Jude's tone was deliberately light and he as turning away to marshal the first of the drinks as he spoke.

He didn't often ask personal questions, waiting for Doddsy to share. If Doddsy had his way no-one would know anything of his business unless he chose to tell them but that was just the way he was. Tyrone, so very different, had already pushed him out of his comfort zone. *I want to tell the world about my new man*, he'd said, when Doddsy had counselled caution. *I'm not ashamed of you.*

'Who wants to know?' If the secret was out, it was out.

'Nobody. I just want you to know that I don't care what you do or who you go out with, and no-one else should, either.'

For a moment Doddsy toyed with letting it go, but his natural curiosity impelled him to ask the question. 'Then why ask?' He looked to Tyrone again, for pleasure and for courage.

Jude sighed. 'It's just a heads-up.'

'It's Tammy, isn't it? What's she said?'

'Only that she's worried about the age difference. Don't worry. I advised her to mind her own business.'

'I bet she thinks he's looking for a father figure.' Though quite what that might say about Tyrone's relationship with his father — a very clever, uncompromising man — was up for discussion.

'I don't know what she thinks, but she's Tyrone's mum. Have a heart. Don't change anything about yourself, mate. But try and understand where she's coming from, for Tyrone's sake at least.' Jude's attitude was apologetic, as if he was taking a rare trespass beyond the bounds of his better judgement. 'I'm right behind you. But we have to work with her.'

Closing his hands round three pint glasses with the ease of practice, Doddsy turned and looked once more at Tyrone, who was laughing uproariously at something one of the junior detectives had said. 'We're just friends.'

'You don't have to justify yourself to me. You can be whatever you want. I don't care.'

'I don't mind telling you. Yeah, I like him. Yeah, I like him a lot. We've been out a couple of times. But we're very different. And she's right, isn't she? He's a hell of a lot younger than me. That makes a difference, too.' Age was a strange thing. In his career Doddsy had come across many people who had engaged in flings with younger partners and it had ended in frustrated violence. Some of them, ending up in court on an assault charge, had excused themselves on the grounds that the relationship made them feel young, good about themselves. Tyrone, with his youth and his humour and his belief that everything was achievable if you gave it enough time and effort, had the opposite effect on Doddsy, even as he moved irresistibly towards the inevitable acknowledgement that he loved him. He made him feel old and tired, as if he had very little to offer so promising a man.

Jude let it drift, dropping the pound that came in his change in the tips jar, picking up the remaining glasses and leading the way across the bar to hand them out. He didn't take a seat at once, but stood back and waited for Doddsy to do the same. 'I'm not going to talk shop all evening. But what do you reckon to Len Pierce?'

'Are you asking me because I'm gay? Because if you are, you're wasting your time. I'm not into the gay scene at all.' Church and folk music were Doddsy's interests, two more things that suddenly made him feel older than he was. The shadow of a mid-life crisis lengthened behind him, stealing ever closer to his shoulder.

'I'm asking you because you're a detective,' Jude said, 'and because I value your opinion. But yeah, Len being gay may be significant.'

'My opinion? Right. Then I don't understand why he was skulking at the end of a lane when there's nothing in the character profiles to suggest he cared what other people think about him.' Doddsy picked up his drink. It wasn't always self-doubt that held people back from being themselves, but doubt about the open-heartedness of their neighbours and friends, unspoken judgement behind a mask of tolerance. 'I'll ask Tyrone. He's much more into that kind of scene than I am. But I think we'll find Len wasn't part of anything. I think he was just an ordinary bloke who met another ordinary bloke and maybe fell in love with him. As you do.'

'My thoughts, too. Okay. Now let's forget about it.'

Stepping away, Jude sat down in the space that Ashleigh had made for him. On the other side of the table Tyrone pulled up a chair and Doddsy sat down behind him and smiled. He'd never hidden his sexuality, never made much of a thing about it and accepted the quiet celibacy that life had placed in his path, and now a strange thing had happened to him, as if Tyrone had somehow led him out of the closet to blink in the daylight.

*

There was a chill in the March night air as Gracie got out of her car, turned her back on it and looked towards the west. Civil twilight, her father called it – daylight was done, darkness yet to come upon them. Only the glow over the Lake District fells and the light from the car headlights offered her any comfort. The lane where Len Pierce had died was bleak and cold.

'This is it?' she asked, to break the silence.

Giles closed the car door and walked round to join her, his body breaking the beams as he walked in front of them. 'Yes.'

He was nervous. Attuned to him in a way she rarely was with others, Gracie could sense it in the tone of his voice. If it hadn't been so spookily dark, if he hadn't had his back to what was left of the light so that his face was a pit of emptiness, she thought she'd have seen him licking his lips.

'Are you all right?'

'Yes.' Again, short and terse.

'You can't see anything,' she said, after a moment during which the soft light faded even further and the harsh beam from the headlights drew sharper, starker lines. Suddenly the world was divided into black and white, all shades of grey departed. 'Perhaps we should have come another day.'

'I don't want to see anything. In any case, there's nothing to see.'

Gracie ran her forefinger around the neck of her coat, hooked her scarf up and tried to seal the gaps, but still that knife-like easterly wind crept in. A man had died here, where they stood. 'You know they'll find you, don't you?'

'Do you think so? They'd have found me by now.'

These things took time. Giles ought to know that. He knew how long it took to get a sample off to the lab and analysed. He must know, too, that if there was no question of saving lives there was less urgency. Would the police be able to accelerate matters when there was murder involved? 'They must have your DNA.'

'They won't know it's mine. They won't have any to compare it with. Because I've always been such a law-abiding sod.'

Sometimes she thought that about herself, how much easier life would have been if she'd had the courage to rebel in the short term and take the hit, for the sake of her own peace of mind. It was hard not to empathise with the bitterness in his tone. 'Then you've got nothing to worry about.'

A pause, longer than was comfortable. 'You think?'

'Yes.' She made herself sound brisk, confident even. And reminded herself that the chill was the wind, not fear. And then, in a moment of pure madness, because if she was going to die at the hands of the man she'd foolishly trusted she was going to let him know, she said: 'Giles. You didn't. Did you?'

A long, long pause. 'No.' His voice cracked. 'No. Why would I? I loved him.'

Giles loved too many people. He loved Janice. He loved Gracie herself, to a degree. One of the people he'd loved, the one he claimed to love most, had died, at this very spot. The thought chilled her.

'Let's go.' She opened the driver's door, slid in and closed it again. Her finger hovered over the lock, just in case, but he made no move towards her, only walking slowly, with his head bowed, back round the car to the passenger door. There he paused for a moment to look at the shadows pooling round them, and opened the car door.

Gracie tightened her grip on the steering wheel. 'Okay?' she said, with false brightness.

'Yes.' He snapped his seat belt back in place. 'Let's get back. Janice will be wondering where I am.'

*

The early evening drinks were done, the group breaking up to go their separate ways. In the ladies' loo, Ashleigh was smartening up her make-up when her work phone, which she'd forgotten to switch off, pinged with an alert of a missed call.

Number unknown. Administering a slash of scarlet lipstick, Ashleigh folded her lips together then dabbed at them with a tissue as she debated the eternal detective's dilemma. To return the call, or not?

'Never off bloody duty,' she said to her reflection, knowing Jude would have answered it, regardless of where he was. He needed to learn to keep his work phone switched off, something she normally did. Closing the cover of the phone, she was about to stash it away in her bag when the voicemail reminder pinged in. So it was important enough to warrant a message. Curiosity won out. She flicked the message on to speaker and listened to it while she dabbed a touch of powder on her face.

'Hi, Sergeant O'Halloran. This is Marsha Letham from the *Eden Telegraph*. We're looking to run a piece alongside our reporting of the A66 murder in the local area. I wanted to talk to someone about diversity and inclusion of the LBGTQI community in the local police operations. I'm told there's a new policy approach being developed. I understand you worked with Detective Superintendent Faye Scanlon at the Cheshire force and wondered if I could chat to you about that. Give me a call if you have a moment.' A pause, and then the cheery voice came back at her again. 'Oh, and no names, obviously. I protect my sources.'

Ashleigh flicked the phone off and frowned at it. Even on a Friday night, even in the ladies' toilets of a local pub, the fallout of her relationship with Faye Scanlon cast a long shadow. Questions about inclusion and diversity? No names? That would only be the beginning of it. The woman must think she buttoned up the back.

I may make mistakes, Ashleigh said to herself as she thought of Faye, the biggest and most damaging of them, but I'm not so stupid as to get involved in something like that.

CHAPTER 9

Once Jude had crept quietly out of the house Ashleigh shared with her old school friend and headed off to work, she couldn't fall back to sleep. Six o'clock was an unconscionable hour to be up and out on a Saturday, but she'd already learned he was a man who couldn't settle easily to anything if there was a major problem to deal with at work. She was as bad. Other people's problems niggled at her, but she preferred them to having to worry about her own.

Except one. As she lay in bed waiting for the warmth that Jude had left behind him to cool and for the dawn light to creep over from the front of the housetop and lift the shadows that lay deep in her bedroom, the message she'd found on her phone the night before nagged at her. Journalists who wanted information on a case went to the press office. If they were looking elsewhere it was either because they didn't think they'd get the answer they wanted or they'd tried and been refused. Whichever it was, she'd steer well clear.

She should have told Jude about Faye the night before, but if she had it would have led her into history she didn't want to revisit. Life was complicated enough without him asking the unanswerable question: *why*?

I should stop worrying about the past, she lectured herself even as she realised she wasn't going to get back to sleep and might as well give up and make the best of the day. It was past seven by then, and she swung her legs over the edge of the bed with a sigh. The plumbing was antiquated and shouted its complaints for all to hear, and Lisa wouldn't thank her for disturbing her so early, so she delayed a shower, slipped on her dressing gown and padded down to the kitchen.

Five minutes later she was sitting on the sofa with the side table in front of her. A mug of strong coffee steamed at one side and her pack of tarot cards, wrapped in purple silk, sat in the middle, inviting her to talk. Moments of silence such as this were rare and the week had given her something to think about. The Queen of Wands, scowling out from the tarot card in Jude's hand. Faye, hostile and antagonistic. Secrets. Jude.

'What I want to know,' she said to the empty air, 'is what the hell I should do about Faye?' Because since that first, frosty, meeting her ex-lover hadn't spoken a single word to her in her frequent — possibly over-frequent — passes through the office.

Faye had always been hands-on. Ashleigh pursed her lips, hand hovering over the cards, as she remembered Faye's close interest in all her staff — irritating to some, flattering to others — and where it had led the two of them. Unwrapping the deck, she dealt out five cards in a horseshoe, face down. 'Should I tell Jude?' But the question was ridiculously obvious. Of course she should tell him. The only decisions were when, and how much?

'I don't expect answers. I never do. But perhaps we can move towards some kind of constructive solution, huh?'

The house rang like a bell with early-morning silence. She must sound ridiculous. She rarely read the tarot for others but when she did so, for Jude or for Lisa, she allowed their scepticism to influence her and she never spoke to the cards. Perhaps that was why those other readings were never quite so successful as those she did when she was alone — because she didn't tune in to the questions she was asking or the answers she received.

She paused before she turned over the first card, the one that would outline the issues in her present, that might hint at the significance of something she'd overlooked. The Saturday-stillness of the early morning frayed at the edges as a car made its way down Norfolk Road. A bird, wide awake and looking for a mate, screamed from a perch somewhere out of sight above the window. The low rumble of a northbound train rattled the windows and died away towards Plumpton.

'The present,' she reminded herself, turning over the card, knowing all too well what the issues were. On the table in front of her the Chariot, with its black and white sphinxes facing in different directions ahead of the stern Charioteer warned of a long and hard fight. 'Who knew?' she said, lightly, though joking with the cards was a high-risk strategy. Was this about Faye, or about life in general?

Or work. Somewhere out there Len Pierce's killer was at large and the only consolation she could draw from it was that the card was upright, indicating eventual success. Was the murderer satisfied with a mission completed, or waiting for another victim to stumble across his path?

She shook the thought off. The cards were for personal problems. You'd have to be a special kind of fool to try and use them to solve a crime.

She stopped for a moment to think what her present expectations might be before turning the card that would shed light on them. She'd arrived in Cumbria an emotional refugee and she hadn't hoped for anything except a new start. The World, a positive card, made her smile, reflected exactly that. It implied a beneficial journey, a new start. So far, so good. Maybe Faye had changed, wanted to wipe the slate clean as Ashleigh herself did, and only a lack of courage prompted her silence and prevented an apology.

Maybe. It had been a short relationship, but she thought she knew Faye's weaknesses.

The next card made her frown. It represented the unexpected, but it was anything but, a card that came up too often in her readings to be a surprise — so often that she'd once checked the deck to make sure there wasn't a duplicate. Jude would have an explanation for its repeated appearance, no doubt — that she'd somehow subliminally marked it so it always came out of the deck, or it was question of perception and it came up no more often than any other. No matter: here it was in front of her, the Three of Swords, a card that spoke too often of Scott, of infidelity and divorce, betrayal and incompatibility.

This time something else struck her about its grim and gaudy iconography. She didn't need the image of its bleeding heart to remind her of Len Pierce, skewered by a six-inch blade.

'That wasn't helpful,' she said, to herself rather than the deck. 'You can do better than that. What am I looking out for in the immediate future?' She turned over the fourth card.

'Seriously?' The High Priestess was one of her favourites, a confirmation of what she thought and believed, that instinct took its place alongside reason as an equal. Jude would have mistrusted it. She smiled at the thought, but the smile faded. In the picture on her card the figure of the High Priestess, like the Queen of Wands in Jude's tarot deck, was looking out with exactly the same steely glance Faye Scanlon turned on everyone around her. *I'm making this up*, she chastised herself, *seeing things that aren't there.*

That bloody woman, living rent-free in her head where Scott used to. Today the negative attributes of the card were there to see when she'd previously only sensed its positive ones — egotism, selfishness and a ruthless drive for success. It dawned on her, then, that after everything that had passed she didn't particularly like the woman who was now very much her senior officer. With this uncomfortable thought, she approached the final card, the long term, with trepidation. The Page of Swords came up, reversed, another figure who was unreliable and unstable, warning of deception. She shook her head at it. More swords. 'I'm in the police. I see people like that all the time. For God's sake, unstable and unreliable probably describes half my colleagues!'

Looking at the cards in frustration, she shuffled the five back into the pack and reached for her coffee. A shadow in the doorway caught her eye and she turned to find Lisa standing there, clutching her shabby dressing gown round her skinny body and staring, a mug of coffee in her hand.

'My God,' Lisa said, cheerfully. 'That was a bit of a show. You could make a better living doing that at fairgrounds than you do catching criminals. Did you realise you were talking to yourself?'

Sighing, Ashleigh folded the pack back into its gauzy shroud. 'There's no-one else to talk to at this time of the morning.'

'Your man's very dedicated, isn't he? I'm sure if I was him I wouldn't want to be sneaking out of a nice warm bed at this time on a Saturday morning, especially not with you still in it.' Lisa came and sat next to Ashleigh on the sofa, peering at the silk-wrapped pack, but if she thought about requesting a reading, as she periodically did, she thought better of it.

'It's not like we never see each other.' A bit of distance was probably a good thing, but Jude's company hadn't begun to grate on her just yet and neither, as far as she was aware, had hers on him. 'We're both off on Wednesday. I'll see plenty of him then.'

'I just love a job that's five days a week.' Lisa watched as Ashleigh sipped her coffee. 'Shall I rustle us up some breakfast? I'd suggest going out but we're such early birds there'll be nowhere open.'

'I'm not hungry.'

'Okay,' Lisa said, after a fractional pause. 'What is it?'

Denial was tempting but it only offered short-term gain. Ashleigh's success as an interviewer relied, to some extent, to communicating to any witness the inevitability of being caught out and the comfort of conceding the truth early. And anyway Lisa was her friend, the best one she had and the one to whom she could trust even the secrets she wasn't yet ready to reveal to Jude. 'I never told you about what happened when I got back from holiday.'

Lisa tilted her head to one side with a questioning look. 'Go on.'

'I met my new boss. And she's my old boss.'

'Faye Scanlon?' Thrusting the cup of coffee onto the side table, Lisa flipped her hands to her mouth in an exaggerated gesture of shock. 'Oh my! Is that what you were talking to the cards about?'

Ashleigh nodded. There was no other source of sensible advice and one thing she knew about herself was that she couldn't trust her heart.

'Did she say anything?'

'No. She pretended she'd never met me.' That cold stare, that unspoken warning, rankled. Faye championed equality and fairness in the workplace but only for others. In personal matters ruthlessness and her own interests held sway.

'That's…manipulative.'

Ashleigh remained silent. It was possible to intimidate without words.

'You've told Jude, though? He can–'

'No.'

Lisa folded her arms, to the grave jeopardy of her cup of coffee. Her wide eyes said everything that needed to be said.

'I know,' Ashleigh defended herself, too quickly. 'I know. And he's not stupid. He knows she came from the Cheshire force and he knows I worked there. He did ask me, once, but I pretended I hadn't heard. It's just too complicated.'

'Not as complicated as it will be if you don't put a stop to it.'

'I know. But right now it's in the too difficult box.'

'God, Ash. Use that finely-tuned detective's brain for once!'

'My finely-tuned brain doesn't work well with my heart, okay?'

'No, you're the worst judge of your own emotional wellbeing of anyone I've ever met. So listen to me. Jude'll be fine about it. He's not possessive.'

He couldn't be, with Scott still so large a presence in Ashleigh's life and Becca in his own. 'He knows some of it already. I told him I had an affair with a woman.' Some men, Ashleigh knew, found that appealing. 'He's already had a bit of a run-in with Faye. They took against one another straight away. I don't want to have to explain how bad it got.' And you never knew with Jude. He might easily take up arms on her behalf against their boss and end by making matters worse.

'Yeah, hiding it make things easier? He's bound to find out at some point. It's much better if you tell him when you're in control.'

Lisa was never short of good advice, though she never seemed to ask for it or to take it herself. Robust common sense was her stock in trade. This time, once again, she was right. 'I will. Later.'

'You should do it right now.'

'He's at work right now. But I'll do it as soon as there's a right moment. okay?'

'That's something.' Lisa spent a moment in thought, looking at Ashleigh, at her coffee mug, at the tarot cards in their purple silk shroud. 'She's not a pleasant woman though, is she?'

'No.' Ashleigh shook her head. That might be what the cards were trying to tell her — that running away from a problem, as she had done, wasn't the answer. The problem had come after her. 'She looked as shocked as I was. I don't think she knew I was here.'

'Oh, but she must have—'

'I don't think she did. And I'm guessing there must have been some kind of scandal after I'd gone, because she's a ruthlessly ambitious woman and she's got a promotion but in a smaller force. That isn't the kind of life plan she had, so something must have gone wrong after I left.' Ruthless individuals made enemies, and there was always someone ready to see an ambitious woman fail. That rang a bell with her, as though Jude's half-hearted interpretation of a cheap pack of tarot cards had held a warning for both of them. 'I don't like her and I'm sure she doesn't like me.'

'Ashleigh O'Halloran.' Hands on hips, Lisa sounded exactly like Ashleigh's mother, exasperated with her when she'd once again failed to make the break from Scott. 'If you don't even like the woman, what on Earth made you get into bed with her in the first place?'

Lisa had been a distant friend when Ashleigh's world had gone dark, when Scott's incurable infidelity had driven her to intense isolation at home and to an almost-catastrophic loss of confidence at work. 'I was lonely.' She was a gregarious soul, a lover not a fighter, a woman who detested the grim echoes of silence, and the one thing she hated more than anything else was loneliness. At the end of the short affair, she'd come out of it with her soul stained with self-loathing and the knowledge that sometimes the open ocean was better than the wrong port in a storm.

'Oh, sweetheart.' The tentative hand that Lisa placed on her arm was a huge compliment, because her friend had never been the touchy-feely type, and in consequence it felt warmer than the tightest hug. 'I understand. And her?'

'I don't know for sure.' Ashleigh paused to think of Faye, capable of offering sympathy and tenderness and then turning the coldest of shoulders. 'I see what she's like but I don't understand why she's that way. Which is weird, because I understand most people.'

After all it wasn't so strange when she couldn't understand herself. She could divine other people's minds but when her own heart was invested her judgement failed her, every time. So it had been with Scott, so with Faye. So, surely, it would be with Jude.

'Maybe she was going through something, too' Lisa offered, a charitable attempt in Faye's defence. 'Maybe she was fighting with her husband all the time and wanted to show him she didn't need him.'

'I don't know. I don't care.' The sympathy Faye had offered her had been short-lived and the moment a whisper of the relationship had emerged at the office coffee machine she'd washed her hands of her junior officer and retreated behind a lofty and distancing coldness. Ashleigh's face flamed scarlet with humiliation. 'If she'd been a man I would have slapped her face and reported her for inappropriate behaviour, but I was stupid enough to think that because she was a woman it made a difference, and it didn't. I trusted her.' As she always did, and always only harming herself.

Lisa, like Ashleigh's family and close friends, like Jude, knew about the affair, something she wasn't ashamed to admit to. It was the crashing misjudgement that had surrounded it, that had led her into a relationship only because she was tired of lying alone at night, that was what she'd kept quiet from everyone. 'I learned a terrible lesson. I'd never been afraid to look at myself in the mirror until that happened, and then I couldn't do it without seeing myself as a fool. And you can't afford to be a fool in the police, can you?'

'Well, I dunno.' Withdrawing the hand as if the measure of comfort she could offer was fully dispensed, Lisa consulted the dregs of her coffee cup. 'It seems to me a lot of people manage it. And in fairness to you, you're only ever an idiot when it comes to your own interests.'

Tears had been creeping up on Ashleigh, but she diverted them into a watery smile. 'Yes. I'll give you that. But most of them don't realise. I knew. I minded. That's why I left. I couldn't have stayed and come face to face with Faye every bloody day.' Now the terrain had changed but this time she was familiar with it, the one established with colleagues and friends. The moment of pessimism passed and defiance reasserted itself. 'And you know why I was so upset? It's because I don't want it to happen again. I don't want it to end in tears and I don't want to have to be the one who leaves.' It was over six months since she'd arrived in Penrith and in that time she'd revived her ancient and comfortable friendship with Lisa. 'I've got new friends. I've got Jude.' And she'd shed all thoughts of Scott, save for the laughing echo that kept reappearing in the cards.

Faye Scanlon could, wittingly or otherwise, change all that but as long as she presented that unrelenting ferocity Ashleigh could have no idea what the woman thought, or what kind of position she was so determined to defend.

*

The chilly morning had turned into a brave one and Lisa had headed off to the gym before Ashleigh set off to walk the short distance into town. On the other side of the road when she left the house a woman sat parked in a car, reading a newspaper. With an eye for everything, no matter how trivial, Ashleigh gave her a second glance. She wasn't surprised to see the woman walking purposefully behind her when she reached the supermarket car park.

There was nothing covert. Her actions were brazen, blatant and determined and, to Ashleigh, spelt only one thing. This was Marsha Letham, the journalist whose cryptic and unwelcome message still lurked unanswered on her phone.

Journalists with a sniff of a story never went away. If Ms Letham thought she'd get something out of Ashleigh she was wrong, but ignoring the message wasn't going to work.

At the pelican crossing she lingered to wait for the lights but the woman, waiting for her, kept a distance. Her pulse raced a little, not with fear but at the possible recriminations if she failed to be sufficiently discreet, or if she was but someone else wasn't. Bugger. She'd have to talk to Jude before she was ready, and it would look as of someone had forced her hand. That, in its turn, made her look guilty and there was no doubt in her mind that if anything came out that Faye didn't like, she'd answer for it.

She cut down the hill into the town centre and doubled back into Little Dockray — a roundabout route, but one that confirmed that Marsha Letham was following her, and not in any way concerned about being spotted. Fine. There would be a confrontation. Ashleigh dropped into a café, strolled to the counter and ordered a coffee and a bacon roll. It wasn't until breakfast had arrived in front of her that the journalist closed in. 'Sergeant O'Halloran, is that right?'

'Hello, Ms Letham.' No point in pretending, and boldness might make the woman think twice. 'I'm sorry I didn't answer your message. I'm not back on shift until tomorrow.'

'I did wonder. Sorry to have alarmed you.' Marsha Letham was in her thirties, with a mannish face and a strained expression. In a mad moment of speculation as the woman leaned forward like a cat scenting a mouse, Ashleigh wrote her off as a journalist challenged to produce a story to justify avoiding redundancy.

The very idea that such a being could have alarmed her was risible. It was a local newspaper. No-one who read it would care, and the story that Faye was scared of was one that no-one would do more than snigger at. A bisexual policewoman? What was new in that? If there was a story it was in the way she'd warned Ashleigh off and finally bullied her off her turf. That would do her more damage than an ill-judged affair; it was the secret she'd want to protect. 'I wasn't alarmed, Ms Letham. I saw you in the car and worked out who you were. But I'm afraid I don't have anything to say to you.'

'You were with Cheshire Police at the same time as Superintendent Scanlon, though? Is that right?'

'Yes, and at the same time as thousands of other people. I did meet Detective Superintendent Scanlon, but I didn't work with her, so I'm afraid I can't help.'

The woman's disappointment was palpable. For the first time, Ashleigh sensed that her secret was safe even if Faye's was teetering dangerously in the edge of the public domain. 'I've heard rumours that Superintendent Scanlon left her previous job under something of a cloud. I wondered if perhaps you'd heard anything—'

'I left last August. If anything happened after that then I wouldn't have heard of it.'

'Aren't you in touch with any former colleagues? Perhaps you could give me a lead there.'

'Only for a few drinks when I'm back down. And obviously I can't pass on details.' Thank God, she'd clawed her way onto the high ground. 'I wish I could help you.' That much had a grain of truth in it, though it would have been more than her job was worth to guide the woman to the conclusion that Faye was unfit for office. Reminded, she covered her back. 'If I did know anything I couldn't discuss it. But I don't.'

Silence. Marsha's big scoop, possibly the biggest headline she'd envisaged since vandals picking the daffodils from the town's churchyard, bit the dust in front of her. 'There must be—'

'The Press Office would be a good place to start.' Thank God, her phone rang, a number she didn't recognise. 'If you'll excuse me…' She turned her back and answered the phone, engaging in a futile conversation with an ambulance-chasing insurance company, and when she turned around Marsha had given up and was strolling along Little Dockray in the direction of the Market Square.

If only every battle were as easily-won as that one. With a degree of relief, Ashleigh ended the call and returned to her coffee and congealed bacon roll.

Chapter 10

'So, now I've outlined the objectives of this session. We've identified areas where we may be showing subconscious bias. We know what the law requires of us in terms of appropriate — and inappropriate — behaviour in the workplace. The first question — exactly what does inappropriate mean? Actions? Words?'

Jude's neighbour, an inspector from the community services team who almost certainly knew everything Claud was telling them and more, hid a discreet yawn behind her hand. She wasn't alone. Aware of Faye's judgemental gaze roaming the crammed conference room from her carefully-chosen seat by the door, Jude took care to keep his body language neutral, though he couldn't quite bring himself to fake enthusiasm.

'The clearest way to help you to know when behaviour is inappropriate is, of course, to show you.' Claud Blackwell, positioned in front of the dozen or so middle-ranking police officers who were the first participants in Faye's new project, raked them with his glance and paused to dwell severely on the yawning offender. 'Natalie and I will act out a scenario between two co-workers and we can discuss whether any element of the scene amounts to inappropriate behaviour. Then we'll try some role play.'

Role play. Jude was sure he wasn't the only one to suppress a shudder, but there was always something he could learn — not necessarily about equality and diversity, but about the Blackwells, so recently the focus of his attention by their proximity to murder. Claud, brisk and bumptious, dominating the room, seemed to have bounced back, but Natalie was quiet and withdrawn in a way that struck Jude as uncharacteristic. The routine background check he'd had run on her had thrown up a complex and varied career, pointing to a talented woman with no staying power. She'd trained as a ballet dancer, excelling as a teenager but giving up on the career before she could pay too high a price in that bruising world of late nights and hard physical work. After a spell as a secretary she'd found the bright lights of the stage irresistible and turned to acting, played a few parts in repertory theatre and made a minor success of it. That, too, ended, this time when she'd run into Claud Blackwell five years before and settled down. When Claud had given up his charity job and branched out on his own she'd taken up a post as his assistant.

'So, first.' Claud motioned to his wife, who stood up and went to the side of the room. 'You're a man. You're a touchy-feely man. You hug people, for whatever reason. Maybe it makes you feel accessible. Maybe you genuinely like people. In your line of work, maybe you think you're offering comfort to someone who's shocked and bereaved. Or maybe you think a hug with a pretty girl is a perk of the job. Most importantly: you mean well. But how do your co-workers see it?' He rolled up his sleeves and placed his hands on his hips, like a peacock displaying. 'Let's begin. Okay, Natalie.'

A pause. 'Natalie,' said Claud again, a touch of impatience in his tone.

This time she responded, walking across the small space at the front of the room, with her eyes focussed somewhere over Claud's shoulder. 'Good morning Claud,' she said, obediently.

'Well, hello Natalie. My you're looking good today. What a lovely top.'

The room shuddered under a collective wince. Jude watched. Claud, with his bright, all-seeing eyes and his sharp mind, was a master of communication. He knew exactly what he was doing – a clumsy, cringe-worthy performance that would have his audience thinking and talking about their real-world experience even as they mocked his examples.

It was astonishing that he'd been looking out of the window for the whole of the period during which Len must have died, and yet had seen nothing.

'Whatever the reason, the key thing isn't whether you hug or not. It's whether your hug is welcome and how you respond if it isn't.'

No-one else had seen anything, either. That was the problem. The checkpoint on the A66 the previous day, a week on from the murder, had yielded nothing but shaken heads from those who'd been crawling along in slow traffic on the day of the incident. So maybe, after all, there had been nothing for Claud to see.

That being the case, where had the second set of tyre tracks come from and how had Len Pierce's killer made their escape? By way of the river? It would be no great challenge for a strong swimmer but a risky one for anyone else. Tammy's CSI team had checked the riverside path and there had been no signs that anyone had been there, but a smart operator would know how to leave as little evidence as possible behind.

'Any thoughts?' Claud demanded of his audience. 'That little scenario Natalie and I acted out. How did you read the body language? Was she happy with that hug or not?'

'Waste of bloody time,' someone muttered behind Jude.

He shifted in his seat. A tap at the door attracted everyone's attention and Faye Scanlon's best scowl. The door opened, letting a welcome breath of fresh air into the crowded room, and Ashleigh peered round it. 'Sorry to interrupt. I need to speak to Jude. Urgently.'

He pushed back his chair. 'Wish I'd thought of getting someone to do that,' someone else muttered, indiscreetly, as he stepped towards the door and out into the corridor.

'Has something come up?' He closed the door behind him.

'Yes.' Ashleigh turned and began walking back down the corridor, as if to imply that whatever it was was, indeed, urgent. 'A man just walked into the police station at Hunter Lane. He says he met Len Pierce in the farm lane last Sunday and that Len was alive when he left him. I thought you'd want to know as soon as possible.'

'Damn right.' It was a lot later than he'd hoped, but the lead had come. 'Do we know any more?'

'Only his name. He's called Giles Butler. According to the duty officer he's sitting there with a cup of coffee, waiting patiently for someone to come and talk to him.' Her smile indicated that her relief at the breakthrough matched his. 'At least it gets you out of that workshop.'

Something in her expression — some slight reservation — implied there was something she was holding back from him. 'It was shaping up to be interesting.'

'Some of us could do with a reminder about sensitivity.'

He could hardly disagree, and shook his head at her as he ducked into his office and grabbed his jacket and bag. 'We'll get down there straight away.'

'You don't want to take Doddsy?'

'No. One of us had better endure Claud's presentation, for form's sake.' He stifled a smile.

133

Ashleigh was by far the most skilled interviewer on his team 'You've got an innocent face and the bad guys all fall for it. I'll play bad cop to your good cop.'

'If he's turned himself in, hopefully we won't need to play games,' she said. 'Shall I drive?'

*

In the half an hour it took the two detectives to turn up at the police station, the courage Giles had struggled so hard to muster seeped away. Someone had found him a cup of coffee and settled him in an interview room and there, in the relatively pleasant surroundings of such a functional space, Giles reduced himself to a helpless specimen, a lost soul. Everything was against him. He'd been with Len. He hadn't presented himself the second he'd learned it was murder. He was a respectable man who kept secrets.

He pulled himself up on that last point, refusing to feel guilty about that, at least. Everyone kept secrets.

'Dr Butler. I'm DCI Satterthwaite. This is Detective Sergeant O'Halloran. We're working on the Pierce case.' The detective was brisk and business-like, hiding his character behind the neutrality of a sharp suit and a crisp white shirt. There was something vaguely attractive about him and Giles, who had taken a long while to acknowledge that it was normal to find men attractive, shivered a little at the thought of how he'd allowed obedience to his parents' traditionalism to lead him into trouble. There was nothing wrong with being gay, he reminded himself, as if there was a chance there might be. It was judging himself by other people's standards that was wrong. That, and lying about it.

He scrambled to his feet, shook the man's hand and then turned to the woman. She was anything but neutral, all vibrant personality the way Janice had been when he first dated her and Gracie still so obviously was, voluptuous and sparkling. She looked as if she was fighting back a permanent smile and despite the sombreness of the situation she did smile, briefly, when she shook his hand.

'Giles Butler.' Sweat gleamed in his palms. They would take that as a sign of guilt, and they must find his carefully-tended image preposterous — pink and plump and tweedy, a countryman from a 1920s seaside postcard, with a thatch of hair that was just too glossily brown not to have had some kind of help from a bottle. Maybe that was why the sergeant was smiling. If you were to cast a country doctor in a stage farce, surely you would cast him. That was all he was — a character living out a lie, but in a murder inquiry not a farce.

The three of them sat down. The chief inspector laid down a pad in front of him and clicked a silver ballpoint pen into action, his hand poised over the pad.

'We'll just take a witness statement at this stage,' the woman said, as reassuring as his practice nurse about to draw blood from a nervous patient. 'I believe you've got something to tell us about Len Pierce. Is that right?'

'Yes.' Giles cleared his throat like a bad actor about to deliver a famous line. 'I imagine you'll have guessed already. I was Lenny's lover.' The phrase screamed, like a bad headline in a red-top tabloid. He threw them an appealing glance, begging them not to judge him too harshly. 'But I swear I didn't kill him.'

His wedding ring caught the light and he turned it over on his finger thinking of Janice, wondering what she'd say when she found out. Their names were engraved together inside the ring, along with the date and a temptation to fate, the words *Happy Ever After*. He'd tried, but he'd failed. Would she understand that?

'Okay,' the man said said, suspending the discussion while the receptionist appeared with coffees for himself and the woman, 'why don't we start at the beginning? Tell us a bit about yourself.' He pushed his chair back and the sergeant sat forward to take over the interview but Giles wasn't fooled. While he was concentrating on what she had to say her boss would listen and watch the two of them, chipping in where necessary, reading Giles's body language and interpreting his nervousness as something deeper and far more sinister, as guilt or fear. And he'd be right in that. Giles was both guilty and fearful.

'I'm Dr Giles Butler. GP. From Kirkby Lonsdale.' He coughed. 'I'm fifty-six. Married.' Because that mattered, if only to Janice. 'Three sons, two at university, one still at school.' He issued the two of them with a pleading look, trying it on one of them, then the other, backwards and forwards and turning to Ashleigh O'Halloran.

'Thanks, Dr Butler. Let's start off with what made you come and talk to us.'

Gracie. It had been her sound common sense, the doubt he'd heard in her voice. That the only person left alive who understood him might suspect him had forced his hand. He couldn't let her think he was a killer and this was the only way out.

'I saw your appeal on the news.' He nodded towards Jude Satterthwaite, who seemed to hide a wry smile. 'I had no idea. I was shocked when I heard.'

'The television appeal was on Monday,' the sergeant reminded him. 'Why didn't you get in touch with us before?'

'I was very busy.' Giles's nerves tightened into nausea. 'But it was on my conscience once I saw the appeal. It was a shock, a terrible shock.' He reached for the cup and the dregs of his cold coffee. 'I didn't kill Lenny — I swear I didn't. But you'll think I did.'

'We don't think anything, Dr Butler.' The woman picked up her pen, turned it over in her fingers and put it down again, a futile gesture since the man was taking the notes . 'We're here to listen. Tell us about how you know Lenny. That's a good starting point.'

He gave a small, huffing sigh, reviewing a prepared speech and trying to remember all the things he had to say. 'I'm gay. I suppose you know that.' Someone in a lab somewhere would already have unpacked the secret he'd kept from everyone but Len and Gracie for the best part of forty years. 'Obviously I hadn't told anyone.'

'Obviously,' she affirmed, without a trace of irony

The difficulty of explaining his domestic situation was too much, though it would hardly be unusual, and she didn't ask. Thank God for that. Janice would be disappointed in him. The boys would be furious or, worse, mortified. His patients, or some of them, would be shocked, either at his sexuality or his cowardice. A few might not care. 'I met him about eighteen months ago, in a cafe in Penrith. He'd been in to see his bank manager and I'd been at the hospital to visit my father. The place was busy so he asked if he could share my table and we got chatting.' Like *Brief Encounter*, or a bad romance. He wasn't sure which.

'You got on well, then.'

What attracted one person to another? It certainly hadn't been his looks. Len had been a skinny man with a sharp expression that reflected his dissatisfaction with the way the world had treated him, but whatever it was some bolt from the blue had taken Giles straight in the stomach and those decades of forcing himself into his parents' expectations had been swept aside. 'I can't remember what, but there was something about him that made me laugh. I took to him straight away.' That was the good side. Len had had a dry wit, not unlike Giles' own. He'd poked fun at him for his staid respectability, teased him about his double life while being the first person ever to understand it. They'd laughed about it, and a whole lot of other, trivial things. In this world it did you good to laugh. 'You know how it is. Sometimes you meet the least likely people and you click. That was what it was like with Lenny and me.' Most of all he'd loved Len's stubborn refusal to care about what other people thought of him. If he had his time over again... *Gay*, he'd have said to the world at large, wide-eyed at the age of sixteen when the possibility had first, briefly, occurred to him, *so what?* But life punished you for being born in the wrong generation and he was trapped in its expectations.

'And you started meeting regularly?'

'Yes. For coffee at first, and to talk. Then later, more.' He couldn't help it. He went scarlet, reached for his coffee again and found the cup empty. 'We didn't always have sex.' In the end it hadn't been about that. 'Sometimes we just talked. Sometimes we went for a walk. On Sunday I met him in the lane as we agreed.'

'Did you always meet there?'

Giles twisted his fingers together. He hadn't thought he could regret his cowardice any more but as the detective forced him to think about Len, talk about him, he did. 'Yes.'

'Isn't it a bit...' She turned the pen over in her fingers. 'Basic?'

'I didn't want to go to his house,' Giles mumbled. 'And he couldn't come to mine. I'm married. People know me. Even in Appleby. They talk. My career.' The lies. The deceit. That was the only thing they'd fallen out about. *Can't you be honest with people*, Len had demanded, and they'd always ended by laughing. 'We chatted for a bit. We made love. And then I drove away.'

'What time was that?'

'I remember it exactly, because I put on the radio to hear the football. It was Liverpool-Spurs. It was just kicking off. So it would have been two o'clock.'

'You didn't see anything around there?' prompted the sergeant. 'Anybody? Any cars?'

'I wasn't looking. I was concerned about getting back home. I'd spent longer with him than I'd intended and I was in a hurry to to get away. I'd told my wife I was playing golf.' He flicked miserably at his top lip. He'd always known he'd be found out, but he'd deluded himself into thinking he'd have the courage to tell her before it happened. Now time had run out on him and his confession was forced.

'You went to a good deal of effort to cover your tracks,' she said. 'Was that entirely necessary?'

'My wife. My patients.' Giles shifted in his seat again. 'It's all going to come out now, isn't it?'

'I'm afraid it'll have to, when the case goes to court. It was courageous of you to come forward. You did exactly the right thing.'

Something about her made him want to confide. 'I wish to God it had never happened the way it did. If I'd admitted to myself I might be gay a bit earlier I'd never have got married, but I never did. God knows, sometimes I think I wasn't gay when I was married. There have been studies that suggest—' He pulled himself up. Poor Janice. What a deception. Had she ever sighed in private about the absence of that passionate something from their lovemaking? 'Never mind. I only realised for sure about ten years ago. There I was. Wonderful wife. Terrific career. I was working in the kind of place where being a doctor means something, where you still have a bit more respect in the community. Very traditional. Everybody was very happy. Except me.'

'Is your wife happy?' she asked.

A strange question. Perhaps a lot of crimes took place behind just such a curtain of perfection, dramas playing out in the heart while the window on the world was one of false happiness. 'I don't know.' He'd never asked her. Maybe she'd guessed and played her own part in his drama, pretending for the sake of the children, or the neighbours, or her own self-respect.

The woman gave a wry smile, as if she was reviewing her own mistakes. 'And then you met Len.'

Belatedly, Giles realised what she was up to, taking him back over the story to check for inconsistencies, looking for things he'd wish he hadn't said. The questioning was innocuous but the path it led him down was full of traps waiting to be sprung and a false step would mean a murder charge. 'I never went looking for a partner. He just walked into my life. But he was my friend.'

'What did you talk about?'

'Everything.' They'd talked about football and politics and work, about the changes in the seasons, about food and holidays and music, about everything except the discomfort of the lives they lived.

'Did he tell you much about his private life?'

'I don't think he had a private life, if I'm honest. He lived on his own, he didn't go out much. He spent a lot of time baking. He loved baking. He made all the cakes for the shop his sister ran.' Giles's voice was wistful. 'I gave him money for the tea shop, once. For new crockery. It was a loan. Interest free. Because we were friends. I always said I'd call in there and try the baking, have a look at my investment, but I never did.' And never would.

The woman wrote it down as if it wasn't at all unusual. 'Can you think of anyone who disliked him?'

'None. I can see he might have ticked a few people off by being abrupt with them, but that's not a crime. And to be honest I don't think he interacted with anyone enough to make an enemy of them.'

Silence bred between them. 'Thank you very much for your help, Dr Butler. It's been invaluable. There are a number of steps we'll have to take to check out your story, of course.'

'I expect you'll want to take my car.' Giles got to his feet, the imminence of disaster closing in on him. 'I don't know how I'll explain that to my wife.'

He got no sympathy from the chief inspector. 'You can tell her it was impounded because the tyres were illegal.' The man pushed back his chair. 'I take it you'll be happy for us to be in touch at a later stage. I've no doubt there will be other questions we want to ask as the investigation progresses. With your permission I'd like to take fingerprints and a DNA sample. In the meantime, if you could read over this witness statement and sign it as a true report of what you've told us…'

'I appreciate your courage in coming to talk to us,' the sergeant said as he scanned his own words, reproaching him in black and white. She must have decided that he'd earned a little soft talking.

'It's in my own interests, isn't it? Because if there's someone going around slaughtering gay people it's in everyone's interests that we catch him.'

*

'What do we reckon, then?' Jude had been silent for most of the short journey from Hunter Lane to the Carlton Hall HQ, drumming his fingers on his knee while he thought it through.

'He definitely has a few more questions to answer, doesn't he?'

'He does. It'll be interesting to see what we get from the car, if anything. Natalie claims to have discovered the body at a little after two, which fits with the information on her fitness tracker. Even if Giles was telling the truth about timings the window in which Len died is large enough for him to have been the killer.'

'It doesn't look good for him, does it?' Ashleigh pictured Giles's round, pink face with its expression of naked fear. 'I know he came to us voluntarily, but I'll bet it was only because he thought we'd find him.' She turned off into the slip road.

'He certainly thought about it for long enough. And it strikes me he's an accomplished liar.'

'I really struggle to understand why people have to get so hung up about their sexuality.' Ashleigh thought of Faye, and how horrified both their husbands had been to discover the place Scott had left in Ashleigh's bed had been filled by a woman.

'My guess is that the doctor cares more about his good name and what's left of his reputation. I imagine he'd have squirmed just as much if Len had been Leona.'

'Do you? Maybe you're right. But I don't think he'd have hated himself quite as much as he seems to.'

'You're probably right.' He glanced down at his watch as the car slowed. 'I'll go up and brief Doddsy. You run and get some lunch. I'll join you there.'

'Can I get you anything?'

'A ham sandwich. Cake. Anything, as long as there's lots of it. I'm starving.'

Ashleigh pulled up outside the entrance to let him out, then parked the car and made her way to the canteen. Over by the window Natalie Blackwell sat forlornly by herself while Claud stood at the other side of the room, deep in animated conversation with Faye.

In the course of the previous week's fruitless investigation Ashleigh had delved into Natalie's background. The overwhelming impression she'd acquired was of a woman who, with her intense and anxious gaze, her defensive body language and her obsession with running, had more to offer than anyone had ever asked of her. Pausing to evaluate her chances of avoiding Faye, she spared Natalie a second glance. Engaging her in conversation involved the risk of being cornered by Claud, whom she instinctively distrusted, or Faye, but curiosity got the better of her. She carried her tray across to the table where Natalie sat with an uneaten sandwich on a plate in front of her and indicated the seat next to her. 'May I?'

'Of course.' Natalie shifted her seat to one side even though there was plenty of room, an indication of her willingness to chat. 'Have a seat.' A pause, while Ashleigh did so. 'I'm sorry the chief inspector had to leave the workshop this morning.'

'I'm sure he was, too.' Ashleigh managed to look at Natalie with what passed for total sincerity and then turned back to her lunch. Natalie's thin frame, her consuming obsession with exercise and the look she gave the two sandwiches and two pieces of cake on Ashleigh's tray implied an eating disorder, either in the past or in the present.

'We'll be doing some more. Claud always tweaks the script as he goes on, to make it more bespoke. He'll have a chance to review what we've done so far. Superintendent Scanlon asked DI Dodd to work with him on it.' With apparent reluctance, Natalie made an attack on her sandwich, taking it apart with a knife and fork and extracting the filling. Limp lettuce and pale ham, shiny with mayonnaise, spilled out over the plate and she lifted the bread and piled the two slices to one side. 'Sorry,' she said, seeing Ashleigh's look. 'It's a ballet dancer's habit. No carbs.'

Aye right, thought Ashleigh to herself. It had been years since Natalie had quit the hard labour of the ballet and her tenure in it had barely lasted two years. Miles run, calories consumed, minutes passed — all were the indicators of Natalie's insecurity, everything trapped and pigeonholed, even the abstract accounted for. 'I should probably cut a few carbs myself.'

'Oh, no. Everyone's different.' Natalie chased a slice of tomato around the plate with her fork before forcing herself to eat it, chewing slowly and chasing it down with a mouthful of thin black coffee. 'Claud always says. Tolerance and diversity extend to the little things in life. It isn't just about colour or gender or sexuality or religion. It's about everyone being allowed to do things their way. If we can't be tolerant of other people's choices, how can we be expected to be tolerant of the things they have no choice over?' Her pale hair had escaped from the grips that held it and dropped around her face like a curtain as she stared at her plate.

Running that over in her head a second time to try and make sense of it, Ashleigh gave it up, a debate for another time, preferably late at night in the pub when no-one would remember what they'd said the morning after. 'Absolutely.'

'So often, too, we resist things in others because we recognise them in ourselves.' Natalie looked at the ham like someone who'd momentarily forgotten they were vegetarian. 'That poor man they found.'

The *they* was telling, a signal of denial and trauma. 'Yes.'

'It's obvious that whoever did it hates gay people.'

It wasn't obvious, but it was possible. It could have been random. It could have been personal. To date there was nothing to indicate which. 'That's an option.'

'Whereas in fact being gay isn't a binary thing. It's a spectrum. Almost certainly people who hate gay people don't hate them because they're different. They hate them because they recognise the same thing in themselves but are afraid, for whatever reason, of admitting to it.'

'That's one theory.' It fitted Giles Butler and his self-loathing too neatly. He'd seemed more uncomfortable about his sexuality than grief-stricken about the loss of the man he'd claimed to love.

On the far side of the room Faye and Claud shuffled towards the door, still in conversation. Faye had a cardboard cup of coffee in her hand and Claud kept drifting away towards them and then heading back, as if whatever she had to say was too important to let go.

'Oh, it's more than just a theory. I saw it a lot when I was in acting. People assume the theatre attracts gay people but that's wrong.' Natalie, too, was watching Claud and Faye, her fork suspended halfway to her lips. 'The culture is more open so they're just less afraid of acknowledging it. I mean, let's be honest. It's a rare individual who's never remotely attracted to someone of the same sex.'

'But that can be to do with personality.'

'Personality is only a part of it. I do believe that if one finds another person attractive there has to be a physical element to it.' Natalie jabbed her fork into the chaos on her plate. 'Many friendships are platonic but that's because of the balance of the relationship. Obviously, heterosexual people don't fancy every person of the opposite sex they meet. I believe every one of us is bisexual to a degree. Even if we haven't had a relationship with someone of our own sex it's usually because we don't understand how we feel, because society has placed a false definition of sexual attraction upon us. We become defensive about it, but that doesn't mean the sexual attraction doesn't exist. And so we feel we're attracted to the wrong people.' She folded a scrap of lettuce into a parcel and popped it in her mouth.

Jude should have been there, listening. There was something so dislocated in Natalie's argument it felt as if she was parroting the words of someone else, without quite remembering them or understanding them enough for them to make sense. In Ashleigh's experience relationships were far more nuanced than that and she didn't need to be reminded of it while

Faye was standing in the room looking severe. That relationship had been an error of judgement, not gender — the wrong person at the wrong time. 'What was it like, being an actress?'

'Fairly grim, if I'm honest.' Natalie considered the debris on her plate and laid her cutlery down. 'Late nights. Hard work. I loved the job, of course. There's something magical about going on stage and becoming someone else for an hour or two. It was all the other things that went with it. I'm not an itinerant. As I grew older I began to value the security of routine, and an actor's life has none of that. The glamour only lasted for a month or so and then I struggled.'

Police work combined the best and the worst of routine. Most of the time you never knew what you were doing other than that the greater part of it would be dull. 'No.'

'That's why I started running. I can control that. I've suffered from depression since my late teens.' Tilting her elegant head towards Ashleigh with a questioning look, Natalie dabbed her lips with a napkin as the few crumbs she'd eaten had filled her up. 'Claud says I'm obsessed by it. I try and run a hundred miles a week.'

A hundred miles a week and no carbs. It was enough to make anyone feel faint. 'Does it work?'

'Yes. Though actually it's been difficult this week. It's been so hard to run. I keep thinking about what happened last weekend, wondering what I'll find every time I run round a corner. But I have to run. I'd run all day if I could. I made myself run past the place where I found that poor man, but only once. Since then I've run in the town.' The sandwich defeated her. She pushed the plate aside and drained the last of her coffee. 'Claud's looking for me. I'd better go.'

Over by the door, Faye and Claud had concluded their conversation and separated, he moving towards them. 'Okay to go, Nat? Chris Dodd can give us ten minutes on what he thought of the workshop. I can manage without you, if you're still eating.'

'Just coming.' Obedient to a summons he hadn't issued, she jumped up. 'I suppose I'll see you again, Ashleigh.'

The relationship between Natalie and her husband played out on their walk to the door, she gazing up at him and he guiding her with a hand on the small of her back, a one-way dependency he seemed to accept without question. Ashleigh finished her sandwich and finally turned without guilt to the slice of cake that had accompanied it, just as Jude slid round the door. She watched, with more satisfaction than she would have admitted to, as he headed towards her. 'Sorry. Doddsy was hell bent on telling me everything he's learned today about respecting other people's differences.' He grinned at her. 'Did you find me a decent sandwich?'

She stifled her amusement. 'It's chicken, all there was left. And thanks to you I've had to endure Natalie sitting opposite me, pretending not to judge me for having two lunches. It just about broke me.'

'I have a stronger heart. Or a bigger hunger. It wouldn't have broken me.' He sat down, reached for the sandwich and ripped it free from its packaging. 'Claud seems very taken with our Doddsy. I thought he'd find him a bit too introverted.'

'They're on first name terms already, by the sound of it.'

'As long as he doesn't seek my opinion.' He paused. 'I saw you talking to Mrs B. What do you make of her?'

'I think there's something very odd about her.' Ashleigh lowered her voice to match his.

'I thought that.' He drained the cup of coffee, already cold, at one go.

'She strikes me as one of those souls who struggles to find peace. You know the sort. Everything they try is the answer, but only for a short time. The only thing that seems to help her is running, or so she says.'

'She runs to live. Some people are like that.' Jude was a runner himself. 'I can't say it gets me that way. I do it to allow myself to think, and I've a suspicion she does it for exactly the opposite reason.'

'You don't go to pieces when you can't do it, either.'

'No. But she strikes me as having an obsessive personality. That's what it's all about. Claud's a brave man, or a devoted one. I think she might be quite hard to live with.'

'Everyone has their peculiarities.' Scott had always left his shoes on exactly the same spot just inside the front door.

'I have mine, too, but I don't get stressed if something disturbs them.' Jude was still staring in the direction in which the Blackwells had disappeared.

'She adores Claud, I think. And depends on him.'

'He certainly seems to have enormous influence on her.' He looked down at his cup. 'I'm going for another coffee. Do you want one?'

If it wasn't for the fact that Faye was lingering near the counter, making herself obvious and accessible as she'd promised she would, Ashleigh would have offered to go up and get it, but discretion was a virtue. It would be wise to keep a safe space between them. 'I'm fine, thanks.'

Faye had other ideas. As Jude joined the short queue for a cup of coffee, she detached herself from her position and drifted over as if he was the one she was keen to avoid. 'Ashleigh.'

'Hi.' Ashleigh waited for her to take a seat, but she stood a clear yard back.

'I didn't know you'd come here when you left Cheshire.'

I'm not hard to find, Ashleigh raged inwardly, but the relationship was over and any leeway had evaporated with it. In work, Faye was a woman who professed informality but practised authority. It wasn't worth taking liberties involved risk. She said nothing.

'It goes without saying that anything that happened in the past…' Faye licked her lips, the faintest, only sign of concern, '…stays there.'

So why talk about it? *Just say nothing.* 'Fine by me.'

'Good. Because if there's any gossip, I'll know where it's come from.' Faye shuffled half a step away and raised her voice, for public consumption this time. 'You're busy on the Pierce murder, I understand?'

'Among other things.'

'And working closely with Jude Satterthwaite. A workplace romance, I understand. Is that correct?'

'That's correct.' Jude put his coffee cup down on the table, pulled out the chair and sat down. His smile was bland, and the expression he turned on Faye gave no clue as to how much of their conversation he'd heard.

'If you'd been able to stay for the rest of this morning's workshop you'd have seen a very clear case study of the pitfalls of that kind of relationships and ways to avoid them. Among other things.'

'No-one's complained so far.'

'Good. I take it there was a good reason for you leaving early?'

'Yes. We had a new and important lead in the Pierce case.' Quite deliberately, Jude helped himself to a corner of Ashleigh's carrot cake and swapped it for a piece of his chocolate brownie.

'Good news. But there are others this week and it's important that you make an effort to attend the next one. I'm sure I can squeeze you into one tomorrow.' And Faye, head held high, swung on her flat heel and stalked out of the canteen.

Chapter 11

'In a hurry, Jude?'

He'd been looking at his watch as he strode down the corridor, already running late, and Faye had emerged from her office showing no signs of getting ready to leave. 'Not particularly. Just off down to join a few guys in the pub. It's Tammy's birthday.'

'I see. And you have to go along to pick up the tab. Very generous.'

Jude enjoyed a drink with friends but he'd have skipped this particular outing if he'd dared. 'Feel free to go along and relieve me,' he said, and laughed. Since Tammy had approached him the previous week they'd brokered a delicate truce, as if having had her say she felt it easier to deal with her concerns, but you never knew what mood she'd be in.

Rather to his surprise, she took it as the joke he'd intended. 'Maybe another time.' And then the smile disappeared and her business face was back. 'Did you find the workshop productive?'

The workshop was the reason he was running late. 'Yes. An efficient use of my time.'

'I don't need the sarcasm. It's a vital part of working with the community.'

'Of course.' He looked at his watch again, to telegraph the message. 'If you don't mind—'

'Any progress on the Pierce case?'

'I'll do some more on it later on.'

'After the works drinks?'

'Yes, I imagine so.'

'Then we can discuss it tomorrow.'

He was due on a rest day the next day but he didn't remind her in case she saw fit to go through the case on the spot, but if she thought of doing that she was distracted by Claud, backing out of one of the meeting rooms in a profusion of goodbyes.

Jude sensed escape. 'Are you heading down to reception, Mr Blackwell? I'll walk down with you. See you out.'

Faye shrugged that off. 'Goodbye, Mr Blackwell. Thank you so much for the workshop. Fine stuff.'

'I'll email the debriefing notes over to you this evening.' Claud bounced off down the corridor ahead of him, the jacket of his brown suit straining across his shoulders. 'Working late to catch our neighbourhood murderer, are you, Chief Inspector?' He fidgeted with the visitor's badge clipped to his lapel, snapped it off the moment they reached reception and headed over to the front desk to sign himself out. 'No nearer laying a hand on him, DI Dodd tells me.'

'I'm doing my best.' He might have been a bit closer if he hadn't had to spend an afternoon in Claud's workshop, but too bad.

'A very fine man, Chris Dodd. And a very useful link on building bridges with the churchgoing community. The feedback on the workshop was excellent, too.'

'Thanks for this afternoon's session,' the devil in Jude made him say, as if provoking Faye wasn't bad enough. 'It was most enlightening.'

When Claud turned injured eyes on him, he knew he hadn't hidden the sarcasm in his tone. 'I know you people resent having to take the time to do these things. I appreciate you have more than enough to do already. But regular refreshment of attitudes and approaches is vital to public engagement and confidence. Superintendent Scanlon knows that. I'm sure your behaviour is impeccable at all times, but to educate people we need to walk a mile or more in their moccasins.'

'Fair comment.' Feeling he'd been too sharp, Jude sought to make amends. 'Is Natalie not with you?'

'She left straight after the workshop. She wanted to run back to Temple Sowerby, but I don't encourage that on country roads when it's dark. So she decided to go down into town, run around for a bit until she's got however many miles she needs today, and catch up with me at the office.'

'You're based in town?' A cold blast caught them as they headed out of the building.

'Yeah. We've just taken on the lease to a new office up in the church close. It's a nice enough place, central, and there's a real community around there.'

'And a great little baker's in the arcade.' Jude, who patronised the bakery on a regular basis whenever he had to buy off the team for some minor misdemeanour, was thankful for something other than murder or diversity to talk about as they headed to the car park,.

'I'll check it out. Nat turns her nose up at cake, of course, but I eat the carbs for her and she runs the calories off for me.' A grin showed Claud's face in a different light, a flash of humour underlying his usually fierce expression. 'I'll head down there and work until she sees fit to turn up.'

'Do you need a lift? I'm heading down into town myself.'

'A wild night out on a Tuesday, eh? You guys know how to live.'

'It's a birthday.'

'Every day's someone's birthday.' Claud laughed again. 'No, I have the car. Nat may like to travel everywhere she can under her own steam, but I don't have the time.'

Jude checked his phone for messages for one last time once Claud had left. At least on a Tuesday he'd be unlikely to run into Becca, and he had the next day with Ashleigh to look forward to. In the meantime an uneasy hour trying to keep the peace between Tammy and Doddsy wasn't something he was looking forward to, and the workshop hadn't offered him any help in dealing with this particular problem. How would Claud have handled Tammy's grievance — as a straightforward case of homophobia or as a mother's badly-expressed concern? And how would Giles Butler have reacted to the challenge that Claud had issued them with, to be true to themselves and honest with each other?

*

In Penrith's Market Square, Gracie stopped for a moment to glance up at the clock. Twenty past six. Giles was due at seven. Perhaps, after all, she should have taken the car.

Too late, now. She'd just have to hurry. The last thing she wanted was for him to turn up and find out she wasn't there. Poor Giles – such a lovely man, such a fragile ego. And so reluctant to confront his problems. His wife wouldn't mind, in the end, surely. Not after thirty years. Surely she'd be forgiving, because she loved him.

She sighed as she stopped outside Barclays, fishing into her bag for her purse and sliding the card into the machine. She had no idea of the real state of Giles's marriage, and what she heard was only one side. *Problems*, she said to herself fretfully. *Other people's problems.* They were much easier to solve than your own.

Giles had been put out with her on their trip to Temple Sowerby, but surely he'd be over it by now. He knew she'd been right. He'd had no option but to go to the police before they came to him.

Well, soon enough she'd find out if he'd done it, and what they'd said. Taking the cash from the machine she folded the notes into her purse, slotted the purse into her bag and headed off.

*

Jude parked the car at his house in Wordsworth Street and walked the short distance to the pub. Recently Adam Fleetwood, no doubt in another attempt to be constantly in his face, had rented a ground floor flat at the bottom of Wordsworth Street, where he sat of an evening with the curtains open and the lights on. This evening Adam was standing with his back to the street, a can of Coke in one hand and the remote control for the telly in the other. At least Becca wasn't there, though it was still early and there was plenty of time for her to head down from work and join him. If she'd been in Adam's living room, or if he were to meet her on the way, he'd have shrugged her off just as he'd done the previous occasion. Jealousy wasn't his besetting sin, and he was almost over her.

But she wasn't there and unlikely to be in the pub. Walking briskly along Meeting House Lane, he dropped down through the church close. The light shone out from the church and a couple of dark figures scuttled across the churchyard and in through the north door. Tuesday night was bell-ringing practice. The daffodils thrashed in the stiff breeze and a starling, disturbed, screeched above his head. On the far side of the church close, Claud's short and stocky figure moved about in a well-lit first-floor window. For a moment Jude watched him as he peeled off his jacket and tossed it to one side, until the church clock, always three minutes slow, struck the half hour and reminded him to move on. An hour in the pub would be enough and then he could decently disengage himself, see if Ashleigh could be tempted back for a bite to eat.

It wasn't quite dark. The rush hour had died down but the square was still busy with traffic sliding around the curves of the A6 as it slalomed through the town centre. Emerging from the churchyard, Jude crossed the road and headed the hundred yards up the hill to the pub.

Inside, what looked for all the world like an uneasy truce prevailed. At one end of a long table, Tammy nursed a tumbler of gin and tonic and at the other, Doddsy stared into the depths of a glass of orange juice. Between them, an assortment of detectives and crime scene investigators, with Ashleigh and Chris among them, kept the peace. Tyrone was notable by his absence.

'Happy birthday.' He gave Tammy a decorous peck on the cheek as she stood up to greet him and then slid into a seat between her and Ashleigh. 'Sorry I'm late. I got held up.'

'No let-up, eh?' Tammy said. 'You need to take more time off, Chief. You'll work yourself into an early grave.'

'I doubt that.'

'We got you a pint. Was that right?' She swirled the glass in her hand. 'I'm not driving. Phil's coming to pick me up when he's finished up at the hospital. We're going out for dinner.'

Jude unbuttoned his coat, laid his phone on the table and took the opportunity to sidle closer to Ashleigh as he took his seat. 'Cheers, then. Here's to many more birthdays.'

'What kept you so long?' Ashleigh asked him.

'I bumped into Faye.'

'Has something come up?'

'Not that I'm aware of. She just doesn't seem able to let me out of the building without a word in my ear.'

She smiled at him. 'Relax. It isn't you.'

'You reckon?'

'I know for sure.'

He lifted a questioning eyebrow.

'I'll tell you later,' she said as his phone rang, and he turned it upwards with a sigh. Claud Blackwell's number, which had somehow found its way into his contacts over the past couple of weeks, flashed up.

'No peace for the wicked, eh?' He picked it up, stood up and stepped away from the table. One day he'd learn to switch it off. Claud had struck him as a man who never let anything go, who worked long hours and never respected anyone else's time off and now, it seemed, he had the proof of that. 'Hi Claud. What can I do for you?'

'You need to come down to the churchyard. Now!' Claud's voice, so unlike his normal hectoring calm, was squeaky with panic. 'Someone's dead.'

'Dead?' Jude needed only a second before he was on his feet, holding the phone away from his ear. 'Doddsy, come here a minute, would you?' He was already moving towards the door. 'Who is it? How? And where?'

'I don't know. There's a lot of blood. It's in the churchyard. A woman. I've dialled 999 but you said you were at the pub. I thought you'd want to know.'

Jude flipped the phone to speaker mode. Equally alert, Ashleigh appeared at his other side and the three of them crowded in over it. 'I'll be with you in a minute. Is anyone else there?'

'A couple of people came by. I—'

'Don't let them touch anything.'

'It's like last time. All the blood.' Claud's self-confidence degenerated into a scared man's whimper.

'I'll be right there.' The churchyard. Not an isolated lane this time. And Claud Blackwell, close to the spot.

A hundred yards or so separated the pub from the churchyard and he covered them in seconds, racing up the opening from the square. The church bells were ringing a strangely cheerful peal. There was already a knot of people in the alley and he shouldered his way through them. 'Police! Let me through!'

'Oh my God,' one of them was saying. 'Did you see who it is? Someone says it's one of the nurses from up at the hospital. Dead.'

Jude's feet overrode his heart, which had somehow stopped while he ran on. Dozens, probably hundreds of nurses worked up at the hospital, but Becca always signed off her rounds there and the churchyard was on her direct route to Adam's flat.

She'd have driven. Surely she wouldn't have walked.

Don't even think that.

Deep darkness lay against the church's north wall, out of reach of the streetlamps and the floodlights that illuminated the square sandstone tower. A shadow moved within the shadow. On the wall someone sat sobbing, someone else talking on the phone. 'Oh God, Mum, I was walking through the church close—'

'Police!' said Jude again, his voice less authoritative than he'd have wanted. No-one moved. He put his shoulder to a gap in the group of onlookers and pushed his way through it. The inner shadow took on a form, human size, human shape.

He flicked the torch on his phone. A sensible shoe, flat, black and comfortable like all the nurses worse, appeared briefly in the light and disappeared again when he turned. Dark trousers, like the ones Becca wore for work. He felt in his pocket for his warrant card, swung it in an arc for anyone to see. 'Police!' he said for a third time. 'Stand back!'

His heart slowed as he bent to the figure on the ground. 'Do we know who—?'

'No.' Claud's face wavered out of the darkness. 'I've never seen her before.'

Jude snatched a look over his shoulder. Doddsy would take the burden from him, even Ashleigh, but he couldn't let them. He had to see for himself. He lifted the coat and looked down.

His heart slowed again, this time in relief. Long hair glinted copper in the artificial light. The face that stared up at him, the eyes wide in shock, their emptiness exaggerated by the lights and the shadows, by the stark whiteness of the skin, was a stranger to him.

Thank God. Not Becca.

A touch on his sleeve. Ashleigh. 'Are you okay?'

'Fine.' She'd seen his moment of weakness and an irrational fury overwhelmed him — with himself for still caring, with her for her ability to see into his soul and know that his first thoughts had been for someone else. He turned his back on her. 'Let's get on.'

Blue lights bounced, strobe-like, off the lights at either end of the churchyard. 'I'll deal with them,' Doddsy said to him. 'You take charge here.' He headed down towards the ground on swift, light steps.

The bells had stopped. The door of the church opened and one of the PCs closed in on it. 'Not that way, Sir. I'm afraid you can't come through here. Use the other door.'

'I'm on it, as well.' Ashleigh turned away, then twisted back to him, her face all sympathy. That just made it worse. 'Just as well we never got started on the drinks.' She stepped away. 'Okay. Everybody. Who saw what happened?'

Jude turned back to the body and the two people who stood by it. A cluttered, contaminated crime scene spread in front of him. Claud should have known better. 'I thought I said not to move the body.'

'I did tell him not to do that. I did.' Claud wrung his hands.

'I had to move her.' A second figure emerged from the shadow. With a weird lack of surprise, Jude recognised him as Phil Garner, Tammy's husband. 'The poor woman was still alive when I got to her, but there was nothing I could do to save her. I'm afraid she's gone. Stabbed. One wound only, I think. Straight to the heart.'

'Do you recognise her?'

'Why the hell would I?'

In the dim light from the churchyard lamps, Jude looked from him to Claud and back again. Both men's hands and clothing were smeared with blood. 'Of course. You did your best. Thank you.'

He'd tried to be neutral but Phil, always quick to take umbrage, bristled. 'I don't need you lecturing me about crime scenes. Tammy never lets up. But it's like I always say to her. I'm a doctor. My first priority is to save life and I'm not going to leave someone to die because of your rules.'

What strange conversations the Garners must share over the breakfast table — a doctor, a policeman, a CSI. 'Mine, too. But now she's dead, it's a crime scene. It's for us to take over.' He glanced over his shoulder. Ashleigh had marshalled the onlookers away from the scene and Doddsy was issuing instructions to the first uniformed officers on the scene, one of whom was already unrolling some tape and closing the churchyard off. Among them he recognised Tyrone, speaking quickly to Doddsy and immediately moving on to join Ashleigh in taking the names and addresses of witnesses.

'Mr Blackwell. You found the body? Did you see anything? Anybody?'

'No.' Claud's voice shook as Jude ushered the two of them away from the scene. 'I just called 999. I called you. I shouted out for help and this gentleman came and went over to her. I told him what you'd said about not moving her but he didn't listen. Jesus. Jesus, I feel ill.'

'It's okay.' Jude steered him away, beyond the boundaries of the churchyard, where they couldn't do any more damage to the scene. A quick gesture brought Ashleigh towards him.

'Arc lights,' Doddsy was saying to someone. 'And for God's sake get all these people away. And tell them all to be bloody careful where they put their feet.'

'Tyrone's taking charge of the witnesses,' she said to Jude. 'We're going to put them in the church to get their preliminary statements.'

'Not these two. I'll speak to them myself. Mr Blackwell found the body, and this is Phil Garner. Tyrone's dad. He's a doctor. I'll speak to both of them just now and then we'll get someone to take them down to the station.'

'What for?' Claud's voice quivered.

'Routine,' Ashleigh soothed him. 'We need to take samples. As you were present at the scene we need to check for cross-contamination.'

'I suppose. Yes. Oh, God.'

'I'll go and twiddle my thumbs until you're done, then, shall I?' Phil looked to Ashleigh for direction and she nodded him to the church. 'I'm allowed to make a phone call, of course? I'd better let Tammy know what's keeping me.'

He marched off, leaving Jude with Claud.
'Okay. I just want you to run through what happened. Let's go into the church and find you a seat.'

'Claud?' Another figure appeared, breaking through a gap that the uniformed officers had yet to seal off. Jude cursed. Natalie, on her way back from her latest run, had once more stumbled on the scene of a crime.

'Don't come any closer, Mrs Blackwell,' he called to her.

She stopped. 'Claud, what's going on? What's happened?'

'Oh God,' said Claud again, a sigh draining his lungs. 'Nat. Where the hell have you been?' He moved towards her like a sleepwalker.

'I was running. You know I was. I said I'd meet you at the office.' She was stock-still in front of them, standing in the doorway that led into one of the buildings in the church close, hands braced on the doorposts like a crucified Christ. 'What's happened? Is someone hurt?'

'I found a body in the churchyard,' he said, wearily. 'I have to go and give a statement. They're going to take me to the police station. Come with me, Nat. I need you.'

'Of course I'll come with you.' She'd remained still as instructed but Claud reached her and she clasped his hand in both of hers, lifting it to her lips. 'Darling. You look awful. So awful.'

'I know what it was like for you, now.'

'This way.' Jude led them around the route one of the PCs directed, away from the body and towards the south entrance to the church. Inside, Ashleigh and Tyrone had half a dozen people sitting on the pews. A further collection sat bemused to one side. The bell ringers, he supposed. Phil sat by himself, tapping blood-stained fingers on the back of a pew and speaking into his phone.

Claud sank into a chair at the back of the church, the nearest place, as if his legs could no longer hold him. 'I need a glass of water.'

'I'll get you one. There must be one somewhere.' Natalie headed off towards the back of the church.

'I know the drill by now.' Claud's natural bumptiousness was returning. 'Quick story now. Full statement later. Why do I have to go to the police station?'

'It's routine. But it won't take long.'

'I understand. Well, mine is a short but bloody tale, I'm afraid. But I'll tell you what I can.'

Natalie re-emerged from the cupboard with a glass of water which she placed in Claud's hand. For a brief moment Jude did a double-take: her fingertips were stained with blood. Then he looked again and saw it was nail varnish, flaming scarlet in the low-wattage light.

'There you go, darling.' Calm words, but Jude noted how she bit her bottom lip when she looked at her husband, and dropped on her knees beside him, staring at him like a devoted puppy.

'It was weird. Horrible. I'd finished with work for the day and I was just waiting for Nat to come back so we could head home. I was standing looking out of the window. Not that you could see very much. It was just getting dark and it's windy, so the shadows of the trees were jumping about. The bell ringers had gone into the church and the place was suddenly really quiet.' He licked his lips. 'I thought I saw Nat down in the churchyard, standing in the shadows by the war memorial. Just standing.'

'But I wasn't—' She stared at him in bewilderment. 'I was running. I didn't run through the churchyard.' She twisted the fitness tracker on her wrist.

'It was dark. It was someone who was tall and thin and in a white top. I thought it was you and so I went down to see what you were doing. Why you were just standing.' His look was a plea for something, or someone, to obliterate the memory of what he'd just seen. ' I was worried. I always am. I needed to know you were all right.'

'And when you got outside?'

'I walked into the churchyard. Whoever was by the war memorial had gone — there was nobody in the churchyard at all, in fact, which is unusual — so I walked across the grass to see if I could see where Nat had gone.'

'Across the grass?'

'Yes, because if she was running she'd have got out of sight in the time it took me to go round by the path. Then I saw someone lying on the ground. A woman. Tall. I thought...' his voice tailed off. 'You don't know what it's like, Chief Inspector, to think someone you care about might be dead.'

Jude, the image of those plain black shoes in front of him, said nothing.

'I saw as soon as I got close that it wasn't her,' Claud went on, after a moment. 'She was wearing a light-coloured jacket. That was where I made the mistake. At first I thought she'd passed out so I tried to help her up but then I realised. The front of her coat was covered in blood. I dialled 999. And I remembered that you'd said you'd be in town so I called you.' He lifted the cup to his lips.

'Did you touch the body?'

Claud hesitated. 'Yes. I remembered Nat had said when she... I remembered she said he was still alive. I thought maybe this woman was but then I was sure she was dead Then I realised that whoever did it might still be around and I panicked. I might be at risk. I shouted for help, and a man came running over and said he was a doctor. I told him not to move her, but he said she might not be dead, even though I told

173

him she was. And then people started coming to see what was going on. The rest you know.'

'Okay. Thanks.' Jude looked around, found a uniformed officer and instructed him to take Claud down to the police station. That done, he turned to look for Phil.

Ashleigh had corralled the witnesses in the church and she and Tyrone were almost through the process of taking their names and brief statements. As Jude turned towards Phil, Doddsy appeared in the doorway.

Phil could wait another minute. Jude headed across to the door, pausing by the noticeboard that rippled with worthiness — Lent lunches, prayer groups, services for Easter, a meeting about the proposed Rainbow Festival. 'Anything?'

'No sign of the weapon in the immediate area. we're still looking. But we know who she is.'

'Oh?'

'Phil recognised her.'

'Did he? He said he didn't know who she was.'

'He must have had a brainstorm, then. She's one of the nurses from the hospital. Name of Gracie Pepper.'

He thought for a moment, running through the names of Becca's nursing friends from three years back, but Gracie's name rang no bells. 'I don't know her.'

They shared a moment's silence. Doddsy would surely be thinking the same as Jude, that Phil was uncomfortably close to a murder scene. Things were difficult enough with Tammy as it was. Up in town she'd be waiting for Phil to come and get her while her colleagues set to imaging and assessing the body of Gracie Pepper, the nurse. 'Okay. I'll talk to Phil now.'

'Good luck,' Doddsy said under his breath as Jude turned away.

Phil, whose lean, spare frame was easily recognisable from the back, was sitting to one side in the nave, in deliberate isolation, staring towards the stained glass windows and the image of a risen Christ. One hand rested on the back of the pew in front and he was tapping his fingers in obvious impatience.

With a nod to Tyrone, Jude stepped across and slid into the pew beside Phil. 'It's not a great time to meet, is it? Sorry about Tammy's birthday dinner.'

With a shrug, Phil ripped his attention away from a bunch of relentlessly cheerful daffodils in a jar on the windowsill. 'Can't be helped. It happens enough in my line of work as it is. Hers too. Birthday celebrations are moveable feasts anyway. You'll know that.'

Jude's rest day the following day, the one he'd planned to spend with Ashleigh somewhere where his phone didn't get a signal, had already gone the same way as Phil and Tammy's evening out. A good night's sleep would make the ultimate sacrifice, too. 'I won't keep you too long. Run me through what happened and we can get the formalities done at the station. Then you can salvage what you can of the evening. And you can always contact me. You know that.'

'Yeah.' Phil took a blood-stained handkerchief out of his pocket, spat on it, and wiped blood from his fingers. The front of his coat was stiff with drying blood. 'Not very hygienic, but I've got hand sanitiser in the car. Fire away, then. What do you want to know?'

The question, Jude recognised, was meant to buy a few seconds to compose himself. It didn't matter how many deaths Phil had attended in the past. He would have had a few moments to prepare for most them, whereas the sudden discovery of Gracie Pepper, haemorrhaging her life out in the churchyard, seemed to have caught him by surprise. 'Begin at the beginning and go on until the end.'

'I'd arranged to meet Tammy at the pub. I finished my shift at the hospital at six, maybe, and parked in Friargate. I was going to cut through the churchyard.' He picked up Jude's questioning look. 'Yes I know there are other places to park, but you know how it is. You do things from habit. I rarely come down through the town, and we were heading up to Roundthorn for dinner so I'd have had to go all the way round the one way system. And I thought I'd probably spend five minutes in the pub while Tammy finished her drink anyway, so I just parked where there was a space.'

He wiped his fingers for a second time, waiting while Jude scribbled down his notes. 'Then the churchyard. I walked from the car park and I cut across the grass to the far side.'

'Rather than go straight up and along King Street?'

'It's six of one and half a dozen of the other. But actually the reason I went that way rather than the other was that I heard something.'

'And that was?'

'A voice. The sound bounces around, you know. And the place was quiet. Usually there's the odd person cutting through, but there wasn't anyone about at that end of the churchyard. I heard someone shouting into the phone about a body.'

That would be Claud. 'Okay. And then?'

'I ran across the grass. There was a man — I didn't recognise him at first — kneeling on the ground next to something. I came running up and I could see that it was a woman and that she was badly hurt.'

'What did the man say to you?'

'He shouted out something like *don't touch the body, don't touch the body*. But I could see she was still breathing. I went through the whole trust-me-I'm-a-doctor routine but he kept on gibbering about a murder scene, so I shoved him out of the way and got on with it. She was bleeding very heavily and wasn't conscious. At that point I couldn't see her face. I tried to staunch the bleeding but there was nothing I could do for her, except hold her while she died.'

His tone was matter-of-fact, but there was the echo in it of the same desolation that had hung over Natalie's description of how she'd failed to save Len Pierce. If Phil couldn't save a life in those circumstances, how could she have done? If, indeed, she'd really tried. 'That was rough for you, Phil.'

'Yes. Then the guy who was there started flashing his torch around. I recognised him then. The Blackwell chap who does those diversity sessions. And I saw who was dead. Gracie Pepper. That was a shock, too.'

Jude allowed himself a slight pause, made a mental note of the inconsistency. 'Didn't you say you didn't know her?'

'Did I? Maybe you misheard.'

'Maybe.' Jude met Phil's challenging gaze, holding it to remind him who was in charge. 'Did you know Gracie well?'

'No, not at all. By sight, only.'

'But you knew her name.'

'The nurses all wear name badges.' His hesitation was fractional. 'I try and remember their names. It's good management.'

Jude allowed himself a moment of reflection. It was too much of a coincidence, surely, that two people should have died within yards of the Blackwells. 'Was anyone else there?'

'As I said before. The churchyard was quiet. When I realised there was a problem and that someone was hurt I focussed on what was actually happening.' He paused. 'I realise that isn't what you want to hear, but I'm not trained to be the eyes and ears of everyone. I have a job to do.'

Phil would pick a fight with anyone over anything but his attitude to Jude, knowing the requirements of the job and the need for immediate action, was one of bolshie entitledness. Briefly, Jude wondered what kind of words might have passed in the Garner household over Tyrone's relationships with Doddsy. Perhaps Phil was just too used to playing God, lord in his own home and his own clinic. 'If you didn't see anything, you didn't see anything. It can't be helped. But at least let me run you through the places you might have seen something.'

Apparently mollified, Phil took a moment to think. 'The library closes at six, so they couldn't have gone there. There was definitely no-one in the entrance to the arcade, but I suppose someone could have got away that way.'

'If they did, someone will have seen them, I imagine. That's helpful.' Jude nodded, a quick stroke of flattery to Phil's ego, a hint that he was adding even more value to his existing public service. 'Nothing else?'

'I didn't pass anyone in the bottom half of the churchyard. Perhaps someone could have got away down to King Street or to the Market Square. I don't know.'

Chris's first task the next day would be checking the CCTV in the Market Square to see who might have emerged from the darkness. 'That's fine, Phil.' Jude proffered his notebook, saw Phil scan and sign and took it back. 'Thanks.'

'The bloody police station now, I suppose.'

'I'm afraid so. And then you can get on with what's left of your evening.'

*

'Come on, darling.' Natalie regarded Claud with anxious eyes as he re-emerged into the reception area of the police station. They'd taken his blood-stained clothes away, as if finding a body made you a suspect, and he was dressed in a jumper and jogging bottoms. God knew where they came from. After all she was glad she'd washed her own clothes. She couldn't have borne being taken to the police station like a criminal and sent home in someone else's cast-offs. 'I'll drive you home. Then we'll have something to eat.' Because although she ate little, Claud was a serious trencherman and there was little she could think of that was more normal to him than food.

'It's okay.'

'It'll be all right.' She felt the weight of his soul, not just the tug of his arm on hers as they made their way along Meeting House Lane. In reality her repeated concerns were as much for her own support as for his and there was room for debate as to which of them was helping the other, but as long as the two of them kept ploughing on, it didn't really matter.

'It's okay, Nat.' He squeezed her arm. 'I'll drive. It was a shock, but I'm over it. Poor girl.'

The fact that he called a mature woman a girl was a sign of his loss of concentration. Proper respect was a central plank of his mission. Her heart warmed towards him even more at this lapse. 'I know. Just like it was at home.' Now they'd been through the same thing together.

'But the worst thing, Nat… For a moment I thought it was you.'

'It wasn't. It's all right.'

'But someone… she was someone's, wasn't she?'

Another non-Claud phrase. People belonged to nobody in his world, though Natalie liked to think that she belonged to him, and he to her, exclusively. 'Yes.'

'It's such a mess, Nat. The things that people do to one another. I realise now, I recognised her. From one of the workshops.'

They slowed as they approached Sandgate. Reaching the car meant passing the eastern end of the church close, where they couldn't avoid the police and the ambulance, the onlookers who didn't understand how shocking it was to cradle the dying. And now a stranger was approaching them, and even this everyday occurrence seemed a potential trap. Natalie shrank back, pulling Claud aside on the narrow pavement to let the oncoming figure pass.

He didn't. 'Mr Blackwell? It is Mr Blackwell, isn't it?'

'Yes.' Shuffling out of the darkest shadows into the streetlight, Claud kept hold of Natalie's arm.

'I thought I recognised you there in the churchyard. It's George Meadows. I was at the meeting after the service a couple of weeks ago.' Impatient to get home, as she was sure Claud must be, Natalie had no time for the concern of strangers, but Claud was different. He knew everyone, never forgot a face. 'Of course! George. We were talking about the Rainbow Festival. Thought your input was invaluable.' He extracted his arm from Natalie's and shook the man's hand. 'Do you reckon it's a goer?'

That was the thing about Claud. No matter what you put him through, the minute you dangled one of his pet projects in front of him he would switch into a different mode. Perhaps it was a defence mechanism. If it was, it wasn't working for Natalie. She bounced up and down on the balls of her feet, impatient to be away from the town and get the corroding scent of death away from her nostrils.

'I know you'll find a lot of opposition to the idea, but there's a lot of support, too. The problem is that we're a very traditional society. But there are plenty of people like myself.' George patted his chest, exactly the point where the knife had struck Len Pierce. Natalie shivered.

'Glad to hear it, George.'

'I'm not gay myself, you understand, but I'm definitely an ally. My late wife was very outspoken on the subject. Love is love. The Rainbow Festival isn't a moment before time and if there's anything I can do to help, say the word.'

'Speak at your church,' Claud responded, with spirit. 'Traditional doesn't explain everything. People need to learn that traditional values are those of inclusiveness. It isn't modern. It's natural.'

'Claud,' Natalie said, 'should we go home? You've had such a dreadful shock. It was Claud who found the body in the churchyard, Mr Meadows. I think I should take him home.'

'You found the body?' That stopped him. She looked at him, blinking under the streetlight. 'I didn't realise. That's an awful business. What a terrible shock. Perhaps you want to come back to my house and have a brandy or something to pep you up? I'm in William Street, not far at all.'

All Natalie wanted was to go home. 'Thank you so much, Mr Meadows, but I really think we need to get back.'

'That's probably right.' Always reluctant to tear himself away from an eager listener Claud picked up the message, but he couldn't quite disengage himself as easily as Natalie would have liked. 'It's great to meet you, though, George. And I'd love to talk to you more about the festival.'

'You know how it is. Folk listen to gay allies like you and me more than they listen to others. It shouldn't be like that but it is.'

'Nat and I'll be going round some of the other churches in the area to drum up support, but we really need people like you — enthusiastic people within the congregations who can change from within and bring them into the modern world.'

Sometimes Claud got carried away. Natalie wasn't a churchgoer herself but her parents had been, and her image of the church was formed in the image of her mother, one of gentle tolerance and a judgement only of oneself. Of course, this wasn't the whole truth, but it was surely no further removed from reality than Claud's view of the organisation as a brake on the advance of modernity. 'Claud. This isn't the time. We need to go home.'

'Yes, you're right.' Once more he turned to her, then back to George. 'It would be so wonderful to have your input.'

'Perhaps you could pop round and visit me and we could discuss it. You could come round one evening. Apart from Tuesdays, when I'm bell ringing,

I'll be in. I don't socialise much since Michelle died. And I'm handy for here. Just on the corner of William Street.'

'I'd love to.' Claud fished in his pockets for a pen.

'Claud!' said Natalie one final time, as he scribbled the address on the back of his hand. 'Let's go.'

'I'll be in touch,' Claud said to the man, and allowed Natalie to tuck her hand through his arm again and guide him down the street. 'Nice bloke. I remember talking to him a couple of weeks ago. He's one of the bell ringers, I think. A really interesting guy. Car mechanic. Not that I know anything about cars. But I'll definitely follow up and go and see him. He's the kind of man we need on our side. And Inspector Dodd, too. I really like that man. Though I can't say I like the phrase *gay ally*. We're all just normal.'

Cars, bell ringers, dead bodies in the churchyard. Natalie would have strange dreams that night. Maybe she should take an extra tablet. 'You're too good, Claud. Far too good.'

'But what a nice bloke he was. And so solicitous. Yes, I'll definitely look him up. Talk to him one evening while you go for your run. He could really help us with the Rainbow Festival.' And finally Claud gave up on the distractions around them and headed for home.

Chapter 12

'Okay. Ashleigh. Perhaps you want to tell us what you've found out about Gracie Pepper?' Jude stifled a yawn and reached for his coffee. He'd stolen a few hours' sleep and hoped she'd done the same, but even making a conscious effort to rest hadn't been much help and he'd lain awake for much of the few hours he'd spent in bed, running things through, thinking of options, trying out scenarios as to how the murderer had got away. Even in his sleep he'd been weighing up evidence. Now the major early-morning briefing was over, the various personnel deputed to their tasks and his concentration was wavering even further as Faye made her way across the incident room. He kept one eye on her as she wove through the desks, stopping occasionally for a word with one of the detectives, towards the table where Jude had assembled his core team of Ashleigh, Chris and Doddsy.

'Okay.' Ashleigh cleared her throat, blinking at the notes in front of her as the only sign of tiredness and spilled a picture of Gracie — long auburn hair in a riot of pre-Raphaelite curls, a serious expression that couldn't conceal a love of life — onto the table in front of her. 'We were able to identify her straight away. Phil Garner knew her. She was—'

'May I interrupt?' Faye reached them at the dramatic moment. 'Thanks for the email update, Jude. I'm sorry I didn't get a chance to speak to you about it earlier on, but I was in a meeting. The local press. It's hardly surprising they're a little over-excited. May I sit in for a moment, to keep myself fully up to date?'

He could hardly refuse. 'Sure. Do you have any questions on the briefing note before we start?'

'Not at all. It was admirably comprehensive.' She bared her teeth just a little as she smiled, a sure sign that the smile was fake, and turned her cool gaze to Ashleigh. 'Do carry on.'

Normally so confident, Ashleigh seemed to crumble under that stare, fumbling with her notes and picking them apart with such violence that the coffee mug at her elbow nearly went flying. 'Her name is Gracie Pepper. Last night Chris and I went to Carlisle to break the news to her parents, and they told us as much as they felt able to about her. They were upset, so it's little more than a broad impression, although I have some officers talking to her friends and colleagues to build up a picture of her. She's thirty-one and she's a nurse at the hospital, where she works in the elder care unit. She's only been there a couple of months. She finished her shift yesterday at four o'clock but stayed on to help out because the colleague taking over from her was held up. She lives up in Greystoke Park.'

For Faye's benefit, Jude got up and indicated the various locations on the map that Chris had pinned on the whiteboard. 'That's here. The hospital is here, up at Tynefield. The churchyard is here.'

She frowned at the map, as if processing the information. 'All right. Carry on.'

'We don't know what she was doing in the churchyard. You can see it wasn't on her way home. Jude's briefing note tells you the sequence of events as regards the body. Claud Blackwell says he left his office to talk to a woman he mistakenly thought was his wife and the woman had gone, but he stumbled across what he thought was a body, lying against the wall of the church near a set of stones known the Giant's Grave.'

'A local curiosity,' noted Jude, aloud. Faye, nodding, wrote that down.

'He was joined by Phil Garner, a doctor from the hospital who, as it happens, knew her, although he says he didn't recognise her immediately. Phil is married to Tammy Garner, who's one of our CSIs, and their son is a probationary constable with us.'

'How very coincidental.'

The gaze Faye fixed on Ashleigh was so steely that Jude felt obliged to intervene. 'It's no coincidence that Phil was there. It was Tammy's birthday. She was having a quick drink with colleagues — all of us included — and he'd arranged to come and pick her up to take her out for dinner. He'd parked at the back of the church rather than get caught up in the one-way system, as they were heading up to Roundthorn for dinner.' Tammy wasn't on the CSI team still working away in the churchyard, and the investigation would be the poorer for it, because she was noted for her thoroughness and her obsession with detail.

'Mr Blackwell said he thought Gracie was dead,' Ashleigh went on, doggedly reading from her notes, 'but according to Phil, when he got to her she was still alive, but bleeding heavily. He tried to staunch the bleeding, with Claud's help, but he describes the haemorrhaging as catastrophic. There was nothing he could do to save her. She died in his arms about a minute after he reached her.'

'There wasn't anyone else in the churchyard at the time,' Chris supplemented. 'Or rather, neither of the witnesses saw anyone in that particular part of it.'

In response to Faye's questioning look, Jude reached for a piece of paper and sketched a rapid plan. 'The church is in a large curtilage, very enclosed. There's no vehicular access to it, apart from about half a dozen parking spaces against the churchyard wall at the north eastern corner. There are buildings at the east end and a footpath connecting Burrowgate and Friargate runs between them and the churchyard. There's a flight of steps that goes down from the south corner into King Street, and a passageway that goes from the west corner into the Market Square.' There were photos on the whiteboard, retrieved by Chris from the internet in the small hours of the morning to give an interim picture of the scene in daylight. Someone had drawn every possible escape route on them.

'It's in the block between those that Claud Blackwell has his office. There are footpaths that cut across the churchyard itself, as well as those that go round it. The configuration is such that it's very easy to be in one part of that close and not see something that's going on in another. The body was found here.' He slid the sketch across to her, and she frowned down at it, before passing it to Chris, who jumped up and pinned it to the board.

'So far, we haven't found anyone who saw Gracie in the churchyard, but she must have cut across one of the paths. Inquiries are ongoing and we may yet come up with someone who can shed light on what she was doing there.'

'You're treating Blackwell as a suspect, of course.' Faye pushed her glasses up her nose and sighed. The rest of the diversity workshops would have to be put on hold.

Under the cloak of his tiredness, Jude bristled with irritation. 'Yes. Anything else you can tell us about her, Ashleigh?'

'I don't yet know if anything's come up from her friends and colleagues that may indicate motive. If there's anything in her private life it's not immediately obvious. She was relatively new to the area, though, so the people we've spoken to haven't been able to shed any light on it. Her parents say she worked hard and came home often. Her mother has been unwell recently. As far as I know she got on with everyone.' She shuffled the bits of paper around.

Faye fidgeted. 'Of course you've enquired about her personal life. In particular her sexuality.'

'We don't know.' Perhaps it was time to shift Faye's attention to himself. Everyone had bad days and the woman could be intimidating, but Jude was surprised at how Ashleigh seemed to have allowed Faye to unnerve her. 'Single, no past relationships that we're aware of.'

'You'll be inquiring further.'

'Obviously.'

'The modus operandi suggests they're linked.'

'But not necessarily a homophobic motive.' He sensed disquiet. On the other side of the table Doddsy, who had remained silent until that point, allowed himself the faintest shrug. 'Until I hear something else I'll keep an open mind .'

'As, of course, you should.' Faye fidgeted with her cuffs.

Jude reached for his coffee and sipped at it, reminding himself who was in charge of the investigation and taking back control of it. 'We have to consider our main suspects.' Chris had already written the key names on the board. 'Those who were on the spot could have done it. There's Phil. We can't rule him out until we find someone who can swear he wasn't lurking round the corner waiting to happen upon the scene.'

'Do you know Dr Garner well?' Faye asked, still fidgeting.

Jude shook his head. 'In passing.'

'I've met him,' Doddsy added, as if for the sake of disclosure, 'but again it was brief and purely social.'

Thankfully she didn't press them. Tammy was furious enough with Jude, as well as Doddsy, and she'd be even madder when she realised they were investigating her husband as a possible murder suspect. 'There's Claud. He was on the spot both times. And Natalie.'

'So the only people we can name as suspects for two possible homophobic murders are someone who's dedicated to saving lives and someone who campaigns in support of gay rights.' Chris sat back.

'There may be other motives. And there were other people in the area as well. We need to cross-check their movements.'

Jude's heart had sunk as soon as Faye had raised the question of sexuality. 'Obviously we rule nothing in or out at this stage, but equally obviously, we have to treat these two killings as linked, and we have to consider the very real possibility they're motivated by hate.' He tapped his pen on the table and the silence that lingered between them had a particular sourness to it. 'But they may be random. I don't want to cause any alarm but I think we need to warn people to take care—'

'They'll all be freaking out over it already,' Doddsy said, 'regardless of any threat level. It's what people do. The risk to an individual might be small, but people don't know that. The last thing we need is panic.'

Faye plucked at her collar. 'Absolutely. Leave that with me. Naturally I reassured everyone as much as I could but it won't help. We'll just make sure there are plenty of uniforms about in the town. That always helps.' She checked her watch and stood up, but she lingered. 'Keep me informed as to what's happening, would you? I have other things to attend to just now.'

'Okay,' Jude said, taking this as a signal to carry on without her. 'Do we know what we're doing? Ashleigh, you'll take on the door-to-door inquiries, as usual. Doddsy, do you want to pop down the road and get up to speed with what's going on in the town? Faye's right. We need to make sure that the public see us about.' Because a murder in an isolated lane was one thing, but there was nothing to put the fear of God into the local population like a violent death on their own doorstep. 'Do your reassuring act. Be as jolly as you can without looking as if you aren't taking it seriously. Chris, I want you to get your team onnto finding out as much as you can about Gracie Pepper. In particular, I'd like to know of she had any connection to Giles Butler. And I want you to find out where Dr Butler was last night.' He pushed his chair back. 'I'm going into Carlisle this afternoon, to

193

attend the PM. I don't imagine there will be many surprises, but you never know. And as always, I'm at the end of the phone.'

He turned to give one long last searching look at the whiteboard, as if its scant information on the previous night's murder might make any more sense, but inevitably his mind was as cluttered and incomprehensible as the material on the board.

*

'I'm off, then.' Jude whisked his jacket up off the back of his chair and over his shoulder. 'Keep me updated.'

'See you later.' Standing up, Ashleigh reached into the pile of small change in her desk drawer and addressed herself to Chris at the next desk. 'I'm heading to the coffee machine.' It would be a quick fix, because there was no time to head down to the canteen. 'Want one?'

'Flat white.' He was already absorbed in the next step of the investigation.

Faye had drifted only as far as the corridor and Ashleigh, leaving the incident room and walking down the corridor, ran right into the trap. 'Ashleigh. There you are.'

Did the woman never sit down in her office and do any actual work? 'Oh, hi Faye.' She turned her back to her boss and slipped a coin into the coffee machine, where it rattled straight into the reject tray. At the close of a briefing meeting her habit was to go to the coffee machine, and it was uncomfortable to reflect that Faye remembered that trivial detail and had used it against her.

'I'd like a quiet word with you. Unofficially, of course,' Faye said, staring down the corridor and picking away at her discreet gold earring.

'Of course.' Because what else could she say?

'I want to know exactly what you've told your boyfriend.'

In their previous shared workplace they'd had the same disparity in rank but this time Ashleigh was in a position of relative strength. Faye's hostility would damage her only if she allowed it. She'd come through all this and was no longer dependent upon the goodwill of a superior officer. 'All sorts of things. We talk. People do.'

'You know exactly what I mean.'

'I didn't think you were talking about whether I take sugar in my coffee.' She rattled the buttons on the machine, glad to have something to concentrate on. She'd allowed Faye's presence to unnerve her during the briefing meeting when there was no reason why it should. 'I told him I'm bisexual. I don't keep secrets from him.' Except that wasn't entirely true. The secrets she chose to reveal would come out anyway. Surely Faye must know this one would never stay buried.

'Very admirable.' Faye's tone crackled with sarcasm.

Aditi marched past them, carrying a piece of paper, as Ashleigh thrust her pound coin back into the machine with added force and this time it dropped with a satisfying thud. When Aditi had disappeared into someone else's office and the corridor had returned to a semblance of quiet, Faye returned to the attack. 'And what else does he know?'

'He knows I had an affair with my boss. He knows my boss was a woman.' Quite how much Jude suspected about the relationship was another matter. Maybe he'd guessed. 'I told him a few months ago. We haven't mentioned it since.'

'It'll be better for both of us to keep it like that.'

Sensible for both of them? It might suit Faye but Ashleigh was already aware that if she wanted the relationship with Jude to go anywhere — if she did — then secrets couldn't be a part of it. The ridiculous affair with Faye could only hurt them if they identified it a problem rather than an incident consigned to history. 'I thought we were having all these workshops to teach us not to be ashamed of what we are and to accept people who are different.'

'The point is not what happened,' Faye snapped. 'Talk about extra-marital relationships in the workplace is distracting and gets blown out of proportion.'

And would damage her career, she meant. 'In which case, isn't it better to be up-front and honest?' But Ashleigh, watching the thick brown liquid tricking into the second plastic cup, knew perfectly well that it wasn't. Faye was by nature defensive and her ambitions were threaded through with an unhealthy paranoia, a conviction that everyone was her potential enemy.

'On the contrary. If an individual's private life doesn't impact on their work they have a right to keep it private.'

The trickle of coffee stopped and the machine sighed and hissed itself to a standstill. 'I'm not going to talk about it. You needn't worry about that.'

'And Jude?'

'I haven't told him yet, but I expect I will at some point. So what? He's very discreet.'

'I daresay. As long as it suits him.'

Lifting the second coffee from the machine, Ashleigh shrugged. Jude didn't covet a Queen's Police Medal for serving time at a desk. He'd made his way up through the ranks because he was good at the job and she suspected he had no ambition to go any further, but Faye's blind spot wouldn't let her see that. 'Why don't you talk to him about it?'

Aditi came out of the adjacent office, this time without the sheet of paper, and Ashleigh took the opportunity to extract herself from the uncomfortable conversation and fall into step beside her junior colleague as they headed back towards the incident room. 'How's it going?'

'Oh, fine.' Aditi held the door open for her, and closed it safely behind her before she said: 'Well, I don't know about you, but I find that woman scary.'

'I imagine she's a pussycat when you get to know her.' Ashleigh set one coffee down on her desk and handed the other to Chris.

'Pussy cat with claws.' Chris said. 'Weren't you in Cheshire before you came here, Ash? Did you know her?'

'In passing.' At moments like this she understood how honest people became liars. It was easier when the consequences of truth were something they weren't ready to cope with. She cared nothing if people knew she'd slept with a woman, but Faye's grim resistance to the facts made it difficult. 'Why do you ask?'

'The Blackwells had a short spell in Crewe so I was running a few things past a mate down there.. He was asking me how we got on with her.'

'She had a bit of a reputation for being fierce.' Every step dug the hole deeper, but really — was it worth telling the truth when a lie was harmless?

'I'll say.' Aditi rolled her eyes.

'She left very suddenly, he said, and no-one seemed to know why.'

'Maybe she had family issues.' Now, at last, Ashleigh found a safe patch of ground on which to rest. There was no sign that Faye had brought her husband with her when she'd moved. Her sympathetic side asserted herself. She wasn't in a position to criticise anyone for falling apart in the aftermath of a breakup.

'Aye, maybe. But they call her Faye Scandal down there, apparently. The gossip is there was an affair and the husband threw her out.'

'Watch out for your virtue then,' Aditi jeered at him, and took herself off over to her desk, laughing.

*

It was four o'clock by the time Jude dragged himself back from Carlisle, bypassing the incident room for the sake of his own sanity and heading up towards Faye's office instead. Outside the spring daylight had faded early and the shadows had gathered in her north-facing room. She was at her desk, frowning at the screen of her laptop and the pool of light from the desk lamp illuminated an empty M&S sandwich wrapper and a half-eaten Double Decker.

When he came in, she looked up. 'You were at the post-mortem?'

He nodded. He must be getting old. There had been a time, not so long ago it seemed, when he could get by on a few hours' sleep, but there had been too many late nights recently. 'Yes. I was just heading home, but I thought I'd stop by and update you.'

'I'm glad you did. There's something I want to ask you.' Silence hovered between them and she reached out for the other half of the Double Decker, peeling down the packet and looking at it thoughtfully. 'I think I can guess how it went. Exactly the same as Len Pierce. Am I right?'

'Yes. A single blow to the heart from a knife. A kitchen knife. Blade six inches. Red plastic handle. One of a set.'

She jumped up, crossed to the door and switched on the light. 'You've found it, then?'

'Yes. And from what I understand there's every indication that it's the same knife that killed Len Pierce.'

'Where was it?'

'In a bin on King Street, just outside Lloyds Bank. It was wrapped in a man's overcoat. The bin caught fire last night, while we were securing the churchyard, and someone living in the flat over the road put a bucket of water on it because they thought it must be vandals, and we had enough on our plate so that they didn't need to bother us. The guys found it last night and sent it off to the lab.'

'I know you shouldn't curse a good citizen, but sometimes I can't help myself. What time was that?'

'The fire was about seven, I think. They found the knife late last night.' He could understand her frustration, had felt just as impotent at the valuable information that would have been lost to flame and water when Doddsy had broken the news to him. 'Just when everything was kicking off. It wasn't a big fire, by any means. The coat had been shoved right down and there wasn't a lot of smother from it. It had pretty much burned itself out by the time they got there.'

'Has it gone off for analysis?'

'It's at the lab now. And the coat looks as if came from a charity bag. There were some open bags in the doorway of one of them.' Now, at least, they knew the route the killer must have taken, another piece of the jigsaw to ponder and slot into place. 'I'll keep you in the loop.' As though she'd give him any chance to leave her out of it.

'Good.' She sat down again, swung her chair round to face him. 'And as I said. There's something else I want to talk to you about.'

Something in her tone caught his attention. Defensive? Yes, that was it. Someone, braver than he, had Faye on the back foot. 'Of course.'

She scowled at him over her glasses as though he was a school pupil answering a teacher back. 'Do you know a woman called Marsha Letham?'

'Yes. From the local paper.' Jude wasn't good with the press and tended to leave that kind of interaction to others, but he made a point of knowing who they were because they could equally be allies as enemies. Chris spent a lot of time cultivating them, but Chris spent time cultivating everyone, a network of people who felt it might be glamorous to play a part in the ongoing process he made look like a fight between good and evil. 'She's very much on the local community side, I think. I'd be surprised if they've put her on anything like the Pierce case.'

'She rang me this afternoon on the pretext of writing up a column inch or two on a new post in the police, asking me why I left Cheshire.'

'That makes sense. Fits with her brief.'

'Does it, indeed?'

'Yes. Nothing to it, I'd say. They're local newspaper and probably desperate for copy.'

'It must be a very quiet day if an appointment at my pay grade is considered newsworthy. Chief Constable, perhaps. Assistant Chief Constable, also possible.'

No doubt Faye harboured ambitions of progress to high office in the police, but something told him that this kind of attitude, rather than her capabilities, would be what held her back. Quiet news day? 'It's certainly not that.'

'Was your appointment in the paper?'

'I don't believe it was. But I wasn't interesting. I was a local boy making my way up, step by step.' By contrast Faye, shipped in from outside to a senior post amid rumours of her predecessor's misbehaviour and with a mission to bring redress, was newsworthy.

'Okay. And we have two murders in the news and half the district in a state of complete panic, and you expect me to believe that the local papers are interested in my appointment.'

'I don't think I said that. But local papers talk to each other. They're asking questions. How you answer them is up to you. I don't think it's a story.'

'I don't need your opinion.'

He was annoyed by that. 'Then what? I speak to the newspapers all the time. It's part of my job.'

'I'm aware of that. I'm asking you to be very careful what you say to them in future.'

For a moment her fragile temper and high sensitivity reminded him of Phil Garner. If she'd been a witness or a suspect he'd have been wondering what she had to hide. Ashleigh's attitude to life was much healthier than Faye's — not flamboyant, not obvious, but an acceptance of facts and an absence of denial when challenged. What happened, happened and you moved on. But Faye, unlike Ashleigh, was the type who made enemies along the way. 'Write the copy yourself if you're that worried. They'd be delighted. But it's a non-story. I'm more worried about what they might do with the homicides. A word out of place and all the speculation starts doing us damage and people get hurt. That's what really worries me.'

Chapter 13

Becca Reid, bending down to place a bowl of cat food beside the back door, knew immediately who was at the door. Jude's taste in cars was expensive and distinctive, and she'd learned to recognise the throaty roar of his Mercedes as it hummed through the village of Wasby when he came to visit his mother. Then the doorbell rang and Holmes confirmed Jude's arrival, interrupting his lunge in towards his supper and performing some particularly improbable contortion to slide around her ankles and head to the front door.

Becca followed his grey shadow into the hall. Animals always knew, and the treacherous Holmes had always seemed to regard himself as Jude's cat rather than hers. Though common sense warned her to avoid her ex for the sake of her heart, she continually fell into the trap of engaging with him in the hope that the persistent tension between them would subside. It never quite worked out like that, and even if their best efforts to be polite fooled other people, the low level tussle they engaged in was profoundly unsatisfying.

It was as well they weren't still together. 'Jude.' She snapped the door open more smartly than she'd intended and Holmes shot through it with a chirp of ecstasy and rubbed round Jude's ankles.

'You don't want to be out on a night like this, old lad.' He bent and picked the cat up. 'Sorry to bother you, Becca. I was passing, and wondered if I could have a word.'

'Of course.' She stepped aside to let him in. 'You know where to go.'

Still carrying Holmes, he headed through to the living room and sat down, stretching his legs out towards the fire she'd just lit. Holmes, on his lap, set about settling, kneading with claws out. 'Busy today?'

'Yes. And you must be, too.' The two murders that had rocked the town were his problem. He'd be worrying at them, digging for information, turning every stone to see what lay beneath. This wouldn't be a social visit. 'Coffee?'

'No, thanks. I won't stay long. I wanted to ask you if you knew Gracie Pepper.'

'Yes. I work out of the hospital. But you know that. She worked in the elderly care ward.' He would know that, too. 'She hadn't been here long but she made an impact. She was very…' She paused to search for a word that fully encompassed Gracie's love of life, and failed. 'Bubbly.'

He nodded, his expression sombre. 'I've just been up in Carlisle. At the post-mortem.'

She tried to read his expression. There had been so much talk. How much of the truth would he tell her? 'Did she suffer?'

'No.' He rubbed behind Holmes's ears, frowning. 'Off the record, of course, but it was fairly straightforward. One knife wound, just next to the heart. Not instant, but very quick. If that makes it any easier to think about.'

'We're all so shocked. She was just so…so alive.' Ten years of nursing, most of it as a district nurse calling in on the old and the terminally ill, had left Becca accustomed to death, sometimes to sudden death, but some lives left a greater echo when they were lost and the shadow of malice aforethought always deepened shock. 'And in the churchyard, too.' She cut through the path at the bottom of it on a regular basis, on her way down to Adam's if she was walking down there from work or if they were coming back to his house after an evening out. 'Right in the heart of the community.' *It strikes at us all*, one of her patients had declared, and Becca had agreed with her even while trying to dampen down the drama.

'Yes.' He was looking at her, his grey eyes serious. 'I was nearby, as it happened. A few of us were having a drink in the Board and Elbow. Someone called us down there and someone else said it was a nurse. For a moment I was afraid it was you.'

She leaned forward and poked the fire, which didn't need it, and when she sat back up again the heat of the flames had brought a scarlet flush to her face and the red glare of the embers danced in front of her eyes. 'We should both be used to dead bodies, shouldn't we? But it never gets any easier.'

'Ain't that the truth? I didn't come here to upset you. I just wondered if you could tell me anything about her.'

On reflection, Becca was surprised how little she did know. That had been the thing about Gracie. In the couple of months she'd been at the hospital everyone had been aware of her whenever she was present, and had talked about her when she wasn't. She'd quickly become the one to lighten the gravest situation with a dash of bitter humour, often crude but always funny, the one whose witticisms were quoted and repeated, central to every anecdote told in the aftermath of a work night out even though she never stayed for more than the quickest of drinks. And yet somehow what she knew about Gracie, other than that, was sketchy, as if she'd kept her real self hidden behind that bright mask.

Lots of people did that. Sometimes she wished it was a gift she had herself, rather than betraying what she thought and she felt to anyone who had an iota of understanding, just as she was betraying herself right then to Jude. 'She lived up in Castletown, I think. On her own. She wasn't married, didn't have a partner or anything.'

'Do you know of any close friends?'

'No. She was friendly to everyone but not especially close to anyone.'

'Do you have any idea what she was doing in the churchyard?'

'Yes, as it happens.' Becca thought again of Gracie, knowing she was falling into the trap of telling dull anecdotes about the dead. She knew, too, that there was sometimes information to be gleaned from the most trite of them and so Jude would listen. 'She liked routine. She'd always drive to work, but every night she would get home and then walk down to M&S to buy her tea. That was her exercise.'

He sat back, amused. 'What a peculiar detail to remember about someone.'

'Well, it isn't really. I came across it when we had one of those extracurricular workshop things we do sometimes. We had to begin by telling everyone something unusual about ourselves.'

His lips twitched into a smile. 'What did you say?'

'I support Arsenal.'

The smile turned to a laugh, and Becca found herself laughing, too. 'What a disappointment. I thought I'd find out something about you I didn't know.'

There was very little that he didn't know, other than the one thing that would alter his opinion of her for the worse. In an effort to protect herself against damage already done, Becca attempted a scowl and failed. It cut two ways. 'I don't have secrets. Most people don't.'

'Most people do,' he contradicted her. 'Half the time it's not something anyone would care about. They just think it is.'

'You sound exactly like the guy who was running the workshops.'

'Yes, because I've had to sit through one exactly the same. It was Claud Blackwell, wasn't it?'

'Yes. What did you confess to?'

'An excessive fondness for this old fellow.' He rubbed Holmes underneath the chin. 'I was almost glad when we got on to the heavy stuff about challenges and diversity. Which is probably what he was aiming for. Anyway. Back to Gracie. You weren't aware of any relationships? I'm not talking about a boyfriend.'

It was the second time he'd asked. 'Do you mean, was she gay?' Len Pierce had been, the papers had said. 'I suppose she might have been. I don't know. Maybe she just hadn't met the right person.' Or she had, and had foolishly let that irreplaceable relationship go. For a second she contemplated whether she'd ever been subconsciously attracted to a woman but it was impossible to be objective with Jude sitting in front of her. She couldn't even think of Adam when he was looking at her like that. The quality of their sex life had been high on the list of points in his favour when she'd made the decision to leave him.

He changed tack. 'Do you know anything about the Rainbow Festival?'

'It was mentioned at the church on Sunday.' A sudden tear rose to her eye, grief for a woman she'd hardly known. 'Bugger. Sorry. I don't normally get sentimental.'

'It's understandable. What's happening is unsettling enough even if it's someone you don't know. It's much worse when it's someone you liked and somewhere you know.'

All those times she'd crossed the churchyard, alone and in the dark, without a thought. 'I know. And everyone's talking about it. Looking over their shoulders, wondering if they're next. So awful for Phil, too, even more because he knew her.'

That sparked his interest. 'Did he?'

'Yes. He was at the workshop, too, and he'd hardly have overlooked her.' To her fury the tear overflowed and she reached for a hanky. 'There's no real danger, is there?' It was an idiot's question. She should have known better than to ask it.

'I've no idea. I wouldn't tell you to be any less careful than I imagine you already are, though.'

He had the gift of saying everything while he said nothing, sharing a secret while keeping it safe. She judged that he thought Gracie might be gay, and she and Len Pierce had been targeted for their sexuality. That meant anyone straight was safe. Her lip curled. Was it wrong to be reassured? 'I'm always careful.'

'Good.' He pushed Holmes off his lap in a easy move. 'I'd better go. Lots to do.'

He looked tired. God knew, he must have the conscience of a saint because whatever things he'd seen, he'd always slept like a child. Her lips pursed as she got to her feet to see him out. Now Ashleigh O'Halloran had the privilege of waking in the night and watching him as he slept. Pain was always greater when it was self-inflicted. 'Will I see you at Mikey's party?'

He was halfway to the door before he answered. 'I wouldn't miss it. Though I'm not sure whether I'll annoy him more by turning up or by not turning up.'

'That's harsh.'

'Maybe it is, but I can never do anything right in his eyes.'

'You know he adores you.'

He turned round on the doorstep. A curtain of rain sluiced the path clean behind him. 'I'm not sure I'd put it that strongly. I did my best for him, and I'll keep doing my best for him. Maybe he'll realise one day, and understand. Or at the very least, he might forgive me if he thinks I've got it wrong.'

It was unusual for him to sound so downbeat. 'Is your dad coming?'

Jude and Mikey's father had walked out years before, when Jude was old enough to cope with it but Mikey was still a child. They'd been together then, at the beginning of their long relationship, and she'd seen at first hand how he'd struggled to be the reasonable figure in the family, and how other people's pain had eventually prevailed. The slight, wry shake of the head told her how much it still bothered him. 'I'd be astonished if he's been invited.'

'I know for a fact he hasn't. Mikey told me. In fact, he must have told me half a dozen times, so there's a bit of me thinks he's protesting too much. You know?'

'Yes. But I don't think I'm the one to make the intervention, and I'm sure as hell not going to risk lighting the blue touch paper by having him burst out of the cake as a surprise guest.'

She struggled not to smile. David Satterthwaite had always had a theatrical touch, his sense of the big occasion not leavened by diplomacy, so that his extravagant gestures often missed the mark. 'That's just the kind of thing he'd do. You'd better not suggest it to him.'

'I'd better not suggest anything to him. But you might be right, because somehow he knows about the party even though I've been careful not to mention it.'

In the end, the complicated and counterbalancing stubbornness of David and his younger son were beyond Becca's powers to move — and probably beyond Jude's, too. 'It was just a thought.' She hesitated. 'Will you bring your girlfriend?'

'Ashleigh? Yes, I think so. She's invited. Or rather, I'm invited with a plus one.'

'Fabulous. Adam will be there, of course.'

There was a moment of stillness, in which they both contemplated the malign influence that Adam Fleetwood had had on Mikey's young life. 'He's turned over a new leaf, you know, Jude.'

'So I believe.'

'I thought you were a supporter of rehabilitation.' It had taken longer than usual for her irritation with him to kick in but his blanket acceptance that the law was always right did the job. This was why they'd split. She couldn't risk him knowing her too well and proving unforgiving of her faults.

'Absolutely.'

'He's working for a drugs charity, now. Helping people to learn from his mistakes.'

'All credit to him.' He stepped over the threshold and out onto the path. 'I'll see you later. I'm heading off back home to catch up on some sleep.'

'Goodbye.' Becca shut the door before he'd even turned, and stood there listening until the bass notes of the Mercedes had died away up the dale towards Penrith. She was already regretting mentioning Adam, but you couldn't avoid facts. Jude had replaced her and she had replaced him, if only temporarily. She wasn't so simple that she didn't understand her new boyfriend's driving passion was a slow-burning determination for revenge on the old. Adam was using her, in his own way, in an attempt to make Jude jealous, but how could that work when her ex had moved on to someone else?

CHAPTER 14

'Mikey. Hi, pal.' Even as he spoke, Jude recognised the false jolliness in his voice, knew that he'd struck the wrong note.

'Hey, bro.' At the other end of the line, Mikey's voice rang with suspicion. Usually they communicated by texts which didn't need to be answered and the bulk of which came from Jude, or via their mother, so the fact that Mikey had picked up the call at all had to be counted as progress. 'Still alive then, with some crazed maniac at large in town? Why haven't you hauled him in yet?'

'I'm doing my best.' Wandering from the well-lit kitchen into the darkness of his living room, Jude stared out into the street. 'And in my few spare moments I thought I'd give you a call. See how you're getting on.'

'Oh, right. So you're handing out a bit of pastoral care to satisfy your conscience?'

When he wasn't busy being angry, Mikey had a more than reasonable grasp of the subtleties of human nature. Jude grinned. 'I hadn't heard from you for a while. I bumped into Becca this afternoon, and she mentioned your party. So I thought I'd phone and check if there was anything you want me to do for it.'

'Just turn up,' said Mikey, after a fractional hesitation that suggested he'd bitten back a smart remark.

'I can manage that.'

On the other side of the street Natalie Blackwell ran past, head down against the blustery rain, running with determination, as if in a race to save her life. Claud must be working late again, and she'd be pounding her way around the town running away from God knew what. It was the second time she'd passed the window that evening. 'Are you inviting Dad?'

'No.' This time there was no hesitation. Mikey's refusal had been out of his mouth almost before Jude had finished asking the question. 'He won't come if I do. I'm not going to give him the satisfaction of letting me down again.'

'I thought it would be nice if—'

'If he rolled up at my party when he's been out of my life since I was a kid? Yeah, Jude. That would be great. Just great. Brilliant idea. Wish I'd thought of it.'

'He didn't want to be out of your life.' When their father's mid-life crisis had proved to be permanent and caused emotional carnage all around him, Mikey had been unable to forgive. David's attempts to make amends had been routinely rebuffed, except for the occasions when Mikey had taken pleasure in arranging to meet him and then not turning up, though he always cashed the cheques that came to him on birthdays and Christmas.

'Then he shouldn't have gone. And it isn't fair to Mum. Because he sure as hell wanted to be out of her life.'

Their mother, who had been an innocent party in the break-up as far as it was possible to separate the issues and allocate blame, was the obstacle to Jude's argument, though at heart he thought she'd reached the state of bliss where she genuinely didn't care. 'You're only twenty-one once. Invite him.'

'He wouldn't come.' In Jude's imagination, Mikey narrowed his lips and set his expression to an exact and unwitting copy of their father's.

'He won't come if you don't invite him.'

'And if I don't invite him he won't have the chance to turn me down. So it's all good.'

It had always been an argument that was lost before it was begun. Jude let it slide. 'Will I see you before the party?'

'Dunno. I might come back from uni tomorrow. I might leave it until Saturday. It depends on what's going on here.'

'Give me a shout if there's anything else I can do.'

'Will do. Cheers then.' For once, Mikey managed to end the conversation without a sarcastic comment, but whether that was a sign of maturity or of something more interesting going on at his side of the country, Jude didn't know.

It didn't matter. The end result was still silence. He stood for a moment, weighing the phone in his hand and dithering over the eternal, knife-edge judgement of how far he should interfere, whom he risked alienating, whether it was worth the gamble to try yet once more to heal a gaping emotional wound.

Mikey would always forgive him. That they were still speaking four years on from the younger brother's experiment with soft drugs and the older's dramatic intervention testified to that. And there was something else Jude had learned throughout his career, and that was that too many people went out one day with rage buzzing in their hearts and a critical word on their lips and never came back, or came back to find that death, natural or unnatural, had taken their loved ones. One day Mikey would grasp that. With that in mind, Jude steeled himself to call his father.

The moment David Satterthwaite answered the phone, the buzz in the background told Jude he'd timed it wrong and the conversation would be short. 'Dad. Hi. How's it going?'

'Fine, Jude. Fine.' He must have covered the phone with his hand, but only partially. 'No, it's only Jude. My round, but give me a minute.'

'Sorry. I didn't know you were busy.'

'I'm in the pub with local history society.'

His mother had been an English teacher and his father taught history, but Jude had never been remotely tempted to hide for the rest of his life in either books or the classroom. Since the divorce, his father seemed to have developed the knack of finding companionship in the pub. 'I won't chat, then.'

'Are you calling to cancel Saturday?'

Jude winced. All too often that was the reason he called, and because a trip to the football on a Saturday or (occasionally) a midweek evening was the only real situation in which father and son were completely comfortable, he never cancelled easily, but David could be as touchy as Mikey, as easily offended. 'No.' But when he reviewed his workload, and the glaringly open case of the the murders of Len Pierce and Gracie Pepper, he backtracked to honesty. 'Not yet, and hopefully not at all.'

His father declined to comment and chose, instead, to condemn him with a very obvious sigh.

'Anyway.' You could love someone and have no patience with them. Even when David hadn't been drinking he was prone to theatricality ,and since he'd ditched the needs of his family he'd become increasingly self-centred. Jude sighed, ran his free hand through his hair and looked out of the window. A dog walker paused on the glistening pavement for a greyhound to lift its leg to a lamppost and on the edge of his vision a light went on in Adam's living room. He turned to look the other way. 'I was calling about Mikey.'

'Is that right?'

'About his birthday.'

David made him wait. 'What about it?' he asked, after a moment.

'His party. I wondered if you might come.'

'I haven't been invited.'

'No. He hasn't invited you because he's afraid you won't come.'

David sighed, so obviously it could only be deliberate. 'I'm not going to come if he doesn't invite me.'

Jude shook his head in frustration. 'Can't we break this cycle, Dad? Can't we try? Just once more?'

'If he invites me, I'll come.'

'Mikey's still a kid.'

'Mikey's nearly twenty-one.'

'But you're the real adult here. You're his dad. You're the one who has to—'

'To make the first move? I've done that before. Time and time again.'

'Yes, and you have to keep trying.'

'When I get the invitation, I'll come. You're a good man, Jude. Thanks for trying. But it has to come from Mikey not from you. Got to go.' And silence.

CHAPTER 15

'All right. Fill me in. What have we all got from our collective labours?'

Jude was in a flippant mood, Doddsy thought, though God knew why. He contemplated his boss and friend. It had been too long since they'd met up for a quiet pint and a heart-to-heart and the thread of close knowledge — how Jude felt about Mikey, how Doddsy himself felt, in love for the first time in middle age — had stretched so that he couldn't divine the source of Jude's light-heartedness. Maybe it was the first signs of spring. Maybe against the odds he'd managed a good night's sleep. Maybe it was the prospect of taking Ashleigh to meet his family and, by so doing, draw a line under the relationship with Becca that Doddsy knew he'd struggled so long to shake off. He smiled at Ashleigh across the table, but she didn't smile back.

'Chris?' Jude prompted. 'Do you want to start?'

'I think we'd better let Ashleigh start.'

The two of them had been comparing notes in a corner before the meeting, while Doddsy had been standing in serene contemplation of the additional information on the incident room board as if they were an aid to meditation. He'd noticed that Chris was looking unusually severe.

Jude must have noticed it, too, because his good mood visibly dissipated. 'Okay. Go on.'

Doddsy abandoned the board and slid into his seat.

'This is a bit of a bugger Jude, if I'm honest with you.' This time she did look at Doddsy and her expression was almost apologetic. 'It's getting a bit close to home.'

'Oh?'

Ashleigh allowed herself a fractional pause. 'You know I had people doing the door-to-doors and talking to people in the town. I also had a couple of PCs down at the hospital, talking to Gracie's colleagues to see if we could pick up any leads.'

'Obviously you got something.'

'Yes. You know Tammy's husband works up at the hospital.'

Jude nodded.

'You might say he's quite outspoken. Hates political correctness. Is a bit right wing. There have never been any serious allegations against him, but one thing I did pick up, from a number of his colleagues, is that he has a reputation for homophobia.'

Doddsy rubbed his chin. Bloody Phil. No-one in their right mind would suspect him of murder but it wouldn't be the first time narrow-minded intolerance had made an innocent man a suspect. He caught himself up for making assumptions. You shouldn't presume innocence any more than you should presume guilt but he couldn't pretend to himself and if asked he wouldn't be able to pretend to Jude. He desperately wanted Tyrone's father to be be innocent.

'Okay.' Jude digested that. 'I take it when you say there were no allegations you mean there's nothing serious, if I dare put it that way. By which I don't mean any derogatory comments are acceptable. I mean he said nothing indictable and nothing justifying disciplinary action.'

'Nothing like that. It was more of a historic thing, an attitude. He's been there a long time — twenty years or so. They came to Penrith just after Tyrone was born, I think. But there are certainly a few people who raised the comment that Phil has made some unfortunate remarks in the past.'

'I hope you weren't allowing your boys and girls to ask any leading questions.'

Ashleigh looked momentarily outraged. 'They asked if they knew of anyone who had anything against Gracie, for any reason whatever.'

'Okay.' Jude must have sounded sharper than he intended, because he lifted his hand in a general apology. 'It just seems very…unusual that they mentioned it.'

'I don't think so.' She turned her watch around on her wrist, unclipped it, clipped it back on. 'I think we all have rather heightened sensitivities to these things these days. Rightly so.'

'Claud took his diversity roadshow down into Tynefield, too, didn't he?' said Chris.

Doddsy spared a thought for Faye's pet project. Good or bad? In the long run it was probably a good thing to talk about your sexuality and he'd been pleasantly surprised by the positive response, but he was a private individual and never welcomed the encouragement to bare his soul. It wasn't as if no-one knew. Tyrone, openly and proudly gay, was one side of that coin. He was the other. Opposites attracted. He smiled.

'Yes, but no-one seemed to think that's what changed it.' Ashleigh pointed out. 'There's nothing recent and nothing specific. It was just that several people mentioned that Phil had always been a bit intolerant of people who didn't fit the mould. Mostly it was in the context that his kind of attitude is the exception these days rather than the rule.'

'I imagine Tammy will have knocked a lot of that sort of nonsense out of him over the years.' Doddsy was losing his objectivity. He knew Tammy well, knew that she was single-minded and determined in her pursuit of what was right and there was no way she would let anyone, even her husband, cause trouble for her child. In his heart he could understand and forgive her hostility towards him.

'Maybe. But Phil lied to me.' Jude looked as if a bad smell had wafted under his nose — not something as nauseous as the stench of death and decay, but an unexpected whiff of the sewer. 'On the night of Gracie's killing he first told me he didn't know who she was, then he said he hadn't recognised her at first but that he knew her by sight only. But according to Becca he did know her, reasonably well.'

'She wasn't the kind of person to slip under the radar.' Ashleigh looked down at her notes again. 'Even after a short acquaintance.'

'No. And they participated in the same workshop.'

'That doesn't look great, does it?' Ashleigh appeared unconvinced of Phil's innocence. 'He wasn't initially in the frame for Len's killing, but I took the precaution of going back and checking what he was doing on the Sunday afternoon when Len died.'

'And?'

'Tammy was at work and so was Tyrone. He was on his own. I asked Tyrone about it, as casually as I could, and apparently Phil had said he was out on his bike. He said he left the house in Stainton, drove to Langwathby, cycled about for a bit and came back again.'

Doddsy pushed his chair back six inches, not needing to look at the map as Chris was doing in order to see the implications. That placed Phil Garner comfortably in the zone where he might, if he'd lied about his route, have been present in the lane where Len had died on the Sunday afternoon.

'There were no bike tyre marks at the scene.' Jude tapped his pen on the table.

'He could have left the bike somewhere and walked.'

'There were no footmarks.' But even as he said it, Doddsy remembered Phil's words to Jude on the night of Gracie Pepper's killing. 'But he knows all about crime scenes. He may not have had any forensic training himself, but he'll have picked up a lot along the way from Tammy. He'll know exactly what to do to avoid contaminating a crime scene.'

'And exactly what to do to avoid incriminating himself, as well.'

There was a short silence. Doddsy felt his own face twisting up in displeasure, just as Jude's was doing. Sometimes crime came a little too close to home, and sometimes they had to remind themselves that circumstantial evidence wasn't enough.

'Yes, that's true,' Jude acknowledged. 'But we need something more than that. As far as I can see, there's no reason at all why Phil would want to harm Len Pierce. I'm not aware of any connection. They don't move in the same circles.'

'Phil's a doctor, though. Like Giles Butler. They could have met.' Chris flipped open his iPad and flicked through document after document until he found the one he wanted. 'Go back to the PM report. Len's medical records indicate that he had specialist treatment for some form of dermatitis. I imagine he'll have had that up at the hospital. What's Phil's area of specialism?'

'He works up at the fracture clinic, I think. There has to be a possibility their paths crossed.' Jude pulled his notebook towards him and wrote down: *check out PG*, as though by writing it, it would magically be accomplished without him having to go through the strain. 'See if Giles Butler knew him, as well. Though I'll be honest with you. I can see Phil punching someone in the face if he disagreed with them, but I can't see him sneaking round the countryside at night with a knife, still less lurking in a churchyard when he knew he was about to pick up his wife from drinks with a bunch of detectives.'

'Bluff and double bluff.' Ashleigh, he saw, was giving Doddsy a sympathetic look. 'Do you know Phil well, Doddsy?'

'No better than anyone else. Bumped into him a couple of times. Nice enough guy.' But that had been before he'd got involved with Tyrone. If he were to bump into Phil now his reception would be a lot less cordial. 'I'm seeing Tyrone later on.'

'Ah, I'd forgotten. You're supposed to be off this afternoon. For God's sake don't hang on here too long. We all need a break.' Jude sighed. 'I'd better talk to Phil, then. Chris. You get someone to follow up on whether Lenny or Giles Butler had ever met Phil. Then we'll see.'

Chris sat back and stuck his pen behind one ear, hands behind his head. 'I think I'd also like to take another look at Giles Butler.'

'Why's that? Did anything come back for the forensics on the car?'

'Nothing that doesn't tie in exactly with what he said. If he'd killed Len you'd expect there to have been blood in the car, either from Giles' clothing or from the knife, assuming he took it with him to dispose of it. There's no trace. But I'm not happy with that.' He paused. 'Not the forensic side. I'm not questioning that. I'm just not convinced that entirely clears the good doctor.'

'Oh?'

'Yes. If we leave aside Gracie Pepper for now, there was always the motive with Giles, wasn't there? He had a reason to kill Len. It might not have been a good one, but it was always there. He was the one who was hiding the affair. He was the one who was lying to his wife. Lenny wasn't open about it and he didn't talk about his private business, but nor did he hide it.'

'Oh, I see.' Ashleigh sat forward, intently. 'Supposing — just supposing — Len wanted to get serious and Giles didn't.'

'That's what I'm thinking. I was reading back through his witness statement. All that stuff about his reputation, his standing in the community.'

'His wife and kids.' Doddsy was more sympathetic than the others. Coming out wasn't always easy. People judged you for it, one way or another. Sometimes they made you into a hero when all you'd done was be yourself, an action as false in its way as making you a villain. 'I get that. It's hard to explain.'

'Yep. And I accept that it's a possibility,' Jude agreed. 'But if Giles is the killer, that doesn't explain how he managed to get the knife, and any bloodstained clothing, from the murder scene down to the bin in King Street.'

'We don't yet know if it's the knife. Though I'll be astonished if it isn't, and if it isn't we still have to find that murder weapon, or explain how he disposed of it, and it doesn't account for the absence of any forensic evidence on the car.'

'Yeah. That's the problem. Leave it with me,' Chris said, with a shake of the head, 'and I'll sort it.'

The meeting broke up. Jude and Doddsy headed back along the corridor to the office they shared. 'Jude. You don't seriously suspect Phil, do you?'

'I have an open mind.' Jude always said that, even when it was clear his thinking was going in a particular direction. There had to be evidence and there had to be good evidence. There was nothing, Doddsy reminded himself, comforted, that firmly linked Phil to the scene of Len's murder and there was no known motive for the death of Gracie Pepper. Even if Gracie turned out to be gay, and even if Phil had objections to homosexuals in general, surely if he was to target someone it would be Doddsy himself. 'Let's see what else comes up.'

Doddsy reached for his coat. 'I'm off.' He wasn't normally precious about his time off, but it wasn't that often that he and both Tyrone found themselves not working on a bright afternoon. For the first time in his life he found himself with a real reason not to volunteer to be the one who stayed on. He had plenty of credit in the bank on that score, and no guilt.

He'd logged out of his computer and cleared his desk before the meeting, knowing the way life had of catching you by the heels on the way out, and someone had left an envelope on there for him. White, a third A4 size, typically bulk-bought office stationery. By post, a typed label that said, in bold capitals, *PERSONAL*. He picked it up. The postmark was smudged.

'One thing you might want to do,' Jude went on, opening a folder and flicking through it, 'is ask Tyrone if he's heard anything about Gracie or Giles on the grapevine. Though you'll have other things to talk about, I imagine.'

Doddsy slit the envelope open with his forefinger and extracted a folded A4 sheet. Jude was still talking to him, but he wasn't listening. All he could see was the sheet in front of him, four words, neatly typed.

DI DODD. You next.

*

'Can we keep it short?' Phil glanced at his watch. 'I'm so busy I can barely manage a lunch break these days. You'll know all about that.'

On the other side of the road an ambulance made its leisurely way on to the hospital campus. Aware of how bad it might look for Phil to be interviewed by the police at work, Jude had acceded to his request to come off-site, but that constituted the single table and chairs near the coffee machine in a petrol station. Phil was still wearing his pager clipped to his belt and kept a forefinger resting on it as if to remind Jude of his indispensability.

'I'll get to the point.' If he hadn't had a dozen other things to do he'd still have wanted to keep the meeting as short as possible, but he was even more keen to do so since the threat that had landed on Doddsy's desk had thrown more fuel on the metaphorical fire. 'I don't think you were quite straight with me on Tuesday night.'

'You think that?' Phil was a big man and he put his shoulders back to make himself bigger.

Used to more direct challenges from more violent men, Jude ignored the implied threat but he made a mental note and it didn't favour Phil. 'I do.

Remember you told me you didn't recognise Gracie Pepper?'

'I didn't recognise her at first. It was dark, and she was covered in blood. And she didn't look like I knew her. Anyway I told you later that I did recognise her.'

'You told me you didn't know her very well.'

'She didn't work in my department.'

'No. But you participated in the same workshop with her a few weeks ago.'

'Ah.' Phil sat back and picked up his coffee cup. 'Of course. Those bloody sessions. Complete waste of my time and of public money. We're stretched enough without having someone making us all fart around telling everybody stuff they'd no desire to hear. Some people buy into that, but not me. I just made something up.'

And thereby confirmed himself to Jude as a liar. Not that Jude fundamentally disagreed with Phil's assessment of the workshops, though the doctor was exactly the type of man they were meant to reach and yet the type who would ultimately remain unconvinced. 'Do you remember Gracie from it?'

'Now you mention it, yes, but I didn't at the time.'

'I understand she was a bit of a star turn.'

'She may have been. I probably spent the afternoon thinking of all the paperwork I'd have to do that evening. If that's all you've got to offer in the way of an interview, perhaps we could just have done it over the phone.'

'You were out on your bike on the afternoon Len Pierce died. Is that right?'

'That's right.'

'Where did you go?' Jude had an OS map in his briefcase and fished it out, unfolding it. 'Can you show me?'

Phil hesitated, just a fraction. 'I don't remember the exact route. Up along the hillfoot villages, anyway. I parked at Langwathby and went from there. Then I cycled down to Knock and back via Newbiggin.' Phil reached for the map and his finger sketched a furtive route, carefully skirting away from Temple Sowerby. 'I left late morning. I saw all your blue lights in the distance.'

'Did you stop anywhere?'

'I had a sandwich in the pub at Langwathby before I started.'

That would be verifiable, but how much of the rest of Phil's route would be? 'Did you have your phone with you?'

'I left it in the car. I cycle where I feel like cycling. I have enough dealings with computers in the rest of my life. I don't need them nagging at me about where to stop and start and where to turn left.'

For a moment Jude thought of Natalie, slave to her own obsession with the fitness tracker as its foreman, shouting orders she had to obey. 'Okay. We'll ask around.'

'Let's hope someone saw me, then, because if you try and finger me for a hate crime you'll be the one who looks stupid.'

'It's murder,' Jude said, folding the map and replacing it in the case, 'twice over. That's pretty serious.'

'Sorry for being inexact. I'm not a lawyer.' Phil fingered his pager again, as if willing it to ring. 'If that was all? I need to get back to my patients.'

'One more thing. You haven't written to DI Dodd recently, have you?'

'No.' Phil got up and leaned forward, a sorry attempt to intimidate. 'I don't write to people. If I have something to say to that man, I'll say it to his face. You can tell him that.' And he turned and headed from the building.

Jude sat for a moment after he'd gone, watching him. Doddsy was right. Phil didn't strike him as the kind of man to pussyfoot around, certainly not the kind who'd kill two people at random before he got to the person who triggered his fury.

And then there was Doddsy. He reflected a moment longer on the note. Faye, when he'd alerted her, had taken it as seriously as he'd expected but her intensity had been frightening. She'd had it off to the lab for assessment within a minute of being shown it, as if the whole thing was personal to her.

So she should. There was a clear and a present threat, now, not only to anyone in the area who was gay but to police officers in particular. But it was personal to him, too. His best friend was gay, his girlfriend bisexual. It had come close.

He was afraid.

His moment of introspection didn't last. As ever, someone else's needs intervened. This time the message that pinged up on the phone was from Ashleigh. *Break-in at Claud's office*. With a sigh, he picked up the phone and called her back.

CHAPTER 16

'I hear my mum's been on your back.'

Doddsy sighed. Tammy's opposition to his relationship with Tyrone had played uncomfortably on his soul since Jude had told him about it, but that was nothing to how he'd felt since the conversation that morning, and the realisation that Phil had been indisputably on the scene of the second murder and within a couple of miles of the first. The threatening message had only made it worse. When there was a right moment he'd tell Tyrone about it, because a threat to one was a threat to the other. 'Not directly.'

'Jude, then. She told me she'd had it out with him. I knew he'd have told you.'

They were coming back into Pooley Bridge along the lakeshore walk. The sun had given up under the onslaught of the rolling spring clouds and a chill breeze had sprung up to whip tiny waves ever faster across the surface of Ullswater and force the Union Jack at the end of the steamer pier to stand out as if to attention. 'Are they giving you trouble at home?'

He was a few steps behind Tyrone as the path narrowed to the gate and he watched the younger man anxiously. Tyrone habitually walked like a policeman on the beat, tall and slightly ponderously with thumbs tucked into his belt, but today he was off-duty and light hearted, swinging his hips through the twist in the narrow gate and turning back with a smile that turned Doddsy's gut and reminded him of his own misgivings. He was looking fifty in the eye, he reminded himself, too old even to justify a mid-life crisis.

'Nah.' Tyrone said, with an easy laugh, and slowed to allow Doddsy to catch up. Out of uniform he went for a look more suited to his age, jeans and a Newcastle United football shirt, a baseball cap defying the faint and declining sun. To the casual onlooker they must look like father and son. 'She knows better. She says what she has to say and that's her duty done. She does think a lot of duty, my mum.'

Doddsy came across Tammy more regularly than most of the other CSIs, largely because of the mutual regard in which she and Jude held one another and the consequent fact that they liked to work together. Her chilliness with him wasn't, he sensed, personal. If it was only Tammy's displeasure he had to think about, he wouldn't have worried. Time would smooth out the wrinkles and eventually, if anything came of what was growing between him and Tyrone she'd get used to it and if nothing came of it her worries and her resistance would melt away like snow off a dry stone wall, her tolerance only to be tested when Tyrone found himself another, younger, man.

The morning's meeting had shown him that there was much more to worry about than Tammy. 'And what about your dad?'

'Let's get a coffee.' Tyrone accelerated away again, shot across the road just before the lights changed from red to green and turned to wave across the stream of traffic that passed between them. When the lights changed again and Doddsy made his more sedate way across the road to join him, he was grinning at him. 'You know what dads are like. They're just like mums, only more macho. Let's get a cake.'

They settled in a seat by the window and ordered tea and cake, Doddsy opting for chocolate cake that he never usually ate and Tyrone choosing the lemon drizzle. It was a strange occasion, Doddsy told himself, feeling like an old maid on a first date. It wasn't the first time he'd been out with Tyrone but his own awkwardness, the lifting of an internal curtain on his own heart, made it different. Suddenly it mattered to him what happened to the Garner family, and whether they were torn apart by criminal activity or an old-fashioned intolerance or whether they made up and stayed together. He'd become invested in what happened to them, purely because it mattered to him that Tyrone was happy, with or without him. For the first time he understood exactly why Jude had been so conflicted over Mikey's struggle between right and wrong, how hard it must have been for him to take the decision that, to an outsider like Doddsy himself, should only ever have gone one way.

'So,' said Tyrone, when the waitress had delivered their cakes and an enormous pot of tea, 'what were we talking about? Dads, that was it. And aren't they strange things?'

Slicing the corner off his chocolate cake, Doddsy allowed himself to remain in a spellbound silence.

'I mean. My dad's a man's man.' Tyrone sighed. 'Rugby and cricket — the men's game, never the women's — and he'd never wear pink. He does the cooking, but only when Mum isn't there. He always drives, unless there's drink involved, in which case he drives there and she drives back. And he'd be appalled if ever saw her drink a pint.'

Doddsy had seen Tammy sink a few pints in his time. He suppressed a smile. 'It's a generational thing. My dad's like that.'

'I thought as much. Though even the metrosexual parents, the ones who think they're right up with it… even those ones are perfectly happy for everyone else to be gay but they can't help questioning things a little bit when it's their boy. In my experience. That's where my dad's coming from.'

'Mine too.' Doddsy's childhood was a generation removed from Tyrone's but it was peopled by the same style of parenting.

'When did you come out?'

'When I was twenty-one. I thought they ought to know.' It had spared his mother the futile exercise of hoping he'd find himself a nice young woman, though not the disappointment of realising she'd have to look to friends for the surrogate pleasure of grandchildren.

'Were they disappointed?'

'That's an understatement.'

'Angry?'

'Not to my face.' On reflection, perhaps they'd taken it well. His father had worked in the shipyards and to him it was a shame, akin to siring a son who was a criminal. It didn't change the love they had for him, only the way it was expressed. He'd no doubt his father had been angry — blamed everybody else, for sure — but the love between them, always unspoken, had been strong enough to survive.

'No. Mine neither.' Tyrone looked beyond him, out of the window and down towards the shallow river to where a couple of smokers, sitting outside, huddled their jackets around them and puffed away in discontent. Following his gaze Doddsy, undertaking a crusade against a quarter of a century of chain-smoking and succeeding only in cutting down, weakened enough to want to join them just for one quick smoke, but Tyrone was abstemious and clean-living so he stayed where he was. 'My mum gave me a hug and told me she was proud of me. She knew, of course. They always do. And I can see why she was disappointed. Not because she minds, not really. It's because they don't have a daughter and she always hoped I'd bring someone home that she could have that sort of relationship with. Optimistic, I dare say. But that's what I think she wanted.'

'And your dad was different?' If only Phil hadn't been anywhere near the site of Gracie's murder, or had arrived just that little bit later, when she was dead, so that he wouldn't have tried to intervene and he wouldn't have disturbed the body and ended up soaked in the woman's blood and looking like her butcher.

'He's a great guy, Dad is.' Tyrone sighed. 'When I told him I was gay he went quiet for a while, avoided me for a week or so, then started talking to me again. Never said anything. Never explained. Certainly never apologised. But he dropped the stuff about poofs and men being real men and so on.'

But had Phil changed his mind? 'And you reckon he meant it?'

'He's a traditional old stick, is Dad. He won't change what he thinks. He might change the way he talks, because he know other people find it unacceptable and every now and then something comes up. You should have heard him when he and Mum were at church and people were talking about this Rainbow Festival. *No place for that in the church. It wants to stop meddling with people's private lives. None of this woke nonsense.*' His mimicry of his father was clever but fond. 'He's traditional enough, thank God, that he still thinks blood's thicker than water.'

'I expect he's wondering what he did wrong.' Gloomy at the folly of his fellow humans, Doddsy in his turn looked outside and the antics of a couple of ducks, scrabbling in the shallows for bread that the smokers tossed to them, cheered him up.

'Yeah, I expect so. But he needs to loosen up.'

'We all do, to an extent.'

Tyrone chopped his slice of cake into neat pieces and Doddsy found himself staring in fascination at his long, thin fingers. 'I don't think he killed Gracie Pepper, you know. But I wonder if that's what I want to think. It's easy to delude yourself. We all do it, all the time.'

'Did he know her?'

'Better than he lets on. I don't understand why people can't be open about their sexuality.'

Doddsy knew. It wasn't easy being an older generation. It made it harder to be at ease with yourself. He had more sympathy with Giles Butler than either Jude or Ashleigh had managed to muster. Sometimes you just wanted to make life easier. And the implications of what Tyrone had just said caught on. 'What did you say?'

'Gracie. She's a lesbian.' Tyrone beamed across the table at him. 'Hey, Doddsy. Don't tell me you didn't know. I just assumed you did but no-one was saying anything.'

'I'd no idea. Where did you hear that?'

'Not so much hear as overhear. I was leaving this morning and Mum and Dad were talking about it. He said something not very complimentary about Gracie being a dyke.' He crinkled his face in distaste. 'Excuse my language. I thought about going back and saying something but Mum tore a rare strip off him for me, so I didn't need to stay and get involved in the aggro. When I went out she was lecturing him about the language he used and he was banging on about political correctness making people think it's cool to be gay when they should just get on with the way they were born, or something like that. I left them to it.'

Gracie, gay. It looked as if Faye had been right after all. And the note, which he'd taken seriously at first and then managed to write off as an ill-judged prank, suddenly became more that that, morphed on the instant into a very real threat to himself and others. 'Quite right.'

Tyrone's anxious eyes searched his face. 'I thought it must be common knowledge. If it isn't that doesn't look good for him does it? If he's right, I mean. But it didn't look good for him anyway.'

The last thing Doddsy needed — the very last thing — was Phil implicated in two murders. He pictured the look on Jude's face when he heard. 'You know I can't talk about it.'

'I'm not sentimental, mate.' Tyrone's anxiety had transmitted itself from face to fingers, and he was

243

mashing the crumbs on his plate. 'If he did wrong he has to answer for it. I don't think he did it. Of course I don't. He's my dad. But let's not pretend he isn't in the frame.'

'Does he realise he's a suspect?'

'He could hardly not, with me in my job and Mum in hers. He knows we're asking questions.'

The truth was the truth and the law was the law. Striving to keep down the importance of what Tyrone had revealed. Doddsy shifted the conversation on. 'I didn't know your parents were churchgoers.'

'The old-fashioned sort. Habit, I think.'

'Does he know Claud then? If he knows about the Rainbow Festival.' It kept coming up. The church meeting about the festival, back on the day that Len had died, had been where he'd first heard of Claud Blackwell. Doddsy himself, a silent listener from the back pew, had liked the idea, seeing it as a vehicle that might somehow lead to his own acceptance of himself. At the workshop Claud had made him feel like a coward for not wanting to engage and choosing, instead, to take on an invisible cloak of celibacy. He'd felt forced into talking about it when he was much more like Jude, someone who was rarely caught out committing the error of showing a stranger how he felt.

But Tyrone liberated him. He understood now that it wasn't about sexuality but about himself and the fact that he'd never before met someone who touched his soul. He'd had to wait far longer than he'd ever thought, but he'd finally found the man who made him care nothing for the opinion of the world around him.

'Claud? I don't think so. He certainly never mentioned it.' Tyrone pushed his empty plate aside. 'We've got the rest of the day. Let's call into Booths and pick up some stuff. Then we can go back to your place and I'll cook you some tea.'

He went off to settle the bill and Doddsy, day off or not, took the opportunity to flick a quick message to Jude.

CHAPTER 17

'This is all my fault.'

Death — any death — was traumatic. Natalie plucked at the skin on the back of her hand but the pain wasn't great enough to distract her. Anxiety bred anxiety, until the smallest thing presaged the largest, the most innocent move assumed the signature of guilt. Deep down she was a rational woman, had read all the books and had all the help that Claud could get for her, but there was an inexplicable and unbridgeable gap between knowing and understanding. No matter what techniques she employed with her rational mind, her eternally anxious soul believed the worst.

'Don't be ridiculous.' Claud was at his desk, looking out of the window just as he must have done when Gracie Pepper had been slaughtered in the churchyard almost under his eyes.

'It is my fault. And they think it's serious.'

'It's routine. It was just a break-in. Nobody died.'

The *nobody died* made her twitch, as if the mention of death was an electric shock prompt meant to keep her sane. And this was after the calming effects of the medication. Without it, she wouldn't have coped. 'If it's routine, why are they sending the chief inspector?'

'They want people to know they're around. It's all about visibility. Or maybe he's got nothing else to do.'

'It'll be because it's us. We're suspects. Me. They must think it's me, because I found the first body.'

'And I found the second.' He'd given in to irritation, as if the strain was beginning to get to him, too, but with those words he turned and smiled at her, as if that was all he could offer in the way of reassurance. 'Of course we're suspects. Dozens of other people must be, too. But just because we could have done it doesn't mean they think we did.'

'At least we aren't gay. So we're safe.'

'For God's sake, Nat. Two dead bodies aren't a scientific sample. They might be random killings.'

Even Claud's nerves were fraying. The tension in her body heightened in response. 'Then nobody's safe.'

'And anyway,' he went on, ignoring her, 'you know what I think. We shouldn't define ourselves as gay or not gay. We're all a little bit gay. It's a spectrum.'

How Claud defined sexuality was irrelevant. It was how the killer saw it that mattered. 'But it's always near us.' She bit her knuckle. How was she going to cope when her rock, her soul mate, was struggling? 'Supposing someone wants to kill you.'

'If someone wanted to kill either of us they'd have done it, instead of taking out the poor guy you found and the nurse in the churchyard. It's coincidence.'

Which took them back to the first question. 'So why are they sending a chief inspector if all that's happened is a break-in?'

'I told you. It's because it's a high profile case and they want the public to know they're on top of it. Or think they are. They clearly aren't, or they'd have arrested someone by now.' He turned away from his position by the window with every sign of relief. 'I'd hoped they might send Chris Dodd, if they were sending a big cheese. Bloody brilliant copper, and so helpful. I really took to him. You know when you meet someone.'

'Like us.'

'Yes, exactly like us. Only different of course.' He squeezed her hand and returned to the issue. 'Anyway, Satterthwaite's here now. You can ask him.'

Natalie stayed where she was, balanced on the more rickety of the two chairs with her knees drawn up to her chin and her arms clasped around them, feet touching the seat just firmly enough to maintain her balance. The damp of her running gear clung to her skin. She shivered, watching Claud as he went towards the door to the office and flung it open, resting his brawny forearm on the wall. In some insane, inexplicable way she was afraid of Jude Satterthwaite. 'Chief Inspector. We're up here.'

The detective paused at the doorway to check a phone message, lifted an eyebrow and pocketed the phone. With enough urgency to show he was keeping a close eye on events but not enough for even Natalie to panic, he ran lightly up the flight of stairs from the ground floor. Claud, who seemed entirely oblivious to potential danger, had left it wedged open for him. 'Good afternoon Mr Blackwell. Mrs Blackwell.' He nodded in Natalie's direction. 'I understand you've had a break-in. Is that right?'

'Yes.' Claud turned his back on the policeman, who was already running his trained eye over the premises to see if there was any damage, any disturbance. 'It wasn't exactly a break-in, though. Was it Nat?' He sighed.

Finding herself the focus of the man's attention, Natalie reluctantly unfolded herself from the secure and womb-like position she'd assumed and sat straight up on the chair to face him. He was looking down at her trainers, as if he expected to find their soles rimmed with blood as they had been after Len Pierce's murder, but if he hoped for some clue to catch her red-handed, then he was doomed to disappointment. The trainers had gone straight in the bin, as had the pair she'd been wearing when Gracie was murdered, and she'd never be able to wear the same brand again. 'No, it wasn't. I'm afraid it was my fault. I let them in.'

'You let them in? So you saw them.'

'No.' Claud interrupted, as if the detective were simple and Natalie herself obstructive, rather than just not quite able to answer the question. 'She didn't let them in. It was carelessness.'

'Mrs Blackwell?'

She wilted a little under his gaze. 'Claud's right. I was careless. I went out and I left the door open.'

'Where did you go? For a run?'

'Of course it was for a run. I keep telling you, Nat. This running is an obsession. You need to break it. It does you more harm than good.' He turned to Jude. 'I wasn't here. I was out at a meeting. At the town council. I'm discussing a program of workshops with them, similar to those we've been running up at your place. And while I was away Nat went for a run.'

His scorn rebuked her. 'You're right. I know I shouldn't have done. But I didn't have any work to do, and I thought if I went out while you were out then I wouldn't have to go out later on.' She stuck a forefinger under the black rubber band of her fitness tracker and tugged at it, but it stayed as firm as a handcuff. 'I didn't have my keys with me, so I left the door open.'

Jude Satterthwaite said nothing either to condemn or reassure her, but crossed to the window and looked out. Natalie stood up, too, so could follow his gaze. A dark grey sky brooded behind the huge sandstone edifice of St Andrew's Church and the green sward around it. In the distance the snowdrops and crocuses that swamped the grass beyond the church in early spring had faded, and the sharp spikes of daffodils threatened to burst out into glorious yellow at any moment. Maybe flowers grew well in churchyards because of the dead below them.

It was reasonably certain that the man wasn't interested in the daffodils but (she shivered) trying to see if there was any spot from which they could have been watched. There must have been a dozen. The north side of the church, the south side, the entrance to the arcade, the stairway into the library, the lane that dropped down to King Street, where she'd appeared to find Claud taking his turn at stumbling on the newly-dead. All of them were vantage points for a casual observer, and that didn't include any passing opportunist who might have spotted her running out of the office leaving the door swinging open, and tried his luck.

Jude concluded his review of the churchyard and turned back, running his eye over the contents of the office. Trying to see it through his eyes, Natalie saw only confusion — a pair of rickety chairs, a desk stamped with the hallmark of Claud's enthusiastic chaos, boxes of marketing leaflets and tee shirts with a rainbow logo. 'Was anything taken?'

'My laptop.' Claud flapped his hand at Natalie. 'It's not valuable in itself. It was an old one. But I keep confidential information on it. If there's a data breach I could lose a lot of business.'

'It's secured, of course?' The grey eyes swept the room again.

'Yes. There are passwords for the laptop, for every package and for individual documents. I dare say your people could break into it in pretty short order, but a casual thief wouldn't be able to.'

'A casual thief would be more likely to wipe the data and sell it on,' Jude agreed. 'I don't see any sign of damage, so my instinct is to conclude that it was an opportunistic theft.'

'I thought we lived in a honest neighbourhood.' Natalie resumed her seat again, bolt upright on the edge of it.

'We do, pretty much. I maybe wouldn't have gone out leaving my door open quite so obviously myself, but if I did I wouldn't expect to be burgled when I got back.' He got out a notebook. 'I'll get someone down here to do a quick sweep for fingerprints, but it doesn't look to me as though there will be many clues. In the meantime, could you just run me through what you were both doing, when you were out, how long and so on?'

Claud took the second seat, running his hand across his brow. 'Shall I start? My version of events is pretty slim.'

252

'Go ahead.'

'I had a two o'clock meeting with the town council. I left here at about half one.'

The detective, who seemed to miss nothing, lifted an eyebrow. 'For a two o'clock meeting?' The town hall was a couple of hundred yards away.

'I like to be early. In my way I'm as bad as Nat.' He smiled at her, a sign that his irritation was thawing. 'Of course I got there far too soon, so I walked back to the square, got myself a coffee to take out and then turned up and drank it sitting on the wall outside. Right under the CCTV cameras, if you want to check.'

'I don't disbelieve you.'

The man would check anyway. Natalie, whose eyesight was good, noticed how he'd put an asterisk beside the word *CCTV*.

'Good. And you obviously didn't take your laptop with you. Is that normal?'

'It was an informal chat, rather than a presentation. I took a folder with some hand-outs and a notepad. The meeting lasted for about forty-five minutes, and I came back via the arcade. I stopped at the bakery for a sandwich — I hadn't had lunch. Then I cut through past the library.' He gave a vague wave in the general direction of the churchyard. 'As I got to the gateway I saw the door at the bottom of the stair was open.'

'It's not a shared stairway, is it?'

'No. This office — office suite, they call it — is self-contained. It may once have been part of a flat overlooking King Street and the square, but it must have been partitioned. The stairs would originally have been the back stairs.'

'And you normally keep the downstairs door open?'

'If we're in, yes. The bell doesn't work. I didn't think anything of it, but I came up the stairs and the door to the inner office was open, too.' He drew a short, sharp breath. 'First up, of course, I thought the worst.'

That was what happened. Natalie felt a surge of pity for her husband. 'But Claud,' she pleaded from the other side of the room. 'I left you a note.'

'Yes, but I didn't see it straight away. When I did see it, of course, it made sense.'

Jude Satterthwaite, she could tell, had already seen and read the note. He struck her as a man who already knew, or suspected, the answer to many of the questions he asked. Nerves rose in her stomach at the idea that the answer she might give him might be wrong, when everyone knew her anxiety made her an unreliable observer, prone to overstatement and always leaning towards the worst possible scenario. Would he understand that when he came to take her statement, or would he silently hold her to account for the inevitable mistakes she would make?

'After that,' Claud resumed, 'I had a look round and saw that my laptop had gone. I guessed what had happened and went down to see if I could find Natalie. She wasn't about, so I waited until she came back to make sure that we actually had been broken into. That must have been about ten past three. Then, of course, I called your sergeant immediately.'

'Okay. Thank you.' He drew a line under the notes on his pad, turned over to a new page and wrote her name at the top. 'Mrs Blackwell?'

Her heart fluttered in her chest. It was always hard to explain herself to anyone who lived by the laws of hard-headed rationalism. Even Claud, who was endlessly tolerant of her many eccentricities, never made the fatal mistake of pretending to understand. 'Well, it's all very simple.' Which it was, but how would it seem to any onlookers? 'After Claud left for his meeting there was very little left for me to do. I'd been for my run this morning as usual, but we were in here early and so I'd cut it short. I wasn't busy so I thought I'd take a quick run to get some of my miles in the bank. I do that sometimes. I always have my running gear with me, just in case.'

She looked at him, uncertain of his reaction. Some people laughed at her obsession and she struggled to sleep if the numbers weren't safely logged, in her head or on the app, but he must have been used to hearing this kind of thing. 'Where did you run?'

'Just around the town. I have a route. It's only a couple of miles. I run along Meeting House Lane, then up Wordsworth Street, along Beacon Edge past the cemetery, down Salkeld Road. Then Scotland Road and Middlegate and back. Sometimes I do it twice. Sometimes more.'

He smiled at her again. 'I've seen you. I do that loop, too, though not often enough. It's the hill that kills you. That's why I always go up first.' And then he moved her on, swiftly. 'What time did you get back?'

'I'm not quite sure.'

'Did you stop?'

'Yes. I used to stop outside M&S to do my stretches but now I think that must be the way the killer got away.' She couldn't do that any more. Not after Gracie. The run along the end of the lane after Len Pierce had died had been hard enough and she had only a limited amount of courage to draw on. 'I stop in Meeting House Lane, now.'

'Okay. It doesn't really matter, as your husband was already back, so we know when the burglary must have occurred. And you left the doors unlocked.'

'Yes, because I didn't have my key.'

'Okay. No worries.' He seemed very cheerful about it. 'If you want my opinion it was an opportunistic theft, but given what's been happening it's probably wise to be extra vigilant. As I said, I'll

256

send a CSI round to look for fingerprints, but it might not be until tomorrow.'

Whoever it was wouldn't have left any. All they'd have done would be to come in and pick up the laptop. And it was a straightforward burglary. Natalie stressed all these things to herself. Eventually she might almost believe them.

'By the way,' Jude Satterthwaite said, as an afterthought, 'I meant to ask you. I don't suppose either Len or Gracie had anything to do with your Rainbow Festival?'

Claud shook his head. It was his project, not Natalie's. She left it to him to do the talking. 'No.'

'Does it go down well?'

'Mostly. there's always some opposition, of course. Every congregation has its unChristian homophobe, and they're always the ones who shout the loudest. But those are the people we're trying to reach.' Claud paused. 'You know one of them.'

'Do I?'

'Yes. I've remembered where I saw the fellow in the churchyard, the doctor. He was one of them.' Claud's lips curled in irritation.

'Fascinating,' the detective said, politely. 'Anyone else?'

'As I say. There's at least one in every congregation. I couldn't tell you their names.'

'I daresay I can find out,' Jude said, standing up to signal the interview was at an end. 'Let me know if anything else comes up.'

'Let's go home,' Claud said, when the detective had got them to initial his record of the conversation and then headed off past the remnants of blue tape on the churchyard railings (whistling, she noted, as though he hadn't a care in the world). 'I suppose in the great scheme of things that wasn't something to make a fuss about, but we're both a little bit stressed.'

He always tried to downplay her nerves. Maybe he thought if he did that his overt calm would rub off on her. She loved him for it, as if her life depended on it. 'Yes.' She tapped her wrist, desperate to run again. 'Are you angry with me about the keys?'

'No, of course not. I know I sounded a bit snappy to start with. But that was because I was worried about you.' He turned around, frowned at the empty chair, where he always left his jacket. 'Bastards!' he said, shaking his head. 'They've taken my coat. To wrap the laptop in, I suppose.'

She sighed. 'It was about time you got a new one anyway.' And he never kept anything worth having in the pockets.

'Yes, you're right. Now come on. Let's get home.'

CHAPTER 18

Ashleigh had been sitting on a desk, running through the results of the constables whose door-to-door inquiries she was responsible for supervising. There were sheaves of notes and the PC who delivered them to her hadn't picked up any obvious connections, but one name caught at her. A tiny thing, but worth exploring. When the constable had gone she jumped down and drifted across the incident room to where Jude was standing in front of the whiteboard. 'Jude. Can I run something by you?'

'Of course.' He stepped back from the board. 'Did the door-to-doors come up with something?'

'I think they might have done. These are the interviews we have from the staff and patients at the hospital. There's nothing in them that helps us directly. No-one has anything you might call a lead. But we talked to some of the patients on the elder care ward where Gracie worked. They all loved her to bits, and nobody can think of any reason why someone would have hurt her. But I think there's something in here that implies that Gracie knew Giles Butler.'

'Is that right?' That stopped him in his tracks, though he should hardly be surprised. It was a small enough world, and people knew of their neighbours and their doings even when they'd hardly ever met. Giles lived in Kirkby Stephen and his paranoia over being recognised suggested he had plenty of contacts up in the Eden Valley.

'Yes, though I wouldn't get too excited about it. It's just that one of the patients she spoke to is a Mr Butler.'

'Not an uncommon name.'

'No, but he mentioned that the last time he saw Gracie was on the day she was killed. He remembers it clearly, because it was the day his son came to visit him. He didn't name the son, but we can check. The son doesn't come too often, because he's busy. He's a GP. In Kirkby Lonsdale.'

'We know Giles went up to visit his father in Penrith hospital. That's where he met Len. How reliable is Butler senior?'

'It's possible he might be mistaken, but if he isn't, that puts Giles Butler in Penrith on the day, though not necessarily at the time, that Gracie was killed.'

'Right. You'll need to get your guys to check that.'

'I've got them on to it already. Butler is working just now, but I expect we'll hear soon enough where he was — or where he said he was — on that day and at that time.' It felt like progress, so much so that she was surprised at his lukewarm reaction to it, but she'd learned to tell when something was nagging at him. 'And what's on your mind? Are you inspired? Or baffled? You must have been standing there for five minutes.'

'More baffled than inspired,' he admitted, tearing his eyes from the maze of information and ironing out his customary frown. I spoke to Claud and he mentioned the Rainbow Festival again. It keeps coming up. Even though it's only a suggestion, it seems to have inspired strong opposition.'

'Can we pin that opposition to anyone we've already covered?'

'Yes. Phil. Claud remembers him from a church meeting, though he wasn't the only one. He said there's opposition in every congregation, though not as great as the support.'

'Okay,' Ashleigh said. 'If we have to go through every congregation looking for the one rotten apple, I'll do it. I don't care how many good Christian folk are upset.'

'The good ones won't mind. But I don't know if we need to go down that route just yet, as neither Len nor Gracie had any church connections that I'm aware of. No. That wasn't what was troubling me.'

'Then what was?'

'It's the little things. It always is.'

'You don't think the burglary at the Blackwells' office is significant, then?'

'I don't know, but that isn't what I meant. There's just something I can't get my head around. It's Natalie and her obsession with running.'

'Is that so odd? She looks to me as if she has a classic obsessive personality. With some people it's arranging the kitchen cupboards or putting their coat hangers the same way round.'

'My mum reloads the dishwasher if Mikey or I load it. Not the same thing, of course, but I do see where you're coming from. I don't have any reason to doubt her. I know she runs the route she says she does. I've seen her do it, even if we didn't have the data to prove it.'

Ashleigh unpinned the map of Natalie's route that was pinned up on the board and spread it out in front of them on the table. 'It seems straightforward, doesn't it.?' Her fingers traced the route. 'All the times. And that ten minute rest she said she had and always does have. It's all there. And the arrival at the crime scene, exactly when she said she was there and minutes after Len was stabbed.'

'I know. That lets her off the hook.' He took the sheet and replaced it next to the one that had tracked Natalie's run on the night of Gracie's murder. 'I don't find it easy to suspect Natalie, I admit, even if this didn't put her completely in the clear.'

'But?'

'But Claud. Here we are. A man murdered in broad daylight outside his house and he's looking the other way. A woman whose body he stumbles on outside his office. Is that too much of a coincidence?'

Ashleigh thought of Claud. If Faye kept popping up in every strong woman in the tarot deck, Claud was more specific, a bull-necked crusading King of Swords, a symbol of action, wisdom and duality. You could add patience to that, too. But somehow the action, and the obvious symbolism of the swords, didn't convince her. 'There are a lot of coincidences going on here, it seems to me.'

'Then they can't all be coincidences.' Jude hated coincidence.

'It's unlikely. We need to look a whole lot more closely at the connections.' Because that was always the message she picked up from the cards, that things were connected at many levels, and sometimes in the least likely way. 'I do agree with you that Claud has to be the main suspect. But he has no motive — almost the opposite. And even if he did, I just can't see him killing anyone.'

'It's not unknown for killers to be in complete denial about their motives.'

He lifted that reproving eyebrow at her, and she laughed. Instinct was a starting point, not an ending, and it was finding the evidence to follow it up that would convict the killer — or killers — of Len Pierce and Gracie Pepper. 'I know what you're thinking, Jude, but we'll get them in the end.'

'Let's hope so.' He turned away from the board. 'I'm done here for tonight. It's nearly six. Let's get away from this place. I spend too much time here, and I suspect you do, too.'

The previous day should have been the one day off they both had in a fortnight. 'Yes. Okay.'

'Are you doing anything?'

'I've no plans.'

'Then why don't we go out for a meal somewhere?'

'That would be fine. Any suggestions?'

He picked up his coat and looked around the depleted incident room, lifted a hand to Chris and turned away. 'We could run down to Askham and get a pub meal. And I can take you in to visit my mum on the way.'

*

They were almost at the village of Wasby when Jude's phone rang. Ashleigh glanced down at it where it lay in the cup holder. 'Unknown number. Should I answer it?'

'Wait for the voicemail.' It was his work phone and he should have switched it off. He'd never learn. The ringing ended and after a moment she checked voicemail. 'Jude. Phil Garner here. Can you give me a ring?'

Jude leaned heavily on the brake, pulling the Mercedes up in a gateway and turning off the engine. Phil. Realising he was in trouble and calling to cover his back? 'This'll be interesting. I didn't know he had my number.'

'I expect he'll have got it from Tammy.'

'Yeah, that must be it.' He picked up the phone and dialled back. 'Hi Phil. Jude here. What can I do for you?'

'I remembered something.' Phil's tone was less confrontational that it had been. Jude had heard that before, always in someone who thought they were at risk and was protecting their interests. Playing along, trying to be one of the good guys. 'It's probably nothing. But it might be.'

'Hit me with it.' Jude stared out of the window. A horse strolled up to the gate and looked down its long muzzle at them, eyes gleaming in the car headlights.

'It's Gracie. Last week I was outside in the car park heading off after my shift. I saw her come out of the hospital entrance with a man. They walked over to a car — her car, I suppose, because she was driving, and they both got in and drove off.'

'When was that?'

'Friday. About four-ish. I can't swear to the exact minute. Hope that doesn't convict me of something.'

Some people couldn't resist a sly comment. Phil was afraid. Rightly or wrongly, and of what? 'Let's hope not. Thanks for that. Did you recognise the man?'

'Can't say I did. And I wasn't close enough to see anything much, other than that.'

'Okay. That's fine. Thanks Phil. Very helpful. Enjoy your evening.' Jude rang off. 'For God's sake. That's not looking good, is it?'

Ashleigh had her phone out, her fingers tapping out a number as they spoke. 'Chris is working late. I'll get him on to that.'

'Friday last week. I wonder how many people Gracie gave lifts to between then and Tuesday? I wonder what the chances are of there being fingerprints still on the car? CCTV is the best bet, and quicker, too, if he's right about it. We should be able to get that pretty soon.'

'Yes. Chris…good. No, don't stay too late. But can you sort a couple of things for me before you go? Can you get a CSI to take fingerprints off Gracie Pepper's car? Passenger side, inside and out. And have a look at CCTV from the hospital car park for last Friday around four… As soon as possible. Like, yesterday… I want to know if she was with anyone and if we know who it was. Yes, brilliant. Thanks.' She ended the call as Jude started the engine and finished the short drive up to his mother's house at Wasby. 'Jude. Imagine…just imagine if it was Giles Butler.'

Chapter 19

When the doorbell rang, Linda Satterthwaite was in the middle of reeling off a list of tasks and the people who would do them and Mikey was looking, Becca thought, unjustifiably distracted given it was his birthday party they were planning.

'Forty-eight hours to go. We should have everything ready by tomorrow night.' Linda tapped her pad with a pen. 'Mikey, go and get the door, would you? But don't go sliding off upstairs afterwards. I'm not having you complaining something isn't right when you can't be bothered to give us your input.'

The moment he'd left the room she leaned forward. 'Have you got the cake sorted?'

Linda must be the one Jude got his organised mind from, because David and Mikey were both scatty, always leaving things to the last minute and trusting in the goodwill of others to get them out of trouble. 'Yes, don't worry. It's in my kitchen. All we need to do is get it to the hall and add the candles. I'll sneak it in when I'm bringing the rest of the food.'

'You're a born conspirator. Though I expect we could carry it in in full view and he wouldn't notice it.'

At least such a casual attitude made planning surprises for Mikey easy. Becca smiled. She'd tried to surprise Jude a few times when they'd been together and never succeeded, though he was good at pretending she had. In fact, when she thought about

267

it, the only time she'd ever caught him out was the day she'd told him it was over.

'Look what the cat's dragged in.' Mikey bounced back into the living room, grinning as if at the idea of some entertainment, and dropped back into his seat.

'Show a bit of respect,' Jude admonished him from the doorway, 'for Ashleigh, if not for me.' And then he was in the room and looking round with the expression that snapped into stillness on the instant to hide what he really thought, and Becca understood why she'd thought of him. The sound of the Mercedes outside had triggered her memories. That was all.

'Shouldn't you be catching criminals?' Mikey's chirpiness was undampened. 'Haven't you heard? There's a homicidal maniac on the loose.'

'Someone else is dealing with that tonight. I have a life.'

Becca made herself as small as she could in the corner of the sofa. He was learning. It was too late, of course, and it was ironic that he was making free time to spend with a woman he must see every day at work. Maybe he cared about Ashleigh more than he ever had done for Becca herself.

'Jude,' Linda said, her genuine warmth covering Becca's more obvious confusion. 'What a lovely surprise. And you must be—'

'This is Ashleigh.' Jude stood back and let his new woman — slightly abashed, Becca thought — precede him into the room. 'Ashleigh, this is my mum, Linda. We were on our way to Askham for a bite to eat and we're a bit ahead, so we thought it was time to introduce you.'

A chilled silence descended on them. 'Hi Becca,' Jude said, to break it.

She nodded towards him, and shuffled up on the sofa, the only space available.

'Mikey,' Linda directed, 'you can sit on the floor and give Ashleigh your seat. Tea, Ashleigh? Coffee?'

'It's okay.' Jude sat in the middle of the sofa and indicated the space next to him for Ashleigh, and then the three of them shifted about until Becca had put a clear two inches between herself and Jude and he and Ashleigh were crushed together in the other half of it. 'We're quite comfortable. And don't worry about tea. We won't stay.'

Becca had met Ashleigh before, in a more formal situation. Trying not to be too obvious, she cast a sideways look at the new light of Jude's life. In fairness to him, you could see the attraction. As an objective observer, it was hard not to be impressed by the sheer lusciousness of the woman, with her bright blonde hair and the inviting curve of her hips, waist and bosom, even though Becca was a little more critical of the startling scarlet of the lipstick and the heavy and expensive scent. 'Nice to see you again,' she said, across Jude.

'You too.'

'We've obviously interrupted the party planning meeting,' Jude nodded at the notepad the Linda had automatically picked up when she sat down.

'Of course you'll bring Ashleigh.' Linda smiled again.

'Of course.'

'You'd bloody better turn up this time.' From his seat in the corner Mikey, in full Goth mode, both looked and sounded aggrieved.

'I'll do my best.'

'You always say that.'

'Yes, and I always do.'

Becca made a face at Mikey, and had the satisfaction of seeing him give a little shrug of acknowledgement. In fairness, no-one could reasonably accuse Jude of letting his brother down, and what he'd done for him was more than anyone should consider he was obliged to. It wasn't enough, because it didn't fill the gap left by an absent father, but why should it? Jude had his own life to live, and it was obvious he was living it to the full. 'It'll be good if you can come along.'

'Yeah,' Mikey said, to Ashleigh rather than Jude, 'it'll be great to see you. We can have a proper chat.'

'If we can hear anything above the music.' Linda steamrollered her way through yet another silence. 'The only thing Mikey's doing for his own party is putting together the playlist. And as I don't recognise anything on it, I'm going to hazard a guess that it'll be far too loud and us oldies will have to congregate in the kitchen if we want to hear one another speak.'

'That's the plan, anyway.' Mikey presented an impudent face to his mother.

'Is there anything we can do to help?' Jude slid an arm along the back of the sofa behind Ashleigh, in a way that included her in the family.

'No, it's okay. We have the hall booked and we'll set it up on Saturday afternoon. Becca's doing the food and I'm going down to Sainsbury's tomorrow to load up with everything else. We'll be fine. All we need is your good selves.'

Another silence. 'If you want us to fetch and carry—'

'It's okay. We're under control.'

Becca looked down at her notepad. *Mac cheese x3* she'd written. *Sausage rolls x 100. Crisps x lots.*

'We should go, Jude.' Ashleigh nudged him, and gave Linda an apologetic look. 'We have a table booked for half seven.'

'Yes.' He heaved himself out of the low sofa and gave her a hand up that Becca was sure she didn't need. 'We were late away from work, or we'd have been able to stop longer. But I thought I ought to make an effort of introducing Ashleigh before

Saturday. Don't bother to see us out. We know the way.'

'Look,' they heard Ashleigh saying as the two of them made their way to the door. 'there's that beautiful grey cat.' And then the door closed behind them and Jude and the new woman — the official new woman — in his life had gone.

*

'I'm glad I finally met your mum.' Ashleigh unwound a thin silk scarf from round her neck and dropped it on the sofa.

'Yes. So am I.' Jude had been rerunning the day's work in a way he shouldn't be doing when an attractive woman was beginning the process of taking off her clothes in front of him. As they'd left the pub Chris had called. It was far too soon for fingerprints, but the CCTV had been easily and quickly available and had confirmed just what he'd expected — Giles, getting into Gracie's car. He'd get him in for questioning first thing next morning. That would make for an interesting session.

'And Mikey.'

Mikey, the little brat. Jude chuckled, turning up his phone to see the message his brother had sent him. *Cool girl. Punching above your weight there, m8.* 'I think you impressed him.'

'Do you think so? In a good way, I hope.'

'Almost certainly. And it was better to catch them informally. Much less pressure on everybody.'

He watched her as she shed her coat, draping it over the back of the chair. 'I hope it wasn't too awkward for you, with Becca there. I wasn't expecting her.'

'Awkward? No, not at all. I only worried that it might be a bit difficult for you.' She fluttered her fingers across the front of her blouse, teasing him.

Sometimes he thought Ashleigh could read minds and if he should ask her to tell him what he thought, because sometimes he didn't know himself. He was learning that getting over Becca wasn't happening the way he'd thought it would. She wouldn't go away. She meant less and less to him every time he saw her, and her obvious irritation with him translated naturally into his irritation with her. Still she persisted, in his mother's life and his brother's and so, by default in his own. At last he was getting used to it. 'Are you having trouble with those buttons? Here. Let me help you.'

Becca wasn't where she once was, in his heart and in his bed. Ashleigh had taken over. And he was getting used to that, too.

'Jude.' She held him off, but not as if she was resisting. 'Just a minute.'

'I'll take as long as you like.'

'There's something I want to tell you.'

His lips touched the top of her hair, an offer he knew she wouldn't refuse. 'Go ahead.'

'It's about Faye Scanlon.'

'Okay.'

'She's the woman I had a fling with.'

At an early stage she'd told him about the affair she'd had, the kicking over of all traces as her marriage disintegrated, and he hadn't turned a hair, but she'd never named names. In his silence, she slid a hand over his heart as if she could trace a change in its beat, or a variation in his breathing, but all she would feel was the quivering of a chuckle. It didn't surprise him, an elegant explanation for every aspect of Faye's behaviour — the defensiveness, the coolness to Ashleigh, the hostility to him. And he hadn't missed the way she'd changed the subject that first day back from her holiday when he'd asked if she and Faye had met. 'That must have been a shock for her when she saw you. Didn't she recognise you? Or was she cutting you dead?'

Ashleigh relaxed. 'The second. She certainly didn't seem pleased to see me.'

'How the hell did she not know where you'd gone when you came up from Cheshire? Surely when you left she would have heard something?'

'I doubt it. And even if she had known, she might not have realised I was here. I was known as Ash Kirby when I was in Cheshire. When I left I took up the Sunday version of my Christian name and went back to my maiden name.'

'I guessed, of course.'

'Of course you did,' she said, her voice bubbling with relief, and she gave up all pretence at resistance and turned willingly into his arms.

CHAPTER 20

'I'll admit to being a cad. I'll admit to being an adulterer. I'll admit to being a coward.' With his back to the wall Giles Butler had finally unearthed enough spirit to come out fighting. His perfect life was already fatally snagged and he couldn't stop it unravelling, but he'd do his best to limit the damage. 'But I won't admit to being a murderer. Because I'm not.'

'Okay. Persuade me.' Jude Satterthwaite, a man whom Giles had down as smart but possibly overzealous, was looking at him as if he believed he was the killer. Under his gaze Giles's gut shrivelled. That was how it went. If you lied often enough, people wouldn't believe the truth. 'Give me a good reason not to have you charged with two counts of murder.'

Colleen Murphy, Giles's solicitor, crossed and uncrossed her ankles and cleared her throat, as if to remind them she was there. Giles had never had the need for a solicitor before, except for making his will, and so had no idea of the procedures, but he trusted Colleen. She struck him as meticulous, and she'd assured him she wouldn't let the police away with the tiniest transgression with regard to his interests, but she'd also advised him, as strongly as possible, that if he was innocent telling the truth was the best way to get the matter cleared up. 'Perhaps you want to help my client by asking him some specific questions, Chief Inspector.'

He accepted the reproof with a wave of the hand. 'I'll begin with the background. Then we'll get on to the questions.' As before he'd brought Sergeant O'Halloran with him and Giles had turned to her with relief, but now they were playing hardball she was respectfully silent. Giles had seen enough TV shows to recognise the good-cop-bad-cop combination and was only faintly surprised that it appeared to be real. 'I'm not going to accuse you of murder, Dr Butler, or not just yet, but I think you ought to know that the evidence that we have doesn't look good as far as you're concerned. Let's begin with the circumstantial evidence. Two people with whom you have an association have been violently murdered. You were on the site of at least one of the crimes.'

At least one. Giles shivered. That didn't sound good. It sounded as if they'd dug deeper, uncovered another secret. 'I understand.'

'I want to go over your previous evidence and ask you some more questions.'

'I understand.' The room was hot and stuffy, and his mouth was dry.

'I have here the statement you gave when you turned yourself in to the police station in Hunter Lane last week.' Jude tapped the printed sheet. 'You initialled it as accurate. I want you to read it through and tell me if there's anything in it that isn't true.'

Giles wasn't a vain man, but he knew his worth. He'd been justifiably proud of that statement because every single word of it had been true. He felt that peculiar pride again, as he read it over. It hadn't been the whole truth, and that was the risk he'd taken, but if he'd told the police everything he would have compromised himself and had no chance of emerging from that little scrape with his reputation intact. Now the pride gave way to a sick feeling in his stomach. At the time he'd known it was a gamble and it had seemed worth it. He'd even thought he was being brave, getting his story in first and establishing himself as an innocent, offering them something that damned him in the hope that they wouldn't see the rest.

The question had been how far he dared gamble on withholding what he knew from the police. It was still the same. The stakes were higher and he had to give them more, and appear to do so willingly. But did he have to give them everything?

He put the statement down on the table. His hand, he observed as if from a distance, was shaking. The sergeant noticed it, too, and pushed a glass of water across the table towards him. The good cop. He wasn't fooled.

'I stand by every word in that statement,' he declared, picked up the glass and sipped.

'Good,' said the woman, with an encouraging smile. 'But perhaps in the light of what's happened since there might something you want to add to that? Something you've remembered?'

What was he to do? What did they know? The must know something. The woman so obviously felt sorry for him and he didn't know why. He sneaked a look at Colleen and was heartened by her encouraging nod. *Even if the truth damages you*, she'd said to him, *it won't damage you as much as lies*. But she'd also reminded him that he didn't have to say anything at all and the way she lifted a warning finger to her lips reminded him of that. 'I stand by my statement.'

Silence. Jude Satterthwaite narrowed his eyes at him. Ashleigh O'Halloran looked reproachful. He might as well already be in prison. He broke, too easily. 'Lenny wanted us to be together. He wanted me to leave my wife.'

'And you didn't want to?'

But he had wanted to. He'd just been incapable of doing it. He nodded, not even sure if that was the right answer.

'Was he putting you under pressure?'

Another nod.

'Did he threaten you?' the sergeant asked.

He was shocked at that. 'He'd never have hurt me.'

'I didn't mean that. But you had a lot to lose, didn't you?'

'He did say he'd tell my wife about our relationship if I didn't. But I don't think he would have done.' Janice would go ballistic when she found out, and she'd be even more devastated if she realised it hadn't changed the way he'd felt about Lenny. Love made you a fool at the best of times and illicit love turned you into a victim.

'Okay. Now tell me,' the woman said with a sigh, 'about how you knew Gracie Pepper.'

They knew. He looked up again. Under Jude Satterthwaite's cool impatience and Ashleigh O'Halloran's interest, he realised that what Janice thought was the least of his problems, but it was still Len who lingered in his thoughts. 'I'm not a violent man. I'd never have hurt him.'

'About Gracie,' persisted the woman.

It was easier to tell her. 'I met her at the hospital. My father has been in and out of there for a long time. Not that there's really anything wrong with him but old age, but he's constantly being hospitalised with infections and for a while he hasn't been quite well enough to go home. I go up to visit when I can. Sometimes I'd combine it with a visit to Lenny. It was a good excuse.'

'Makes a change from golf,' said the chief inspector, his voice dripping with criticism.

Giles addressed himself to the sergeant. 'You know Gracie worked in the elder care unit. Dad thought the world of her from the minute she arrived, and she did of him, so I made a point of seeking her out to ask about him. We found out we got on, straight away.' Like the sergeant, Gracie had been someone it was easy to talk to at a time when Giles had needed to talk. More than ever he wished he'd been honest. 'It was an entirely innocent relationship.' He smiled, wryly. 'Ironically, of course, if my wife had found out she'd have thought I was having an affair. But I think she'd have forgiven me more easily for an affair with a woman than she would have done for an affair with a man.' It was about margins, how wrong you could be and salvage soothing from your mistakes.

The woman was looking at him in a strange way, as if she'd like to disagree with him but didn't dare. 'You weren't interested in her, sexually?'

It was a roundabout way of asking a question. 'No. I might have been, I suppose, but I always assumed she preferred women to men, though she never said.' He took out a handkerchief and wiped a bead of sweat away from his brow as he thought about Gracie. 'To be be honest with you, it was a relief to have an uncomplicated relationship.'

'Okay.' Satterthwaite snapped back into the discussion. 'Let's ask you some additional questions. Did you see Gracie Pepper last Tuesday?'

'She drove me to the lane at Temple Sowerby,' Giles said. Heat prickled under his collar and he didn't even have the courage to flip his shirt button loose in case it somehow incriminated him.

'Why?'

'Because I needed—' A tear pricked his eye, the final humiliation. 'I needed to find closure.'

'Gracie knew about you and Len,' the chief inspector went on. 'Did she threaten to tell your wife?'

'No!'

'Did you ask her to drive you to the lane with the idea, perhaps, of murdering her there?'

He thought of Gracie, standing in the lane in the fading light, of a cloud of starlings wheeling above their head, of a moment of fear when she'd accused him of killing Lenny. 'No, I never did! It was sentiment. That was all. Sentiment.'

The two police officers exchanged glances. 'When did you last see Gracie?' DCI Satterthwaite asked him.

He sat back, shoulders straight. 'On Tuesday afternoon.'

'Tuesday was the day she died.'

He bowed his head.

'Where and when did you see her?'

'At the hospital. She was just going off shift as I arrived. I spent an hour with my father and then I left.' He drew a long breath. 'She invited me back to her house for supper.'

'Why was that?'

He looked across at Colleen and her closed expression told him this didn't look good. 'I've been struggling. It was bad enough when Lenny was alive, but since his death I've realised how close I came to dying, either at the same time or in his place. Gracie understood.' Rather like he sensed Sergeant O'Halloran did, and that must be why Satterthwaite had muscled his way back into the interview. Resenting that, he turned away and back, once again, to his more sympathetic interrogator. 'She knew how conflicted I was about Len. I loved him but sometimes he made me feel like a coward and a hypocrite. But with Gracie I never felt judged. She never judged anybody. So when I'd finished with Dad, I went round to her house as we'd arranged, but she wasn't there.'

'What did you do then?'

'I knew I hadn't got the time or the date wrong, because we'd spoken about it just that afternoon, but I didn't want to hang about, so I left the car and walked back into town. I thought I'd give it half an hour and then go back. I walked down to the Market Square and along to the New Squares. Then I walked back along King Street, and I was there when I heard sirens and saw blue lights.' And he'd seen these two detectives, running down the hill as if someone's life depended on it. Now he knew where they'd been heading.

'Okay.' Satterthwaite sat back, unclipped the buttons at his cuffs and pushed his shirt sleeves back up to his elbows. 'Can we just confirm that? You're telling me you were in King Street when Gracie's body was found.'

'Yes.'

'But not in the churchyard.'

'I never went into the churchyard.'

'And is there anyone you can think of who might have seen you, and be able to confirm exactly where you were at that time?'

Giles licked dry lips. 'No.'

'Okay. Another question. In your walk along King Street did you notice any bags outside any of the charity shops?'

He shot a despairing look at Colleen, who returned it and then focussed her attention back on the chief inspector. 'I think there were some outside the shop on the corner of the square.'

'Okay. Open?'

He closed his eyes and tried to remember. 'One of them was torn, I think. I think.'

'Another question. Do you smoke?'

'No.'

'And do you ever carry matches? A lighter?'

Giles felt a net tightening round him. They'd already have picked up the car, Janice's, that he'd taken to drive up to Penrith. They'd know. 'My wife smokes. She keeps a lighter and cigarettes in her car.'

'Thank you.' He flung a look at his sergeant and then turned back. 'Okay. I'll run through this again and you can tell me if I'm wrong. Because it isn't looking very good for you, is it?'

*

Giles Butler looked like a man on the edge. The very edge. But of what? A confession or a breakdown? Jude allowed him a moment of silence in which to think, if he was guilty, about admitting everything. Surely the evidence against him was convincing. Even Colleen Murphy, doing her job with skilled but silent determination, looked as if she knew that Giles's was a lost cause.

Damn. A tap at the door broke the silence, and the tension within the room snapped like an overstretched elastic band as all four turned towards the sound. Giles's shoulders slumped and the breath he'd been holding slipped out.

Ashleigh jumped up, flicking the door open and stepping outside. The voices in the corridor were tense, but he couldn't make out the words. He waited.

She half-opened the door. 'Jude. Can you spare me a minute?'

'If someone needs you, Chief Inspector, perhaps we can halt the interview to allow my client a break.'

'Of course.' He got up and stepped out into the corridor where Doddsy stood with his hands in his pockets and a troubled expression on his face. So it was serious. 'What's happened now?'

'History repeating itself,' said Doddsy, nodding his head in the general direction of the town, 'only backwards. We've found a knife, covered in blood and wrapped in a coat. In a bin on on Fell Lane. Whoever it was hadn't set fire to it, though. They probably didn't want to draw any attention to themselves.'

Jude froze. Behind him in the interview room Giles might be in a state of panic but this changed everything. 'Fresh blood?'

'Relatively. A dog walker found it.' Dog walkers always seemed to find the bad things. 'Whoever shoved it in there must have been in a hurry and hadn't wrapped it up properly. Our man was putting the poo bag in the bin, and the dog got all excited over it, and he looked in and saw the blade. Fortunately he had enough sense to dial 999 and not touch anything.'

'No body?'

'No sign of one so far. I needn't tell you the Super is doing her nut over it, and I've got everybody out combing the area. Because it's the same MO as Gracie Pepper and nearly the same as Len Pierce, so I'll be astonished — astonished — if we don't find another body somewhere nearby.'

'But Giles—' Ashleigh rolled her eyes back towards the interview room. 'We had him on the ropes in there. Len was putting pressure on him to come clean to his wife. He knew Gracie. And he was in King Street when she died. He admits it.'

Jude stilled. Giles had every reason to be glad of Lenny's death and who knew what kind of argument he might have had with Gracie? It was tempting, so tempting, to get the CPS to charge him but this new discovery cast enough doubt to prevent laying charges. 'He could have committed both of those killings.'

'He could. But he couldn't have committed this one, if it's been committed. And if the blood is fresh — or even relatively fresh — he couldn't have dumped the knife. Because he was in Kirkby Lonsdale at nine o'clock this morning and he's been in custody ever since.'

'Jesus.' Giles was so smug, so clearly implicated, that Jude couldn't bear to let him go. 'No. We'll keep hold of him just now. Apart from anything else, if this is connected to the two other deaths it could be safer for him that way.'

'You want me to take over here?'

'Yeah, go and break it to Colleen, if you wouldn't mind.' Jude was already on his way along the corridor. 'Tell her I've been called away. Ashleigh, do you want to come along with me?'

With her in his wake, he raced up to the incident room to find Faye standing by the whiteboard. She turned as she saw him, hands on hips. 'Jude. This isn't great. You've hauled in the wrong man.'

'I don't know if I have.'

'I can tell you. You have. There's been another murder and it happened in the past couple of hours.'

So they'd found a body. 'Who is it?'

She looked down at the scribbled notes she'd tossed onto the table in front of her. 'His name was George Meadows. He was fifty-five and ran a garage out on the Gilwilly estate.'

'Gay?' Jude asked, the second question to spring into his head.

'Not that I'm aware of. He was widowed, though of course that needn't preclude it. We found him in a house in William Street about half an hour ago. The postman noticed blood seeping under the front door and dialled 999. The body was in the hall. We don't have any details yet, but the officer on the scene says it looked like a single wound to the heart, and he might have been dead for a couple of hours.'

Jude paused to think. Was it conceivable the dead man knew Len Pierce, or Gracie, or Giles? 'Do we know of any connections to the other deaths?'

'There was a leaflet in his kitchen about the Rainbow Festival. There may be something else. They're still looking over the house.' She scowled at that, a woman who hated situations that got away from her, who couldn't abide a shortfall in knowledge. 'We need to find out, though.' She hesitated. 'Phil Garner's already a suspect. We need to find out where he was. And Claud Blackwell and his wife.'

'Let me check the details and get down to William Street. In the meantime I'll get Chris to follow up on Claud.'

'Good idea. And get him to check up on Garner while he's at it.' She looked down at her paper again. 'One more thing. I hadn't had it down as a priority but now I wonder if it might be. We've found Claud's laptop.'

'Where?'

'In the stream behind the Tourist Information Office. It was wrapped in a plastic bag, but it was still pretty wet. I've passed it on to the appropriate department to see if they can salvage anything from it, but I don't have high hopes.'

CHAPTER 21

Two minutes of your time, please.

Faye, who liked to see everything that was going on, didn't normally text and when she did she was rarely terse. Jude had scarcely had time to take his coat off when he got back to the incident room after visiting the scene at William Street, but the tone of it couldn't be ignored. 'Back in a minute, Doddsy. That's Faye. Must be important.'

'I'll keep in charge here.'

Jude lingered. The threat that had come to Doddsy hadn't been reported, hadn't been talked about in the office. Doddsy might have told Tyrone but that was it. The three of them, and Faye, when the latest killing had been reported, must have had the same thought. Who would be next?

Faye had been waiting for him. When he went in she was sitting straight up at her desk with her hands folded on a copy of the local newspaper. 'Jude. Thank you for coming by.' She pushed the newspaper towards the edge of her desk as if it disgusted her. 'I have today's local paper. Hot off the press.'

Time to read the paper? Faye didn't have enough to do. He'd thought he'd be expected to update her on the important things, like the note he'd just received from the CSI team and which Faye had been copied into. George Meadows had had a warning note just like the one that had come to Doddsy.

He reached out for the newspaper, which had been folded over to display an article — less than a quarter of a page in the bottom right hand corner of (he picked it up to check) page 7. The headline, if it could be called a headline, announced *New Superintendent's Equality Crusade* and the six column inches contained a brief resume of Faye's career, an outline of her stated intention to improve equality and diversity and a reference to the ongoing story of the local murders, concluded with the line that *Detective Superintendent Scanlon, who is separated from her husband, reportedly left the Cheshire force after an affair with a female colleague.*

He read it a second time for any subtext that he might have missed, then turned the newspaper over in case he should have been looking at something else. 'Is this a problem?'

'I'd trusted your discretion.'

'What the hell does that mean?'

She exaggerated her sigh. 'I'm glad you're so sanguine about it. Did any of this information come from you?'

'No.' He unfolded the paper and refolded it to its normal state. The front page had gone big on the real news, a third murder, and that was where the journalists had let their imaginations run riot. It reminded him, if he needed reminding, that there were three people dead and whoever had done it had actively threatened others. Faye flattered herself.

'Who's interested in what a police officer once did in their private life? No-one's going to read that article with all this going on. I wouldn't let it bother you. No-one cares, Faye. No-one.'

'I'm glad you think so,' she said, though she could hardly have expected that any published article would be so anodyne.

'I've seen stories about serving officers that were a lot worse and a lot less accurate.'

'You don't seem remotely surprised about the content of it.'

'I'm not surprised. Ashleigh told me about it.'

Her lip quivered. 'I thought as much. I asked you in here to give me your reassurance that you have nothing to do with this story.' She looked down at the local newspaper with contempt.

Most of it looked as if it had been culled from Faye's own press releases. 'I've nothing to do with it. It's way more than my job's worth.'

'Indeed it is.' Her eyes narrowed.

'Right. My advice would be to let it slide. And we could usefully spend our time working on more important things. Like trying to see if we can stop anyone else being slaughtered like a pig in the street.' He could hear contempt in his voice. His opinion of Faye had been low and now it slipped further.

'Thanks for your input.' Her tone was dry. 'I haven't forgotten what's going on. But I think you and I are diverging on this investigation. As a straight white male you carry the baggage of privilege. I want you to focus much more closely on the victims and their sexuality.'

Jude might have privilege but Faye had a chip on her shoulder. And she might be right but his gut told him there was more to it. 'There's no evidence George Meadows was gay.'

'He had a leaflet about the festival.'

George had had a wife, too, but so did Giles. 'We can't assume he's gay because of that.'

'Not can we assume he isn't. But perhaps even if he wasn't someone thought he was. And there's this warning note. At which point, I must add a footnote to this story. Or rather, a forenote.'

'Oh?' Jude calmed himself.

'Yes. I didn't mention it to you because it isn't something I want widely known but I received a similar warning to the one that came to DI Dodd.'

He drew in a long breath, as if he needed reminding that the killer who had come to the Eden Valley had extended their shadows right into the corridors of the police headquarters. Perhaps after all Faye's concerns about the newspaper article weren't so self-serving. 'Did it come here?'

'No. It came to my home address, which is a matter of concern in itself. Nevertheless.' She turned to her computer as if the interview was ended, 'I'm telling you that for information only, but I'm having the papers analysed.'

'Get the tech people to copy me in,' Jude said, and headed down the corridor.

*

'Excuse me, Doddsy.' Tammy, bristling with chill hostility, shouldered her way past him as he moved towards the desk where Jude was in deep conversation with one of the constables, his body language demonstrating his sheer frustration at the turn the investigation had taken.

Doddsy understood. Just when they'd been so sure of the case against Giles Butler, with a name and a reputation he was so desperate to protect and a perfect motive for murder, along had come an indication that either he wasn't the killer, or that he was and there was a copycat case.

'If we hear any more on his movements,' Jude was saying, 'I want to know straight away. Okay?'

'Jude.' Tammy's hostility extended beyond Doddsy. She must have guessed where Tyrone had been when he hadn't come home the night they'd gone for their walk up by Ullswater, but he sensed she knew her own powerlessness. 'May I interrupt?'

Tammy was sensible and she would get used to the idea, in time. But what might Phil have done, or what might he have threatened to do, in the first heat of his fury? And if there was a threat to Doddsy, then there could also be a threat to Tyrone.

Jude sat back. From a distance, Doddsy thought he could sense yet another in what seemed to be a series of sighs, and moved a little closer. 'Is it important?'

'I think so.'

'Fine.' Jude turned to Chris. 'Good work so far, though. Let me know if anything comes up. Okay, Tammy. Is something wrong?' *Something else wrong*, the slight rebuke in his tone seemed to imply.

'Yes. I haven't been called in to look at the crime scene up in town. The murder. Why's that?'

With his colleagues Jude was a poor liar, unable even to reproduce the bland expression he kept for witnesses. 'I couldn't say. I wasn't the one who called the CSI team out. I was interviewing a suspect when the body was found.'

'You know it makes sense for me to be out on that job. I was available. I know the other two scenes. It's possible that there are things I could find out from there, more quickly than some others, just because I know what to look for.'

'Yes, I know that. And you know how highly I think of your work.' Jude smiled, one that was meant to reassure her and which, judging by the little shift of her shoulders, failed. 'Whoever sent out the team must have had their reasons.'

'If it wasn't you, who was it? Doddsy?' She turned to scowl at him. 'Did you decide to cut me out?'

'It wasn't me. I imagine it was Faye.'

'And should I go and ask her reasons, or are you going to tell me what you think they are?' Tammy turned her hard stare back to Jude, then over to the far side of the room, where Faye was sitting listening intently to what one of the detectives had to say.

Jude had been fidgeting with a pen, and at that he put it down. 'I haven't discussed it with her, but I imagine she thought it wasn't entirely appropriate that you should be involved when it was Phil who found Gracie Pepper's body. That's all. You can imagine what fun a defence counsel would have if that piece of information came out.'

'Are you seriously suggesting Phil is a suspect?' Her look would have frozen a lesser man. 'For God's sake, Jude. Phil? He's a doctor.'

'I'm not suggesting anything. I'm only pointing out that we have to observe all the protocols. We've hardly started eliminating people from our inquiries, let alone finished, and until then we can't make any assumptions without evidence. I do hope you understand that.'

She stared down at him, the hard, curious stare of a woman determined to defend her family, placing them above everything else, without question. 'Well, hurry up and rule him out, then. I don't need this hassle hanging over me, and his career won't stand being accused of murder.'

'Nobody's accusing him of anything.' Jude stood up and turned away from her, in a gesture of dismissal. 'Doddsy, I'm glad you popped by. We can pool information. You probably know more about this than I do.'

Doddsy pulled up a chair and inspected his spotless fingernails for the half a minute that it took for Tammy to realise that, as far as Jude was concerned, the interview was over. It was with relief when the door closed. 'Awkward, that.'

Jude resumed his seat. 'As if we didn't have enough to do.' In the half minute the notifications in his inbox had pinged half a dozen times. Is that what you wanted to talk to me about?'

'Among other things. I take it she's right about the reasons for her not being involved.'

Jude spread his hands, in a gesture of hopelessness. 'What choice do we have? She must know Phil's a suspect, even if she won't admit it to herself. And even if she does admit it, she won't believe he could be guilty. I don't believe it myself, but we have to look at everything and we have to approach it with an open mind. I can't afford to rule him out without proof. And if I'm wrong and he did do it…too bad. He gets charged.'

'There's no evidence Phil was on the scene at the time of this latest one, is there?'

'I don't know if there is. We haven't yet definitely established where he was. We do know he was in work late because he was at the dentist, in Stricklandgate.' Jude shook his head, because it was only the slightest detour from Stricklandgate to William Street. 'Until we get the PM results we won't know the time of death, but we can be pretty certain that the window is going to be wider than for either of the other two, so everyone's going to have to account for their movements for a bit longer than five minutes before the the discovery of the body. At the moment I have to say it's possible that he was.' He paused, an uncomfortable moment for them both to dwell on the possibility of Phil's involvement. 'What's your take on it?'

'I had a chat with Tyrone about it.'

'It must be tough for him.'

'Very, but he's hard-headed about it. Far more so than Tammy. He knows his dad's dislike — even distrust — of gay people goes very deep. People like me.'

'Not just you. Tyrone, too.'

'Maybe. But I know that sort of mind set. I come across it everywhere. And look at how folk care so much about their kids. They'd die in a ditch for them. They'd kill for them. Other people are different.'

Jude narrowed his eyes slightly, as if this information, difficult as it was for Doddsy to give, was unwelcome to him.

'You've seen how Tammy reacts,' Doddsy went on. 'She doesn't seem to mind who Tyrone sees. It's whether it makes him happy. Phil isn't any different, except that he probably has it in his head that some twisted queer had perverted his kid. But you know what?'

'What?'

'Phil knew Gracie was gay.'

Jude sat back, his face fixed in thought, but only for a second. He reached immediately for his phone and dialled. It rang for a moment and then there was a click and Phil Garner came on the line again. Jude flipped him onto speaker. 'Phil. Glad I caught you. I just remembered something I wanted to ask.'

Even at a distance, Phil's discomfort was obvious. As always, he resorted to bullishness. 'Remembered something else I've done wrong, have you?'

'No,' said Jude, his voice entirely neutral. 'It's just a question. Gracie Pepper was gay. Did you know that?'

The pause was so long you could almost hear the cogs whirring in Phil's brain. 'Now you mention it, I think I did.'

'You think?'

'All right. I did know it.'

Doddsy's heart sank.

'It wasn't common knowledge,' said Jude, tapping the fingers of his free hand softly on the desk. 'How did you know?'

'She told me.'

'Okay. When was that?'

Another pause. 'Jude. Don't mess me around.'

'It's just a simple question.'

'It was after that bloody workshop.' Phil heaved a gusty sigh, one they were obviously meant to hear. 'I said something. Can't remember what it was but she seemed to think it was disrespectful. *You're talking about people like me*, she said. I asked her what the hell she was on about and she said she was a lesbian and walked off. Is that enough?'

'More than enough. Thank you.'

'If you're trying to set me up for this, you won't keep your job.'

'If I was, I wouldn't deserve to. Thanks, Phil.' Jude ended the call and turned back to Doddsy. His laptop nagged at him again and he hit the mute button. 'Well, well. Interesting.'

'Faye's right, isn't she?' Doddsy frowned at the phone. 'I know you want to keep an open mind but you can't look beyond the connection. I wonder if Claud knew.'

'We could ask him. Or rather, you can ask him, since you're such good mates with him. I'll be interested to see what he says.'

Doddsy took out his own phone and put the call through. Claud, when reached, was anxious. 'Such a shame about George. Lovely man. A great friend of our community. I spoke to one of your constables this morning, told him all about it. I don't know what to do, now. People are scared. I've already had them wanting to call off the festival.'

'We're doing the best we can,' said Doddsy, retreating into blandness and noting Jude's amused lift of the eyebrow. 'Did you know Gracie Pepper was gay?'

'Oh, of course. Everyone's a bit gay.'

Jude was shaking his head.

'You don't know for certain, then?'

'Oh God, yes. She came up to me after the workshop we did and said she'd always preferred women to men but she'd never thought it a big deal. I told her there was nothing to be ashamed of, and she said I was right and she'd be a bit more open about it in future.' At the description of such a successful outcome to the workshop, Claud's voice seemed to swell with pride. 'You only have to ask. You can encourage people to be honest. There's never any harm in it, and a lot of good. I'd invited her to come over one evening and talk about it, if it would help. I think she'd have come.'

For a second Doddsy thought again of the threat that had landed on his desk. *You next.* But he hadn't been. Some other innocent had been next. 'Okay, Claud. Thanks. That was all.'

'Right,' Jude said. 'What do we make of that? Two people now who knew Gracie was gay. Three if you include Claud. But not George.'

George had been outspoken on social media and argued loudly for equality. His avatar bore a rainbow and a pinned tweet proclaimed that love was love. 'You don't need me to tell you. Sometimes when it comes to motive it isn't about how things are. It's about how you think things are.'

'Yes. I know.'

'And there might be other lives at risk.'

'There almost certainly are, I'd say. I'm no psychiatrist, but I can't see how these particular killings can be anything other than the product of a warped mind.'

In an unguarded moment, Jude was silent, staring across the room. Following his gaze Doddsy saw that it went beyond Faye and to the far side of the room where Ashleigh was sitting with her head down over a pile of papers. 'You reckon?'

'Yes.' Jude turned back, as if he hadn't even realised that his mind had jumped from the job. 'Which is what makes it so difficult. I don't know where this leads. I don't know who else is targeted. Which is perhaps why Faye is so jumpy.'

Everyone's a little bit gay, Claud had said, and now it made sense. Doddsy had seen the newspaper that morning and though his mind had been too busy racing on to more important things than tittle-tattle it had registered with him. So Faye was bisexual and now Jude was looking towards Ashleigh with that slight crease of the forehead which signified concern. Cheshire.

Ashleigh had put the papers down now, and was sitting back as if a revelation had come upon her. A ray of sunlight crept onto her desk, fingering the sheet of paper on top of the pile. She picked it up, put it to one side, sorted through the pile — witness statements, he presumed — and extracted two. Then she jumped up from the desk and, carrying the three pieces of paper, crossed over to the desk. 'Jude.'

He motioned to her to sit. Faye, now seeming more interested in what was going on at the table beneath the whiteboard than she was in the conversation in which she was engaged, gave up pretending and also got up and moved towards them. A briefing meeting convened itself, uncalled for, around the table.

'Do you have any updates for us, Jude?' Sitting down, Faye directed a frosty stare at Ashleigh. Until that moment her obvious dislike had puzzled Doddsy, but now he thought he understood.

'We were just discussing that.' In a few words he outlined the calls with Claud and Phil. 'Anyone got anything to add before we discuss things?'

'I have.' Ashleigh spread the three sheets out in front of her. All were witness statements, typed up and signed, and all had Gracie Pepper's name at the top of them. 'The latest victim. I knew the name rang a bell. We've spoken to him.'

'Have we? When?'

'He was one of the people we interviewed after Gracie's death. He's a bell-ringer. They do bell ringing practice in the church on a Tuesday evening from six thirty until eight. He was early and he was already in the church. He didn't see anybody or anything suspicious. I took a chance just there and called Claud to see if he knew him and he did.'

Jude picked up his pen and began making rapid notes. Faye's expression was chilly.

'George spoke to Claud and Natalie when they were leaving Hunter Lane on Tuesday night. He'd given his statement to a police officer — Tyrone, as it happens — and he was on his way home. Claud says he'd didn't recognise George at first, but when George introduced himself, he did.'

'Recognised him from where?'

'Church. George is a regular churchgoer and very keen on Claud's proposal for a Rainbow Festival. He'd been at the meeting Claud had held in the church. '

'The Rainbow Festival,' said Jude, still busily twirling the pen. 'That keeps coming up, doesn't it? And yet from what I heard about the idea it was barely formed enough for anyone to know what it was, let alone develop a murderous objection to it.' He looked towards Doddsy and Faye, who seemed tolerant of everything except other people's religious beliefs, shook her head as if this mumbo-jumbo was too much for her.

'It's early days but it's still causing a stir.' Doddsy was the one to whom Jude was looking for comment. Tyrone had been right. You couldn't hide things. 'I understand Phil was opposed to it.'

'Dear me,' Jude said, playing the whole thing down as far as he could and convincing no-one. 'Strongly opposed?'

'I think so.'

Faye sniffed. 'Did Claud and Natalie say anything about that?'

Ashleigh referred to her notes. 'Yes. Natalie couldn't remember his name, though she did remember what he said. Claud somehow managed to give chapter and verse of the encounter. He's one of those people who remembers that sort of thing.' She put the papers down on the desk. 'So as far as I can see that's three people who died, all of whom have some kind of connection to Claud Blackwell. Len died within sight of his house. He found Gracie dying in front of his office. And George Meadows introduced himself to Claud two days before he was found dead.'

You could make a case — a looser one, admittedly — for all three of them having a connection with Phil, too, if you took into account the vagueness of his whereabouts on the day that Len had died and the even vaguer possibility that he and

George had somehow fallen out over the Rainbow Festival. Doddsy saw that both Jude and Faye had made notes to that effect, though neither of them seemed to want to pick up on it just then. No doubt they'd leave it until Doddsy was absent and chew to over then. He'd feel his ears burning, no doubt.

'Let's talk about Claud.' Faye sighed.

Doddsy liked Claud but he sensed a certain shiftiness behind his bumptiousness. 'I've something to add, too. An update from the CSI team. They gave me a description of the jacket in which the knife had been wrapped. It came from a brown suit. I don't know the exact measurement, but they said it looked as it it would fit a short, broad-shouldered male.' He flicked up the picture that had come through on his iPad and laid it on the table.

'We'll know for certain when we get the results from the lab, of course,' said Jude, after a moment's consideration, 'but that certainly looks like the suit Claud was wearing for the workshops.'

'It also ties in with some information I've had back from the Intelligence Unit about his laptop.' Faye wasn't, Doddsy sensed, a woman who ever took particular pleasure in the process of delivering information, unlike Chris, who had a theatrical streak and liked a bit of drama, or Ashleigh, who uploaded new knowledge as swiftly as possible to the relevant person. Faye's approach was more measured, more logical, adding information onto a stream where it became relevant, rather than a random fact or where it would distract from something equally important. 'They were able to retrieve data from the hard drive. God knows how. Claud was a regular contributor to activist forums and some more general ones.'

'Okay.' Jude was leaning forward, a look of keen interest on his face. 'Is there any connection with Len? We don't know that he used dating websites, but it's possible. I don't think we've got the full analysis of his laptop yet. It's unlikely Giles did, under the circumstances, but you never know.'

'That I don't know. They sent me that piece of information as soon as they had it. I'll let you know both minute I hear anything else from them.'

'I don't have Claud down as gay.' Doddsy rubbed his chin. 'I don't know why not, because although he's married that doesn't rule it out.'

'And devoted to Natalie,' contributed Jude, 'though of course you're right. Just because he's fetched up in a stable relationship with a woman doesn't mean anything, in itself.'

'He's so very gay-friendly. I'm pretty damned sure that at one level he'd quite like to be. Although of course it would equally suit his purpose to make a stand for gay rights from the perspective of a straight man. He's so keen on making out that we're all equal.'

'Of course we're all equal,' Faye said, accusing him with her gaze.

'Yeah. Sure. We are.' And Doddsy shook his head and let it go.

Chapter 22

'What, is your man off to work already?' Lisa was in the kitchen when Ashleigh let herself into the house. 'It's barely nine o'clock. Still, I'm glad you're here. I had a couple of sherbets too many last night so you can make me a cup of coffee to kick-start me.'

'Make it yourself. It's a matter of boiling the kettle.'

'Oh, Ash.' Lisa sank down at the kitchen table, running hands through her rumpled hair, rolling her eyes to the ceiling. A routine hangover acquired the panache of a Greek tragedy. 'It would save my life. Be a pet. It's Saturday.'

'I'm making it for myself anyway.'

'Great. Lifesaver. Thanks.' Lisa unfolded the newspaper and leafed through it while Ashleigh filled the cafetière. 'I see your mate at the newspaper has rumbled your friend Faye. You don't fancy rustling me up a full English while you're at it, do you?' She winked.

'Don't push your luck.' Ashleigh put the cafetière down and tried not to look at the newspaper. 'I wouldn't call either of them my pal. Just as well the newspapers are more interested in corpses than scandal.' She looked out of the window as a jogger ran past, but it wasn't Natalie.

'They're not exactly short of them just now. Three in a week. And bloody ones.' Despite her self-inflicted misery, Lisa managed to find some sympathy. 'Gruesome for you. Are you okay?'

'I'm fine.' But Ashleigh scanned the newspaper with distaste. 'I don't think it's helpful making a song and dance about it. And Faye's background has nothing to do with it.'

'It's all about bread and circuses. They rely on these things to keep their circulation up.' Lisa was an archaeologist by profession, but her fascination with history was as broad as the world itself.

'You think I don't know that? I suspect this story is a journalist trying to make a name for herself and this is the only angle she can think of that someone else hasn't covered.'

Lisa looked into the depths of her cup as if she were reading the coffee grounds. 'It's just as well you didn't talk to her. At least your conscience is clear.'

'Faye's already looking poison at me.' But then, she looked poison at everyone, with the sole exception of Claud Blackwell. Perhaps, after all, it wasn't personal. 'Remember, I did talk to her.'

'Only because she cornered you, and then again, you gave a flat *no comment*. It's hardly the same.'

'True. But if she does come up with anything else, you can bet your life the finger will point at me. Especially with that call on my phone.'

'You didn't answer it. That'll be logged too, won't it?' Lisa was already on her second cup of coffee, and the world obviously seemed a little brighter and what little light there was less painful on the eyes.

If Faye stopped thinking about work and started brooding on how unfair life was there was only one way it would go. On Monday, Ashleigh would have Professional Standards breathing down her neck. 'I expect so.'

'And even if you had told her something, it's not like you're leaking details of a case or anything.'

'No, but she's my boss.' Over the past couple of weeks Ashleigh had come to terms with Faye's constant and invasive presence around the office. It was good that she was so actively involved in the investigation, but she didn't need to make the woman into an enemy when having her as a hostile presence was enough. 'On a purely practical note, I don't want to get on the wrong side of her.' In her mind's eye she could see the headline Marsha Letham might wish she'd written. *Top Cumbria Cop's Gay Fling With Detective*. She shuddered. It had been a narrow escape.

'Well, if you don't name names and Faye doesn't tell, who else can tell? Who else knows it was you?'

'Jude.' Ashleigh picked up her coffee and took comfort from it.

'He won't say anything.'

'No.' If he wasn't discretion itself, it was more than his job was worth, as well. 'There were people back in Cheshire who knew. One of them might have left and felt able to be indiscreet. There were plenty of people on the wrong side of her back there.' Now she was catastrophising, just like poor Natalie Blackwell. 'Other people might guess.'

'I see your problem.' Lisa was a thinker, a woman who teased a problem until she came up with a creative alternative. It was a very different skill set to that of a detective, and much more aligned with reading the tarot cards. 'And the solution is pretty obvious, too.'

'Yes,' Ashleigh said, with misery creeping in to the back of her mind at the thought. 'I know.'

'You know you're going to have to have it out with her. You should have done it as soon as you realised she was here.'

Being so controlling meant Faye could be hard to talk to. When she felt threatened she could hiss like a snake and she could strike like one, too. Any discussion would only ever be on her terms. 'I know. But—'

'But if she's making your life difficult you have to say something. You don't have to put up with it. It's not appropriate behaviour in the workplace, certainly not for someone in her position. And certainly not after what she did last time.'

'I'll think about it.' The previous time Ashleigh had moved on rather than stand her ground and make a complaint. That had been a mistake; but the right thing was no easier to do than the wrong.

*

Faye's arrival had turned her personal life as well as her professional one into a minefield. When Lisa had gone, heading up to Carlisle to lunch with a friend, Ashleigh stood in the kitchen and stared out, knowing her own weakness, knowing she shouldn't let Faye's insecurities impinge on her own and at the same time finding herself powerless to stop it. Turning, she headed upstairs and withdrew the cards from their gauze wrapping, the only place she could think of to turn for the answer.

Jude would have laughed at her, as he so often did, and pointed out that what she was looking for was the wrong answer, the answer that offered her a chance not to do the right thing. And he'd be right. She really didn't need the cards for that.

Complicated issues required complicated spreads, but the answers she was looking for were fairly straightforward. 'What should I do about Faye?' The question asked, she shuffled the cards, dealt five of them into a horseshoe on the table in front of her, and turned them up, one by one. The King of Cups, hinting she should take wise advice from those who knew better than she did. The Five of Pentacles, to reassure her like a beacon on a stormy night. The Eight of Wands, so predictable she could have guessed it, and offering her catharsis through talk. And then the Fool, the card that somehow always came up when she told the cards for herself, and almost always signalled the conclusion of the reading. Carefree, foolish and optimistic — all of them words that applied to her in some element of her life.

She smiled. There was something about the depiction of the King of Cups that reminded her of Jude. The image had a smile of amusement lurking on the lips, a querying look in the eyes and a handsome face that seemed to stare out at her. 'You win. I get the message. I need to stop worrying and sort it out.' After all, she didn't know what was going on in Faye's head. Maybe her ex-lover's concerns were as great as her own, and maybe none of them were well-founded. 'So that's that settled, isn't it?'

But it wasn't. The answers to all her questions had been delivered, accurately, at speed and in exactly the form she'd expected them, and there was still a card left, face down on the table. She contemplated the abstract design thoughtfully. It was a little faded, but it had once been bright and exciting. 'Okay. You've dealt me a wild card. What's this one about? Something I haven't thought of?' But the cards didn't play like that. They addressed your specific concerns. Like the most cunning criminal, like a member of the public with some other guilt to hide, they never answered questions you hadn't asked.

She held her hand over the card for a moment before she turned it upwards to reveal the Queen of Cups. An emotional card, a disturbing one. It radiated feelings and, the card being upside down, they weren't good ones. They were feelings of loss and introversion, of misunderstanding.

Ashleigh thought of Natalie, running, running, running and never escaping something when it would have been so much easier to turn and face it. Then she remembered the purpose of the whole reading, the answer to her questions and the confirmation of what she'd known to be the truth.

At least this time there were no swords.

She shuffled the cards away, packaged them up, and called Faye.

*

'I've arranged to go and see Faye this afternoon.'

'Good idea.' Jude sat back and smiled at the sound of Ashleigh's voice. There were a few people working on the Saturday, though nowhere like the full complement, and he knew he did his share and more of weekend work. He should change that. He should make more time to spend with Ashleigh and try and have a bit of a life, stop letting his dad down so they could go to the football every second Saturday and sink a pint or two afterwards, make himself more obviously available for Mikey, if he were ever needed, and just spend a bit more time with him if he wasn't. 'It's the only way to sort things out.'

'Yes, you were right about it. So was Lisa. But I was the one who had to decide to do it.'

'Who said you weren't?' he asked, amused. An email pinged into his inbox. On a Saturday. Someone else was working then, too. Wonders never ceased. 'So that's this afternoon. I'd offer to give you some moral support, but I'll be at the football.'

'We can talk about it over drinks tonight, if you like.'

'Sounds perfect.'

'If it ends horribly, you'll back me up, won't you?'

He took a moment before answering trying to work out whether the question was a serious one. Faye hadn't been around long enough for him to get the hang of the way she worked, other than that it was very much in-your-face, but he thought her bark might be worse than her bite. 'Of course. But it won't.'

'But it might. You saw the story in the paper.'

'Faye's diversity and inclusion agenda is all very newsworthy,' he said, as if he were speaking to Claud. But Faye herself was over-sensitive.

'But what if the journalist comes back for more? She specifically said she wanted to talk to me because I was a former colleague of Faye's.'

'Don't answer, and tell me. She can talk to Faye herself, if she's brave enough.' Jude doodled a series of circles on his pad. Saturday was a working day and normally he never took personal calls at work, but somehow he'd forgotten this particular rule he'd made for himself. Maybe loosening up a little wasn't a bad thing. 'Have you enjoyed your morning off?'

'Yes. I walked up the hill and along Beacon Edge.'

'The views are stunning up there, aren't they?'

'Yes, particularly today. Isn't OCD a weird thing? If I was Natalie and I was going to take my ten-minute break somewhere, I'd definitely do it up there rather than in some dark alley in Drover's Lane.'

'I think it's to do with how far she is from home.' Another email pinged in, this time from Claud. 'I'd better get on. Good luck with Faye, and you can tell me all about it this evening.'

'See you then.'

He waited for a moment after she'd ended the call, thinking. The last thing he needed was to get involved in an internal row with Faye, but there was a line that had to be drawn.

'Taking a breather, Jude?' Chris, who'd traded a Friday in the future for a Saturday when he had nothing else to do, came back from the coffee machine. 'We don't often catch you staring into space.' He bounced across the room and sat down at his laptop.

'Just thinking,' Jude said, as if he needed to justify himself and turned his attention back to business and flicked on Claud's email.

As a follow up to my earlier comments to you, Claud had written in what felt like an unusually circuitous and possibly defensive manner, *you'll want further confirmation of where I was when the latest unfortunate victim was killed. I was at work on my own. Natalie, as usual was running. Obviously I had no computer so I have been working from my phone. I attach a screenshot showing a list of emails sent from my phone during the relevant time period.*

Either Claud was innocent and doing the police's work for them, or he reckoned he'd found out some way of establishing a fake alibi and was so sure that it was foolproof he was prepared to take on the risk that the police were smarter than he was. They might not be, but they had better resources at their disposal. They could trace the position of the phone, but Claud could have left it in the office while he made his way to William Street. Could he have faked the time stamp on the emails? That was one for the tech team. He fired off an irritable query, in case one of them was about and answering questions.

I can also establish Natalie's whereabouts, Claud had written, *and attach a screenshot showing her running route at the time in question. You will see that it takes her nowhere near William Street.*

The screenshot, when he opened it, showed exactly that. Natalie had run her usual route, taken her usual ten minute rest in Meeting House Lane. Weird. He shook his head over it. Something about the case was staring him in the face and he couldn't see what it might be.

Yet another email pinged in. This time it was a message from the intelligence unit, informing him that they'd have a look at the issue he'd raised. *And we've just had this back.*

This was a forwarded email headed: *source of printed material.* He opened it up. *The printed sheets you sent us have been scanned and the source is the printer with the following ID. The printer is registered to the business Blackwell Ltd.*

He sat back, looking at it. 'Chris. Are you busy?'

'Do I look busy?'

'I think we need to go out to Temple Sowerby and have a chat with Claud Blackwell.'

'Sure.' Chris bounced to his feet and stretched. 'Anything more on him? I was just going back through those interactions he had on the local forums. Did you know Len Pierce was on one of them?'

'Is that right?'

'Yes. He never commented but he liked the odd post. One or two of Claud's, in fact.' Chris lifted his jacket from the back of his chair. 'You want to send Doddsy, if you want to get anything out of him. Or Faye. He likes those two way more than he likes the rest of us. If I was Mrs Blackwell, I'd be getting jealous.'

Jude had been turning towards the door, but at that, something clicked in his mind. He spun back on his heel and strode over to the whiteboard, stared at its confusion of maps and tracks and photos and the black dots on the tracks that marked the stops in Natalie's complicated, obsessive runs.

If I was Mrs Blackwell I'd be getting jealous.

Of Len Pierce, if the two had ever met. Of George Meadows, so keen to help with the Rainbow Festival. Of Doddsy, to whom Claud had taken such an improbably liking, and of Faye, whom he so clearly admired.

'Right,' he said. 'Let's get moving.'

Chapter 23

The sun had made a belated appearance in the Eden Valley. From the living room window, Natalie watched Claud as he moved among the roses that grew up against the fence. He was late pruning them. He'd been talking about doing it, she remembered, on that afternoon when Len Pierce had died in the lane.

It seemed so long ago, so distant. The image of the man, lying dead at her feet before she'd turned to flee to Claud floated across her mind like a cloud. Now even the last of the police tape had gone, and only the occasional tractor trundled up and down the lane. The cars that had stopped there for their owners to meet up and couple and leave no longer came, as if there were still a threat.

Eventually, no doubt, they'd forget all that and come back. People did.

She'd showered after her run and dressed, and towelled down her hair. The fitness tracker, heavy on her thin wrist, irritated her so she unclipped it and laid it on the kitchen table while she cleared up after the previous night's supper. Claud had cooked a beef casserole and she'd barely been able to manage a few mouthfuls of it. He always cooked, she cleared up, but she'd been worryingly distracted and hadn't been able to face it. On another day Claud would just have done it, but these days he seemed to tiptoe around her as if her emotions were too deep and too dangerous for him to disturb.

She rearranged the mess prior to washing it up. The curved blade of the kitchen knife Claud had used in his preparations troubled her, the beads of congealed red on the blade bringing up images of the dead — of Len, of Gracie, of George, who'd been so kind to them on the night of Gracie's murder. Eventually time would close over them and their killings, unsolved, would be forgotten.

Or would they? Bending her head, she squeezed her eyes tightly together. It couldn't go on.

Out in the garden, Claud moved along the line of rose bushes, clipping them back and dropping the cuttings in a bucket. Placing the carving knife on the table next to her fitness tracker, Natalie strode out through the conservatory and across the soft spring grass towards him. He was whistling. 'Claud.'

'Are you okay?' He looked up, alarmed.

He was in a constant state of alarm these days. Every time she spoke to him he seemed to be expecting something, some bombshell that had burst in her mind, some new fear he alone could soothe. Claud did so much for her yet somehow that patience, that commitment, that consideration was never enough. She needed everything. 'We need to talk.'

'Of course.' He straightened up and dropped the sprig of rose bush, with fresh green leaves on it, into the bucket. His face framed the ready smile it always took on when she was needy. 'What about?'

She took a deep breath and met his questioning gaze. Sometimes Claud's expression was thoughtful, sometimes it was concerned. Sometimes it darkened into an approaching storm, and those were the times when she was irrationally afraid he might hurt her. As if he would. Claud could never hurt anyone. 'Who is your lover?'

His eyes widened in astonishment. His silence condemned him.

'Claud.'

'You're my lover, Nat.' He dropped the secateurs he'd been holding into the bucket, stripped off his gloves and tossed them on the grass next to the secateurs. The traffic hummed on the A66, the tractor rumbled in the lane. Startled by the sudden movement, a robin skidded from tree to hedge, its breast as scarlet with feathers as hers had been with Len Pierce's blood. 'Listen. We need to talk about this.'

At his ringing failure to deny it, an invisible knife sliced into her heart, just as a real one had ripped the life out of Len and Gracie and George. 'I knew it.'

'No. Listen to me. It's you. You only.' He drew a deep breath. 'What made you think otherwise?'

She flicked a dry tongue around her lips. So often she'd rehearsed what she'd say to him when she challenged him, and already it was playing out in a way she hadn't envisaged. Claud was lying – he must be, because a man who loved his wife would have wanted to spend all his time with her instead of seeking the company of others when she needed him — but his shoulders were set. He'd never admit it. 'All those other people.'

'Natalie. Darling. This has all been a bit too much for you.'

Claud was a liar. He'd say whatever was expedient to keep her quiet. 'I saw it on your laptop.'

He lifted his chin, not quite in defiance. Claud never usually felt the need to be defiant, too entrenched in his own position so he only ever needed to indulge in self-justification. That kind of moral superiority was what irritated other people about him, unjustly, because Claud was a very good man. 'I knew someone had been looking at it. I didn't think it was you.'

That must be why he'd disposed of it. She'd seen him, carrying it through the church close, shadowed him when he dropped it into the beck. A manic laugh curdled somewhere in her brain at the thought of what Jude Satterthwaite would say when he realised that Claud had faked the burglary. 'You were hiding it from people. You're a fraud.'

There was fury in his eyes, but he subdued it. Claud was good at that. He could control his feelings, hide them, but now she could see what he was really thinking. Her breath came, short and ragged, the precursor to a panic attack. 'It isn't the way it looks.'

'You went on gay websites.'

'But not to date people. Why the hell would I want to date anyone else when I have you?'

'Why would you go on those websites? The clue's in the name. Dating. Dating, Claud!'

'Christ, Natalie. You don't think I'd do that, would you? But I find people interesting. That's all. And we have a cause. I thought you were on board. It's really important. I just wanted to talk to people. Not just men, either.'

That made it worse. 'Talking is how it starts. Isn't it? And what about Gracie Pepper? What about that bloody bell ringer, picking you off the street and inviting you to his house to discuss the Rainbow Festival?'

He was bewildered. 'But what's wrong with that? He invited you, too.'

'But I didn't want to go. I didn't want you to go. I wanted the two of us to be together, with no more of you spending all evening on secret sites and emailing God knows who, and always finding ways to see someone else. Anyone but me!' She paused for a snatched breath. Her heart raced. There was no way through Claud's self-righteousness.

'Oh, Nat. Come on.' His eyes flicked nervously from her to the secateurs, as though he thought she might pick them up and lunge at him.

He was hers and hers only. Sharing him with anyone meant less of him for herself. Eventually he would leave her and she would go under, drowning in the airless horror of her own inability to cope. 'What about Faye Scanlon?' she asked, breathlessly.

'Faye Scanlon?'

'Yes. And Inspector Dodd.'

He kept his eyes on her face. She used to trust him but now she knew she couldn't. 'They're colleagues. That's all. Maybe I've spent a bit too much time working. I'll take a few days off. Take a day or two and think it through. All the things we've been saying. All the things we've been teaching people. That matters. That's why I'm talking to people. You have to network.'

'They all think you're a bit weird, you know that?'

'Maybe they do. It doesn't mean I'm wrong.'

'That sergeant. Ashleigh O'Halloran. She thinks you're very weird. I bet you think she's attractive, too, but she doesn't care about you. She's just mad for her boss.' And just as well for her. But if she said that Claud would look at her the way he had done before, measuring up in his mind how unhinged she might be and then saying whatever he thought necessary to deflect her.

'Did you take your tablet this morning?' He laid a hand on her arm.

She shook it free. 'What's that got to do with it?'

'Just that you don't sound like your normal self. You don't really think I'm having an affair.'

'How dare you tell me what I think?'

'I'm sorry, but every rational conversation I've ever had with you, you've understood. I'm sorry if I haven't shown you how much I love you, but I have to see other people. It's my job. It doesn't mean anything. And I'm sorry about the laptop. I knew you'd been looking, and some of the content on those chats wasn't really appropriate. That's why I got rid of it, and I see now it was stupid, and not only because the police started looking at it. I was afraid you'd get the wrong idea. And you have.'

She took a moment to breathe, a moment to listen, knowing he was right. She was being irrational and when these moments came upon her, she struggled to keep control. But because she thought differently some times from the way she did at others, did that mean that what he called her irrational mind was wrong? 'I'm not a good person.'

'My gorgeous girl. Let's go inside and talk about it, shall we?'

When they got inside he'd be checking to see she'd taken her drugs and probably putting in a sly call to a doctor to have the dose increased. Maybe he'd try to have her locked up. Yes, that was it. And then he could do whatever he wanted with whoever he chose and she'd lie alone in some narrow room in an institution, for the rest of her life. A thin tear overflowed her eye and trickled down her cheek, dropping onto the roses and gathering like a raindrop at the base of a leaf. 'You don't love me any more.' She set off back towards the garden with him trailing in her wake.

'Christ almighty, aren't you listening? Of course I love you. You're gorgeous. Don't you understand?'

Yet he'd disposed of the laptop when he'd realised she was looking at it. No-one with a clear conscience did that. 'Why didn't you tell me you knew Len?'

'Because you'd have got the wrong idea. And you have got the wrong idea, haven't you?'

'What about Gracie?' She was shouting at him. 'Did you have sex with her?'

'Gracie was gay!'

'So? Anything goes with you, doesn't it? Except fidelity.'

She strode into the house and he caught her in the kitchen and grabbing her arm, pulling her back so that she faced him. On the table the knife gleamed next to the dull black rubber of her fitness tracker. Her heart hammered.

'Listen to me!' He stepped right up to her, and the echoes of his shout rang in her ears and shocked her into silence. 'Natalie, this can't go on. I love you, but I think you need help.'

All the things she'd run away from were in front of her. Claud, whom she adored, for whom she would have done anything, for whom she would have sacrificed everything, no longer loved her. She was suddenly immensely tired, her legs shaking. She shook her head again.

Her breath tore in her chest. Her fury, higher than it had ever been, flashed across her eyes like a kaleidoscope of red and black and silver. 'Now say you love me!'

'I love you, Nat.' She opened her eyes to see him smile. 'When you're calm, you'll understand.'

When she was calm, if she was ever calm again, maybe she would. 'Yes.'

The knife gleamed at her on the table. 'I'll make us a cup of tea. Then we can sit down and talk about it. And perhaps if you aren't feeling well I can take you down to the hospital.'

'You think I'm mad, don't you?'

'No,' he said, too quickly.

They stared at one another, a crisis, and she saw his integrity crumble. He was afraid of her emotions, would say anything to reassure her and she could no longer tell his truth from his lies.

But would he be faithful to her in the future? How could she ever trust him again? 'You made me do it, Claud. Because I love you and I want you only to love me.'

'Made you do what?' Fear flickered in his eyes. 'I'm sorry if I've hurt you, Nat. But let's sit down and talk this through. And maybe call a doctor and see if they can help.'

And lock her up so she'd never get out. *Never, Claud. Never.*

She reached behind her for the knife.

Chapter 24

'So you reckon it's Natalie, then?' Chris turned to look towards Rainbow Cottage as Jude manoeuvred his way off the A66 and doubled back through Temple Sowerby towards it.

'I don't know. There's still a lot that doesn't make sense. The fitness tracker, for a start. She wasn't on the spot. But I want to talk to both of them again. They have some questions to answer.'

'If either of them has been sending threatening messages to investigating officers, they're going to have to have some very good answers.'

Jude thought, briefly, over some of the answers he'd already come up with. There had been nothing on Claud's laptop to incriminate him when it came to murder, but there was plenty to rouse the suspicions of a spouse. 'I'll be interested to know what she has to say for herself.'

Claud's car was parked outside the cottage, and there was a line of washing — most of it running gear — blowing in the breeze on the line at the side of the house. The door of the conservatory stood open. 'Looks like there's someone at home, at least.'

'I wonder what her explanation will be.'

'We'll find out.'

They got out of the car and Chris strode up to ring the doorbell. It jangled in the depths of the house and there was no sound or movement in response. He rang a second time.

After another long silence, he turned a troubled expression towards Jude.

'Let's have a look around.' Jude stepped off the path and around the side of the house, scanning the scene. A scarlet bucket lay abandoned in the middle of the empty lawn. He gave that a second look before he turned elsewhere, walking rapidly towards the open door to the conservatory, with the radio still playing inside. He followed the sound through the house to the kitchen.

They were too late. The first split-second glance showed him Natalie's fitness tracker, abandoned on the table. The second revealed the slumped figure of Claud Blackwell, sprawled beside the table in a pool of congealing blood.

Chris turned a puzzled face to Jude. 'How the hell…?' I mean, weren't we sure it was him?'

Jude, staring down at Claud's appalled expression, saw the conformation of his fears. 'No. It was Natalie.'

'Oh God. Do you think she's okay? Should we look for her?'

'Sure as hell we should look for her.' Jude was reaching for his phone. 'She did it. She killed them all.'

'But you said, about the tracker. She can't have done. This one,' he gestured at Claud's body in horror, 'yes.'

Jude was through to the control centre. 'Police and an ambulance to Rainbow Cottage in Temple Sowerby. Homicide. Yes, and we're looking for a suspect. Natalie Blackwell. Mid forties. Driving a Honda Civic, silver. I don't know the reg number, but you'll find it. Cheers.'

'Jude. She can't have done it. She wasn't at any of the locations.'

'She was near every one.'

'But not at any of them.'

'We don't know that. We know that her fitness tracker wasn't at any one of them. We know that at every one it shows she'd stopped for ten minutes or so within a couple of hundred yards of the scene of the murder. Look on the table.' Before, he had suspected. This clinched it. 'The fitness tracker she swears she's so obsessed with that she never takes it off. It's there. So we can't conclude that because the tracker was somewhere Natalie must have been there too. As an alibi, it's busted.'

He paused, waiting for the lights of the patrol cars that would descend on the scene. 'There's no knife. She's taken it with her.' What else did Natalie know, and where was she heading?

He could ask her.

*

Natalie's phone rang as she bumped along the track out of the woods where she'd parked up. She knew whom it would be. She'd seen the car going up the track and the figures moving in the garden of Rainbow Cottage. It would be Jude Satterthwaite, and he would know what she'd done.

Only for the sake of a human voice, because she'd never hear Claud's voice again, she answered it, fishing her phone out of her pocket and clamping it to her ear as she headed towards the village. A walker gestured to her, an imaginary phone in his own hand and a scowl on his face, but she ignored him. What was another law broken?

'Natalie,' the detective said, as calm as she'd have expected of so cold a man. 'It's Jude Satterthwaite here. I'm calling to make sure you're all right.'

'Yes. Thank you. I'm perfectly all right.' She would never be all right again. At some stage, later, she'd understand the implications of what she'd done and it would break her, but for now she cherished the strange moment of calm that always followed the madness of self-destruction and, latterly, the destruction of others.

'Where are you?' He kept his tone even.

'Oh, just out for a run.'

'Are you driving, Natalie? In town?'

She didn't answer.

'Natalie? We're at your house. I'd very much like to talk to you. Where are you?'

More silence. She'd driven out of Temple Sowerby and could just see the low roof of Rainbow

Cottage on the far side of the A66. It would be so easy to turn round and hand herself over. Then she thought of Claud and the pain of his interest in people other than herself, and drove on.

'We've found Claud, Natalie. I need you to be sensible, here. I need you to give yourself up. So I want you to drive to the police station, or tell me where you are and I'll come and find you. You have to do the right thing.'

'The right thing? What's the right thing? I hate people, Chief Inspector. I want to love them. I want to be good to them. But they let you down. They're liars and they're cheats.' Like Claud. And then the people who loved them — genuinely loved them — were left with nothing but a broken heart. 'They all deserve to die, you know that? Because I only had Claud and they would have taken him away from me.'

'Who deserved to die?' There was an edge to his voice.

'All of them,' she said, sharing her voice rising to a wail. She was going mad, and the recognition was relief. She could do whatever she wanted to ease the pain of jealousy and loss. When you were mad, no laws or morals bound you. 'They all deserved to die. They tried to come between me and Claud. They'll all pay. All of them. Even DI Dodd. Such a lovely man. So kind.' And Claud had been so so taken with him, bland and ordinary as he was, so that surely he must have felt an attraction to him that he didn't feel for her. 'I hate him, too. I want Claud back. I only want Claud.'

'Natalie. Tell me where you are, and let me get you some help.'

She flicked the phone off and dropped it in the foot well. Inspector Dodd and Len and Gracie and George. Faye Scanlon, too, all over Claud, all those cosy little tête-à-têtes in her office. She hated them all.

She turned into the estate. Detective Inspector Dodd lived in one of the new houses on the edge of Temple Sowerby, behind the medical centre. She'd seen him a couple of times, driving out of the new estate, but she wasn't entirely sure which house it was. Being a detective wasn't so difficult after all. His car, or one very like it, was parked up on the drive outside one of the houses. It would be easy. He was as tall as she and much stronger, of course, but so had Len Pierce been, and George Meadows. It was the element of surprise that had proved fatal. She would ring the doorbell and before he had the chance to react she'd plunge the knife, still wet from Claud's slaying, into his heart. It had worked so well with George. Push him inside, shut the door and escape. Then the superintendent, who was responsible for it all. She knew where she lived, too. Natalie had dropped a document off for Claud one evening on the way past on her run.

She watched as DI Dodd moved about inside, straying occasionally to the window as if he was expecting someone. If he saw her, her chance would be lost. He'd be bound to look twice, bound to raise an eyebrow and, now the secret was out, to call for help.

With that in mind, she drove the car to the far end of the estate. She shouldn't have mentioned the man to Satterthwaite. The first thing he'd do would be to send a car round.

A car drew up outside the house and the policeman who'd taken charge in the churchyard got out. He walked up the path and rang the bell. DI Dodd answered the door, ushered him over the threshold. They hugged, and the door closed.

A wail of a siren alerted her. Natalie flung the car into gear and shot out of the estate without looking, turned right, turned left and dived up a side road, and down a farm track. When the blue lights had turned up towards the estate and a second and third car had headed up towards Rainbow Cottage, she drove out of the farm track and began to thread her cautious way through the network of narrow country lanes towards Penrith.

Chapter 25

Faye lived in a tall sandstone terrace in Brunswick Square, a location Ashleigh noted with a certain degree of discomfort. It was halfway between her house and Jude's, so that when she moved between one and the other she'd have to be prepared to bump into her boss.

Once she'd done what everyone had gone on at her to do and cleared the air, there would be no need to care about it. Nevertheless, her courage wavered. A bird sang in the trees and an early and confused butterfly hunted for scant pickings, a bright spot in the dull greys and greens of a flower bed. *Nothing scares me*, she reminded herself, but it wasn't true. What had always scared her was her own capability for screwing up every relationship that mattered and Faye, through the part she'd played in the final rift with Scott, had precipitated the ruin of the most important one of them.

But it was done. Her marriage had already been on course for the rocks. All Faye's intervention had done was give Scott another grievance and make Ashleigh feel foolish when she preferred to think of herself as smart, modern and intuitive. With that thought in mind, and the knowing images of her tarot advisers in her head, she pushed open the gate and walked up the short path.

Faye must have been as much on edge as Ashleigh herself, and let her sweat for a moment on the doorstep. Her footsteps inside the house were slow and deliberate, and the blurred signs of movement visible through the opaque glass pane in the door showed her crossing the hall and back again before she answered. When the door creaked open it did so without welcome. 'Ashleigh, hi. Come on in. Sit down.'

It was an unsettled house. Ashleigh glimpsed piles of plates and lines of wine glasses on the table in the dining room and when Faye showed her through to the living room it was overflowing with boxes of books piled up next to empty bookshelves, with pictures stacked up against the skirting board. Faye's taste in art was mainstream, good quality prints of well-known landscapes and the books that showed themselves on the top of the boxes were paperback fiction and hardback popular history.

Ashleigh sat on the edge of a hard, new sofa and tried to look as if she was comfortable. 'Thanks for finding the time to see me.' As if she were a supplicant.

'Coffee?' said Faye, an offer which begged refusal since there was already a steaming mug by the armchair opposite the television.

'No, thank you.'

Faye sat down, lifted her mug, prolonging the pause until it generated tension, exactly as Jude sometimes did with a reluctant witness. 'Tell me what you want.'

She always cut straight to the point. That was something, at least. 'This interview that was in the paper. It's nothing to do with me. You've nothing to fear from me.'

Faye raised an eyebrow. 'I should hope not.'

How had she ever found this woman sympathetic. 'Can we clear the air?' That was what she'd come for. 'Right. We had an affair. We both thought it was a mistake. It's over, but it happened. Let's not pretend it didn't.'

'I'm pretending nothing.' That was a twisting of the truth. 'But I prefer not to talk about it.'

'Me, too. But that's not the same as hiding from it. That makes us look guilty of something. We aren't. At least, I'm not.'

'Ashleigh.' Faye turned the mug in her hands. If it was hot enough to hurt, she gave no sign. 'I'm in a senior position. I can't afford to compromise it by having people talk behind their hands. Gossip does nothing but damage.'

But people never paid any real attention to gossip, and Faye herself could hardly have listened to a word of the ill-fated workshops she'd insisted would make them all kinder and more inclusive. In the office, her behaviour towards Ashleigh had come closer than Claud would have considered acceptable to bullying. 'Claud's quite right. It doesn't matter. If we hide what we are it's tantamount to being ashamed of it.'

'I'm not ashamed of anything.'

Her attitude was cold, her tone clipped and hostile. 'Nobody cares what we did in bed.'

'If nobody cares, why are you here?'

It didn't need to be difficult but Faye would make it so. It was in her interests to set up a situation in which one partner was subordinate to the other. Ashleigh fidgeted with the cuff of her shirt. 'Let's at least admit we knew each other before we came here?' That would have been the easy option, in the first place. 'Someone will find out about it.'

'I know you've told your boyfriend,' said Faye, freezing her with a look.

'I'm entitled to tell him.'

'You aren't entitled to tell anybody my private business.'

God, the woman was even more stubborn than Ashleigh had given her credit for. 'I should probably tell you. The journalist who ran that article.' A ridiculously trivial article, too, in the end, not worth the trouble. 'She did call me before she wrote it.' She raised a hand to stop Faye's intervention. 'I refused to speak to her. I'll do the same if she rings back. I just thought I'd tell you.'

'I wondered. She called me, too. I didn't ignore it, but I told her I had no comment. Except for my standard response about trying to improve the tolerance of our force for those of different ethnicity, gender and sexuality both within the force and in the wider community, etcetera, etcetera.' For a moment, Faye exhibited a trace of humour.

'It's so hard,' Ashleigh burst out, impulsively. 'Don't think I don't understand. When everything goes pear-shaped in your life you do stupid things. And when it comes down to it, it was the same for both of us, wasn't it? We were both lonely and we both needed help. It's not weakness to admit it.'

'I'm trying to make a new start.' Just like Ashleigh herself had done. 'The last thing I need, at this stage in my life, is a newspaper coming in and looking for something sensational.'

'But it's only a local paper.'

'It's a local force and we work in the local community. So yes, local matters.' Faye reproved her.

'What they printed was nothing. Even if she does come back with more it'll be a flash in the pan and the next week people will be talking about the plans for the roundabout or whether they should allow any more houses to be built, or anything. They might even be talking about Claud's Rainbow Festival and how wonderful it is. And at the end of it, people will respect you for the job you do.' Faye's defences were up. It was obvious. There was no point in wasting any more time.

Pointedly, Faye looked towards the door. 'I hear what you say, Ashleigh. thank you.'

Ashleigh got up. Faye was trying to shame her into apologising, but she wouldn't. Honesty was the only thing if they were to work together, and she wasn't going to be the one to give up and move on if it all went wrong. If Faye was going to make life difficult for one of them, it would be for herself. 'Goodbye, then.'

'Thank you for calling round.' It was enough of a concession. 'I'll see you in the office.' Faye got to her feet and shepherded her to the door, as if she couldn't be trusted to pick a safe route through the teetering piles of boxes and bags still unpacked.

'Ah, damn. I'm sorry.' As she reached for the door, Ashleigh's bag caught on the small side table in the hall, sideswiping the contents to the floor. She swooped to pick up what she'd knocked over. A picture in a clip frame, a younger Faye with two small children clinging at her knees and a bespectacled, slightly older man staring down at the three of them in adoration. She handed it back.

'Get out,' Faye said, and slammed the door behind her.

*

The door to Faye Scanlon's house opened and closed, and Ashleigh O'Halloran, in a scarlet shirt and blue trousers and with her blonde hair loose and blowing in the wind, stepped down the path and onto the pavement. Turning sharp left, she headed away from the house and up the hill.

Faye Scanlon and her bloody workshops. If her enthusiasm for equality hadn't been so strong, the equal to Claud's, he might have spent less time enthusing about this woman's capabilities and behaved differently towards the wife who only wanted him to love her. Shivering, Natalie reached out her hand for the knife, slid it out from under the passenger seat and put onto the seat.

She didn't enjoy killing, but there was no other way to purge her life of the poison that had taken Claud from her but to rid the world of all the others Claud might have grown to love.

Time was her only ally now she'd given herself away to Jude Satterthwaite. She drew her finger along the edge of the blade, the knife that Claud had used to cut the meat the night before. Her blood mingled with his and dripped down onto the seat of the car.

She got out, concealing the blade inside her coat, and paused for a moment in the empty square. The wind whipped against her face and a bad-tempered cloud passed overhead, spitting rain upon her. She turned her face up to the sky, and a rainbow slipped down from the sky and hovered over the house that Ashleigh had just left.

As if she'd needed a sign.

*

Before she was at the top of the hill, Ashleigh knew she'd given up too easily. She'd been humiliated and there had been tears pricking at the back of her eyes as she left, but in reality Faye's mistakes weren't all that different to her own. It was the picture that had given her away. Chris had said something about Faye's husband having thrown her out in the aftermath of the affair and that was what Ashleigh herself had done to Scott, still regretting the bitter necessity of it. A mistake like theirs, a joint lunge into misery and self-pity, could cost you the earth but you healed it only by confronting it.

I never took it out on Scott, she reminded herself. *I ended it cleanly.*

It was the injustice that got to her. Jude would counsel caution, with any action going via the proper channels if Faye's behaviour in the workplace verged on intimidation, but that wasn't enough. Faye still loved her husband, perhaps, just as Ashleigh loved Scott, but you moved on.

For a moment she'd thought she'd got through, and there was still something that nagged at her in Faye's face, as if the woman had been desperate to be persuaded to do the right thing and Ashleigh had failed to give her the nudge in the right direction. Faye had children. Did that make a difference? She turned and headed back down again, in time to see Natalie Blackwell get out of her car and stand for a moment on the pavement, staring up at the sky, with one hand inside her coat.

Always alert to the unusual, Ashleigh reached for her phone. 'Jude.'

'Ashleigh. Good.' His voice was terse. 'Glad to hear from you. Where are you?'

'I went down to see Faye. I've just left. But I've just seen something really strange. It's Natalie. She's here. Not running.'

'Here?' He almost snapped at her. 'Where?'

'Brunswick Square. Outside Faye's house.'

He turned away from the phone and she heard him issuing muffled instructions to someone. 'Don't approach her. Unless you have to.'

Fifty yards away, Natalie stood erect, staring at Faye's house from the other side of the street. 'Has something happened?'

'She's killed Claud, and it looks like she killed the others, too. I spoke to her on the phone and she mentioned Doddsy and Faye before she cut me off.'

'Is Doddsy—?'

'He's fine. Can you see if she's armed?'

Moving as carefully as she could, Ashleigh manoeuvred herself so that she got a better view of Natalie. 'She's got something under her coat.'

She almost heard him groan. 'Call Faye, if you can, and warn her. Tell her not to answer the door and then get somewhere safe as fast as you can. I've got someone on the way, and I'm coming along myself. Ten minutes, with the blue lights.'

Natalie waited, still staring at the sky, her brows concentrated into a caterpillar of thought. Above Faye's house a rainbow intensified, its vibrant colours deepening against a bruise-grey sky. Aware of Jude's warning, aware of the danger and the close presence of an unbalanced mind, Ashleigh nevertheless sensed that the woman cared for nothing except what was behind the front door of the house. She moved along the pavement towards her, as casually as possible. Her fingers slipped on her phone as she dialled. Impatiently, she swiped the number and dialled again.

Thirty yards away, Natalie still stared at the sky. Ashleigh checked her watch. Ten minutes? One, maybe two, of those had already ticked away, but would Natalie really stand staring the sky for all that time?

As she paused, her pulse racing, the rainbow spread to a double bow, throbbing with light. The phone rang and rang and went to voicemail. 'Faye. It's Ashleigh. Natalie's outside and she might be armed. Don't answer the door.' Would she pick it up, or ignore it?

She was beginning to type a text when Natalie gave up on the rainbow, strode up the path and raised her hand to the door.

Over Faye, she'd have the advantage of surprise. Over Ashleigh, she would not. And against the two of them, she had less chance of doing whatever her unbalanced mind intended. Ashleigh dialled again. *For God's sake, Faye, answer!*

In her hand, the phone rang and rang and flicked to voicemail. Faye must have seen her number and chosen to ignore it.

The first wail of sirens split the distance. Natalie raised her hand to the bell again. If Faye didn't answer the door what choice was there but to intervene?

The figure moving behind the glass pane in the door — thank God, slowly, as if again she was afraid it might be Ashleigh — forced her hand. She broke into a run and arrived at the gatepost as the door opened and Faye appeared on the doorstep.

'Faye! Look out!' She lunged up the short path as Natalie's elbow drew back prior to a strike, grabbed at the arm, gripped it, lost it, hurled herself at Natalie and brought both to the ground to one woman's screams of fury and the other's of pain and shock. But the scarlet-bladed knife spilled from Natalie's hand and onto the path and Ashleigh pinned the killer down as the first police car screeched to a halt beside them.

Chapter 26

'All right,' Jude said, trying not to scowl at Natalie, knowing that if he gave her solicitor any cause for argument there would be trouble, because this time he wasn't dealing with Colleen Murphy but with some bumptious young man who was barely out of law school and felt he had something to prove. 'Can we go through this again? I want to be clear. You are confessing to four murders and one attempted murder.'

Natalie was sitting opposite him at the table in the interview room, bolt upright, and with her hands folded on the table. She didn't look at him.

He sat watching her, always conscious of the clock which had somehow ticked on past seven. Mikey's party would be getting under way. He'd had no chance to call and cancel and his phone, when he switched it back on, would bombard him with messages of reproach — from Mikey, from his mother, even from his father who'd once again ended up watching the football with an empty seat beside him and no explanation for his elder son's no-show that afternoon.

'Natalie.' Ashleigh was in coaxing mode now, and he sensed that even in the aftermath of four lost lives, she'd been able to mine some vein of sympathy for a killer. Such sympathy might not be entirely professional, but a sideways look at the solicitor showed he was sufficiently taken aback to accept it at face value. Fine. If Ashleigh wanted to play the good cop, let her. Maybe it would get them out of the place earlier than otherwise. 'It's better for everybody if you tell us why you did it.'

The stubborn silence with which Natalie had begun the interview was giving way. In front of their eyes she resolved to tell the truth. 'I need help.' Her eyes filled with tears, but she stayed upright and made no attempt to wipe them away. 'I'm so sorry. I can't believe I did it. Oh God. I can't believe I killed Claud. But I was so angry. I don't know. I can't remember. But he hurt me so much.'

'He hurt you? You mean—?'

'He didn't hit me. No. Not that. But there are so many ways of hurting people.'

'Is that really what made you do it?' Ashleigh sat forward as if she were coaxing a child to admit to mischief. 'Because he upset you? But what about the others?'

'Shall we start at the beginning?' Jude repeated, mindful of obtaining some kind of a narrative, but he made sure he learned from Ashleigh and moderated his tone. In any case, his anger wasn't directed at Natalie but life in general and at himself in particular. 'Tell us about Len Pierce. What had he done to you that you wanted to kill him?'

'It's so complicated. It's so difficult. I don't know—'

'Chief Inspector. My client is clearly distressed and needs medical help.'

She turned on her supporter, like a chameleon snapping up a fly. 'I told you. I won't see a doctor. Now I want to explain. I want somebody to listen to me. Let's get it over with and then we can all go home.' And then, as if she realised that she was the one of the four of them who wouldn't go home that night, she finally dabbed at the tears that rolled down her cheeks.

From the depths of her pocket, Ashleigh produced a packet of tissues and handed them over. With blood-red fingernails, Natalie unpicked the packet and drew one of the tissues out. Now it was obvious why she'd polished her nails so vivid a scarlet — to hide any traces of blood that would have lingered there, a lesson she must have learned after the death of Len Pierce. 'Tell us about Len.'

'Shall I tell you about Claud, first?' She dabbed at her cheeks with the first of the tissues, but the tears were already drying. 'You won't believe me, but I loved him. I adored everything he did. I met him when he was working with the repertory company I was with. It was before he set up his training workshops, and he was working for another company. They did the same sort of role-play, for different sorts of training. Customer-facing, mainly.'

'You weren't an actress for very long, then?' Ashleigh leaned in towards her.

Jude exchanged glances with the unnamed solicitor. It was going to be easier for everyone to let the two women carry on with a private conversation.

'Only a couple of years. I loved acting, but I didn't like the lifestyle, all the things that came with it. I hated the late nights. I hated not knowing what I was going to be doing six months ahead. I didn't like the people. They were self-centred and unpredictable. I'm like that too, I know that, but they thrived on it and I don't. I need stability and security. Then I met Claud and I fell in love with him.'

'He seemed very charismatic.'

'I know what you really think of him. He was bumptious and determined and he had a prickly side. He liked a fight. But he was never like that with me. He was always so protective, so tender, so loving. We moved here because I didn't like living in the city. He set up the business so that we could work together and he'd always be there for me. He understood what anxiety was like, and he helped me through it. Always. I adored him. He was my man.' She reached for a glass of water.

'And then?'

'It was the business.' Her voice quivered. 'He was obsessed with it. He'd always been championing someone's rights for something but for some reason this seemed to touch something inside him. He talked about work all the time. Everything he did was about equality, about rights. We went to marches. I had to wear some silly costume and pretend I was enjoying myself. That was bad enough. But I did it because it was the only time I got to see him. He was so lost in his work. He loved people. He thought they were so interesting. Far more interesting than me.'

There was a period of silence.

'Anxiety's an awful thing.' She replaced the glass on the table, in exactly the same place that she'd picked it up from. 'You always see the worst coming. You always believe the worst and you keep believing the worst is going to happen. It's only when the time's passed and it hasn't happened that you really believe you're safe, and by then there's something else for you to worry about. Life is such a strain. If I didn't have Claud with me, I knew I wouldn't be able to cope, and everywhere I looked I saw reason why he'd leave me.'

The solicitor, Jude noticed, was looking perplexed. Ashleigh helped herself to a tissue and began picking at it. 'I see how that would happen. But what did Len have to do with all this?'

'There were always couples in that lane. It didn't really bother us, because we didn't have to look at them, but I knew some of them were gay. I came home one day from my run and Claud was chatting to one of the guys in the lane.'

'Are you sure about that?' Claud had said he hadn't met Len, but they couldn't ask him now. Maybe there had been something he was afraid of.

'I'm quite sure. I asked him about it afterwards. He said he was just chatting to him. And it could have been true. That was so like Claud. He was interested in everybody. But it wasn't the first time.'

'You were jealous. Is that it?'

For a moment, Natalie considered. 'I didn't think of it like that. He was at work so much, and there were hours at a time when I didn't see him because I was running. I began to wonder if he was seeing someone, and eventually I became obsessed by the idea that Claud was seeing this man. The man — Len — was there often, with another man, but the other man never stayed. Len did, though, and he and Claud would have a chat and a laugh. And then I realised that if I killed him, everyone would think it was his lover. You'd never think it was me.'

There was a long pause. Claud had never mentioned meeting Len. Maybe he'd guessed it was Natalie and he'd tried to protect her. Maybe he was afraid he'd incriminate himself. They'd never know.

Jude pulled out a chair and sat down, leaning over to join in the conversation. 'The tracker. That was clever.'

'Did you work it out? I am obsessive about it. That's true. I'm obsessive about everything.' She looked down at her bare wrist. 'Especially running. But I don't suppose I'll be able to run in prison, will I?'

'I wasn't smart enough to get it straight away,' said Jude, reviewing all the evidence with the benefit of hindsight, 'but I might have seen it sooner. It was those stops you made. That was strange. You were convincing about the obsession, but there was no logical reason why you'd stop where you did, about half a mile from the end of a thirteen mile run.' It was Ashleigh who'd put the idea in his head, with her observation about the view. That was only that morning, but it seemed like days before. 'What did you do — take the tracker off and leave it somewhere?'

'Yes. I'd been trying to break the habit. That was why I stopped when I did my stretches. I used to take it off and put it on the wall and walk away from it, sometimes run a hundred yards or so and back, without it.' Natalie paused and looked down at her bare wrist. 'Then I realised. It meant I could be somewhere and seem like I was somewhere else and that meant I could kill that man. I'd been planning it for a couple of weeks. I'd bought a knife in Carlisle and I hid it by the lane, for when I needed it. The first time I ran past the two of them were there and I didn't dare stop, but the next week it was different. Just as I was in sight one of them drove off and the other one stopped for a cigarette. I got the knife and I ran to where the man was, next to his car.' Her wide eyes turned uncertainly from Ashleigh to Jude and back again. 'Please don't ask me to… but I did it. I did do it.'

'And the knife?'

'I hid it in the garden shed. Then I went and told Claud what I'd found.'

Silence surrounded them as they contemplated the crime, and then Natalie reached for another tissue and folded it in half.

'And when that was done,' Ashleigh said, with her voice very carefully controlled, 'what did you do next?'

'I got scared. I was scared about everything. I was scared about being caught, and although Len was dead, I was still scared that Claud would leave me for someone else. There was always someone else he was talking about, always someone who wanted a piece of his time. That bell-ringer. He was so keen to see Claud.' She folded the tissue again, and again, and again. In reality, Jude thought, there was every chance that Claud had talked about these things for only a fraction of the time, but they were all she ever registered. 'And Claud kept saying how normal it was to be gay. I thought it was a coded message to me, that he was preparing me for him leaving. I was sure he was having an affair. I started looking at his laptop, and I could see he'd been on some sites, but I couldn't get access to them.'

'Did you take his laptop?'

'No. He faked the burglary and threw it away. He must have suspected I was onto him, and of course that just made me more suspicious. I didn't know what to do. But there was that woman, Gracie.'

'You must have met her at one of the workshops, then,' Jude said. 'But they were before you killed Len, weren't they? Why her?'

'Claud was always talking about her. He wanted to invite her round for supper and when I didn't want to he said he'd take her out somewhere without me. I'd seen her walk across the churchyard and back every evening after work. I'm sure if I wasn't there they must have met.'

'Same plan, eh? With the tracker.'

'Yes. I found a coat in a charity shop bag, and I wrapped the knife in it. I didn't know poor Claud would find her. He was so upset. He said he thought she was me. He'd been worried about me.' The tissue would fold no smaller. Unfolding it, she began to tear it in half, in half again. 'On the way back from the police station we met that bell ringer. He came up to help us and he was lovely. And I remember him saying to Claud that he'd have to come round, and he gave him his number and address. And that's where I went completely mad. I thought he was inviting Claud round because he wanted to have an affair with him.'

'Was the invitation only for Claud?'

'He said *you must come round*.' She paused, ripped each half of the tissue yet again. 'I hear it differently now. I see he must have meant both of us.'

'But you knew where he lived,' Ashleigh said, sounding to Jude's sensitive ear as if exhaustion was beginning to kick in, as if her capacity for understanding was becoming strained. 'And it was just handy that it was on your route.'

'Yes. I ran past his house and there was a light on, so I rang the doorbell,' Natalie said, breathlessly, 'and when I…he fell backward into the house I pulled the door to. Then I ran off and left him.'

'And was it Claud's jacket you wrapped the knife in, this time?'

'It was so handy. I'd known I'd have to kill him, too, because he had his eye on Claud, and when I came back to the office after the burglary I took the coat and put it in my bag and pretended it had been stolen, too. That time I had to run a bit further. You'll see I stopped a bit longer there, if you've had time to check the tracker, but fortunately I never met anyone.'

'But what about Claud? Why kill Claud?' Ashleigh was shaking her head in perplexity.

Natalie turned to her, lifted her hand to her breast, an actress in a moment. 'I don't know.' A tear, unquestionably a real one, rose to her eyes. 'I asked him if he was having an affair and he told me he wasn't, but I didn't believe him. I could see it in his eyes that he thought I was mad. I told him I still loved him and when he came to hug me, I was brave. I killed him because if I hadn't, he'd leave.'

Silence, while they digested this tale of tainted love and self-delusion, and Jude risked another look at the clock. Half seven. 'And after that?'

'After that I don't remember.' She hung her head, and the red fingernails closed once more on the tissue paper. 'I don't remember anything else. Anything at all. It's all a blank. I wish I didn't remember killing Claud.'

There was a tap on the door. 'Shall we take a break?' Jude asked. He glanced at his watch again. 'I think we all need one.'

'My client needs a rest.'

'I told you, I want to tell everything—'

Jude got up and answered the door. Faye stood outside it, her left arm in a sling, her fingers bandaged. He joined her in the corridor, with Ashleigh behind him. 'Well, Jude?'

'She's confessed. To all four killings. Not in her right mind, if you ask me, but the experts will be the judges of that.' He indicated the hand. 'Are you okay?'

'I've been worse. Maybe this will offset the newspaper article that Ms Letham will no doubt produce as a follow-up. Maybe I'll get points for bravery. Do stitches compensate for a bad reputation?' Her eyes glittered like obsidian. 'I hope so. I have seven of them in play, and some very strong painkillers to see me through.'

Faye, Jude thought, was exhibiting her own signs of delusion. Nobody really cared what stories ran in the local paper. The woman was mad even to be in the office, but he might as well take advantage of her folly. 'Brilliant. Could you take over here? Ashleigh and I were supposed to be somewhere else.'

Her eyes widened. 'I beg your pardon?'

'My brother turns twenty-one today. I'm supposed to be at his party.'

'Am I hearing you right? You're proposing to walk out of an interview to go to a party?'

'Yes. I'm not supposed to be working today. I worked my last day off. I missed spending the afternoon with my dad. I'm done here.' It was probably too late to salvage anything from the evening, but at least he could try. And if the worst came to the worst, he could offer Mikey the sacrifice of his career, in a way he hadn't been able to offer Becca.

'You can't leave—'

'I must have worked seventy hours this week.'

'We're all expected to put in long hours.'

'I know that. I do it regularly enough. It's cost me in the past, and I'm not having it cost me again. Take it up with my union, if you have a problem with it.' He took three steps down the corridor to signal his intent. If only Mikey was there to see him make a stand.

'Chief Inspector.' Faye's voice cracked like a whip. 'That's dangerously close to insubordination.'

He turned back.

'I appreciate your difficulty,' Faye observed, maintaining her steely calm, 'but let me remind you of your priorities.'

Ever since he'd lost Becca he'd vowed to change his priorities. 'No-one's ever accused me of neglecting my duties before.'

'Then don't make me do it now.'

Silence. Ashleigh broke it, stepping forward, laying a hand on his arm. 'It isn't worth it. It really isn't.'

If the circumstances had been different, if Mikey was in trouble, he might have carried it through, but what was the point when all that was required was his presence, when the party would carry on fine without him? It would be another grievance for Mikey to chalk up against him. That was all. 'All right. Let's get on with it.' And the sooner they finished, the better the chance he had of salvaging something from the evening.

Chapter 27

The party was well past its peak when Jude finally arrived in Wasby. A knot of revellers crammed the pavement outside the village hall with plastic pint glasses and lit cigarettes, and a few of the guests were beginning to drift towards their cars. Behind him, a taxi pulled up and a few of Mikey's more boisterous friends piled into it, no doubt away to carry on carousing in their own places, or in a club in Penrith or even Carlisle.

He parked the Mercedes outside his mother's house and walked the hundred yards or so back to the hall, sliding in through the doors just as someone else came out. Inside, the lights were dimmed and the wooden walls throbbed with Mikey's eclectic taste in music as he shuffled along to the side of it, past a couple of recklessly drunk dancers, and towards his brother, who was standing next to the trestle table at the side with a can of beer in his hand. 'Mikey. Sorry I'm late. But I said I'd be here.'

It was the blackest of looks he got in return, one that implied the half an hour he'd managed to salvage was a worse insult than his absence would have been. 'Good of you to make the effort.'

'Something came up.'

'Something always comes up.' Mikey turned his back.

Jude hadn't eaten since the middle of the afternoon and the promised mass of food had all but disappeared. Picking up a paper plate, he helped himself to the few edible treasures among the remains — a curled sandwich, a distressed-looking sausage roll or two, a crumbling slice of salmon and broccoli quiche. The dishes that had contained Becca's famous macaroni cheese had been scraped clean. He strayed over to the drinks table and helped himself to all that was left there for a driver, a can of warm lemonade.

He didn't even like lemonade. There was no sign either of his mother, so it looked as if he'd arrived so late she'd already gone home, probably disappointed in him, or of his father who, had he come, would definitely still have been there, propping up the bar.

'You made it, Jude. Good for you.'

The hand on his arm surprised him, but not nearly as much as the lack of sarcasm in Becca's voice. She was balanced on a pair of heels that were far higher than she was used to, so that when he turned he found himself almost looking directly into her eyes. 'I would have been here earlier, but I couldn't get away from work.'

'You never can, can you? But I'm glad you're here. I told Mikey you'd turn up. I was beginning to think I couldn't rely on you.'

What was he to say? He wanted to explain to her just as he wanted to explain to Mikey, but even if it was professionally appropriate, would any of then have understood how important it was, how the law had to be followed and the woman who'd killed four people and tried to kill a fifth should be put through due process? He remained silent, thinking of Natalie. That was why he struggled to summon up any kind of a smile, even as everyone else around him was having a wild time. Or maybe it was less complicated than that. Maybe it just came with the territory of being the only sober man at the tail end of a party. 'I've seen him and he knows I came. That's what matters. Maybe I should head off again.'

'Not without a dance.' She grabbed his arm, regardless of the can in his hand. Left with no option he slid the plate down on the table and the can of lemonade after it, and followed her out onto the dance floor. He did it, he told himself, because it was probably the last dance they'd share. By then the playlist had moved in from the blcak, dark stuff that Mikey favoured, so obscure that he couldn't even name its genre. Someone had got on to the oldies.

'Love a dose of Elvis.' Becca grabbed his forearm and swung him round to face her. She was drunk, and he couldn't say he wouldn't have welcomed a shot of the hard stuff himself, but if he had done he'd have had to stay over at his mother's and wake up the next morning to face Mikey's hangover and his fixation on all the times Jude hadn't been there.

'Steady.' He caught her as she stumbled.

'Love a dose of Elvis,' she said again, an echo from her own mind. 'Remember this one? It was in the charts when we first went out. They were playing it in the restaurant. Remember?'

It always amazed him how selective memories were. He could remember a lot about their first date, but not that. She'd been wearing black jeans and an asymetrically-patterned top, scarlet boots with heels as high as those she was wearing that night, and her hair, which had been much longer then and blonde rather than brown, had been twisted up into a knot that hadn't lasted the evening. They'd gone into Carlisle for a film and a Chinese and he'd kissed her when he brought her home. But he didn't remember Elvis singing *Are You Lonesome Tonight*. 'Don't be daft. The King was dead before we were born.'

'It was rereleased.' She laughed at him, not realising it was a joke.

Three minutes of Elvis passed in a few seconds, or so it seemed. 'Brilliant. Thanks for the dance, Becca. I'm going to head off now. I've done my duty.' He headed for the door.

'Duty?' She came tottering behind him. 'I'm coming out, too. I need some fresh air. Is that all it was? Duty?'

Jude stepped out into the chilly night. 'No. It was important. What do you want me to do? Walk out on my job? I got myself in enough trouble getting here. I don't need any more from you.'

'I'm not thinking of myself,' she said, as though that was what he'd accused her of. 'I'm thinking of Mikey.'

'Yes, and so am I. I came. For God's sake, what more do I have to do?'

They were outside, in the fresh March air, and he stopped, turning to face her. 'I try, okay? I try my hardest. If my best isn't good enough, then that's too bad. It's all I've got.'

She stared at him for a second longer, shaking her head. 'Oh, Jude.' She reached out a hand and touched his cheek. 'Oh, Jude.'

He lost his mind. Maybe it was Elvis after all, coursing through his blood in a way he hadn't remembered, or maybe it was tension, or maybe it was the memory of a dead woman's shoe in the darkness of the churchyard and the overwhelming, irrational fear that Becca was dead.

But she wasn't dead. She was alive and looking at him as she used to do, with the open eyes of a lover. He leaned down towards her and kissed her.

The hand that had touched his cheek slid around to the back of his head and pulled it down towards her. Almost at the same time, her other hand pushed him away. 'Jude. No. We mustn't.'

'Why mustn't we?'

'It's not that I don't want to. But you have a girlfriend. Stop.'

It was the word 'stop' not the mention of Ashleigh that made him pull away. Thank God she'd stopped him. 'Okay. Okay. I'm sorry.'

'Is he bothering you, Becca?'

'No.' She swivelled on her high heel and wobbled off back towards the hall.

'My fault,' Jude said, though it wasn't. He didn't like and didn't trust Adam Fleetwood and he knew the man he'd once called his best friend well enough to have good reason for it. He backed away, justifying his behaviour. 'She's maybe had a bit too much to drink.'

'It's a party,' she called back over her shoulder, but she was smiling as she carried on her way.

Jude was left eye to eye with Adam, in a way he hadn't been, and hadn't wanted to be, for years. 'It's probably time I went.'

'It probably is, Judas. Glad you worked that out for yourself. Or I'd have had to make you.'

Adam wasn't that drunk, certainly sober enough to spin a line and see if his prey was foolish enough to bite but Jude had too much to lose. It was worth his while to allow Adam to humiliate him. 'I expect I'll see you around.'

'Oh don't worry. You will.' Adam trailed him to the Mercedes, just far enough from him not to be too obvious a threat. 'Just as well Mikey's got me to keep an eye on him. You're not doing a great job.'

'I'm sure he's grateful to you.'

'What kept you away tonight? More blood on your conscience?'

Jude opened the car door and slid inside, but Adam's hand flashed out and closed on the side of the door before he could shut it.

'One more thing, Judas.' He leaned inwards, eyes narrow, breath heavy with beer. 'I'm watching you. One step out of line, one tiny mistake. You'll be inside like I was. See how you like that.'

'Let go of my car, Adam' Jude brought out the sharpest tone he had, and it surprised Adam long enough for him to let go of the door and for Jude to drive away.

It was no surprise when blue lights flashed in front of him as he drive onto the roundabout that joined the A6 to the A66. Just off it, he obeyed their instruction to stop and got out of the car. PC Charlie Fry, an old acquaintance, was regarding him with grim horror, and the young female PC who was with him was looking rather more enthusiastic. 'Sorry to stop you, Sir. We've had a report of this vehicle being driven under the influence of alcohol.'

'Sure.' He should have known. Adam had been out of prison for six months and it had been only a matter of time before he'd pounced. 'That's okay. Whatever you need to do.'

He breathed into the tube the Charlie offered him, not bothering to look down. His conscience was clear but for the breath of warm white wine he'd somehow harvested from Becca's kiss. On the A66 the traffic hummed and somewhere, a few hundred yards away, Natalie would be lying in her cell, playing back the chain of events that had led her to kill.

'That's all in order, Sir. Sorry to have stopped you.'

'That's okay, Charlie.' Jude moved back to his car. 'That didn't surprise me, after the night I've had.'

'Got on the wrong side of someone, have you?'

'Looks like it.' Jude got back into the car and sat for a moment while Charlie and his partner headed off to apprehend some real wrongdoer. Adam had laid down a marker and it was one he'd do well to take notice of. This was what it was going to be like, every step of the way, until Adam's bitterness ran out of steam or Jude had enough of it and left.

He could cope with Adam Fleetwood, because he no longer cared about him. But as he started the car and headed on towards home, he kept on thinking of Becca.

THE END

More by Jo Allen

Death by Dark Waters
DCI Jude Satterthwaite #1

It's high summer, and the Lakes are in the midst of an unrelenting heatwave. Uncontrollable fell fires are breaking out across the moors faster than they can be extinguished. When firefighters uncover the body of a dead child at the heart of the latest blaze, Detective Chief Inspector Jude Satterthwaite's arson investigation turns to one of murder. Jude was born and bred in the Lake District. He knows everyone... and everyone knows him. Except his intriguing new Detective Sergeant, Ashleigh O'Halloran, who is running from a dangerous past and has secrets of her own to hide... Temperatures – and tensions – are increasing, and with the body count rising Jude and his team race against the clock to catch the killer before it's too late...

The first in the gripping, Lake District-set, DCI Jude Satterthwaite series.

Death at Eden's End
DCI Jude Satterthwaite #2

When one-hundred-year-old Violet Ross is found dead at Eden's End, a luxury care home hidden in a secluded nook of Cumbria's Eden Valley, it' not unexpected. Except for the instantly recognisable look in her lifeless eyes…that of pure terror. DCI Jude Satterthwaite heads up the investigation, but as the deaths start to mount up it's clear that he and DS Ashleigh O'Halloran need to uncover a long-buried secret before the killer strikes again…

The second in the unmissable, Lake District-set, DCI Jude Satterthwaite series.

Death on Coffin Lane
DCI Jude Satterthwaite #3

DCI Jude Satterthwaite doesn't get off to a great start with resentful Cody Wilder, who's visiting **Grasmere** to present her latest research on Wordsworth. With some of the villagers unhappy about her visit, it's up to DCI Satterthwaite to protect her – especially when her assistant is found hanging in the kitchen of their shared cottage.

With a constant flock of tourists and the local hippies welcoming in all who cross their paths, Jude's home in the Lake District isn't short of strangers. But with the ability to make enemies wherever she goes, the violence that follows in Cody's wake leads DCI Satterthwaite's investigation down the hidden paths of those he knows, and those he never knew even existed.

A third mystery for DCI Jude Satterthwaite to solve, in this gripping novel by best-seller Jo Allen.

Acknowledgements

There are too many people who have helped me with this book for me to name them individually: I hope those I don't mention will forgive me.

I have to thank my lovely beta readers – Amanda, Frances, Julie, Kate, Katey, Liz, Lorraine, Pauline, Sally and Sara – who not only read and commented but also produced support and suggestions throughout the process.

Rebecca Bradley kindly commented on aspects of police procedure; and Julie Cohen spent time and effort on a sensitivity read – something necessary on such a tricky subject. Julie, I hope I have managed not to allow the unpleasant views of some of my characters to take over too much!

Finally, I owe a huge debt of gratitude to the eagle-eyed Keith Sutherland, for the most thorough and detailed piece of proofreading I have ever experienced!

Printed in Great Britain
by Amazon